Libraries and Information

CRI

This book should be returned by the last date stamped above. You may renew the loan personally, by post or telephone for a further period if the book is not required by another reader.

292397 Designed and Produced by Wakefield Council, Communications 04/23 ♻recycle

www.wakefield.gov.uk

D1440165

7000000290309

Rebecca Bradley

1

The noise unnerved her as she tried to shift her body in an attempt to ease the pain. Instead, the slight movement caused every bone and fibre of her body to howl out in objection. She could no longer tell where the pain was coming from, but the receptors in her brain kept up their constant transmissions. The shrieking of her nerve endings blended into one mindless assault on her senses. The stench of her own urine was sharp in her nose as it burnt her bruised and bleeding body.

As she shifted, it creaked and rattled again. She froze, the sound reawakening her terror, returning her to the reality of her surroundings. Her eyelids felt heavy and hot, drawn down and protective, but she forced them open. Just to check.

Her body throbbed. Blood crusting on dry and broken skin added to the acrid smell assaulting her nostrils. It tasted bitter and vile in her mouth. The room was unlit, a faint light sneaking under the door at the far side of the room casting shadows, playing with her mind. She could make out shapes in the gloom, furniture she knew was there in the daylight, shape-shifting in the dark. It was quiet. She strained for any sound of someone else in there with her.

She tried to turn her head to check he wasn't there, watching from the corner. Pain seared through her skull like hot metal rods. She was alone. Slowly, she lowered it back down onto the damp, sticky plastic base and let her eyelids close. The dog cage surrounding her was left behind for the blackness that now enveloped her.

2

Blue and red lights sliced through the night as I approached, the rotations casting eerie signals of death around Nottingham's city community. I parked in front of a beautiful three-storey terraced town house, which had probably been broken down into several flats by now, the insides a distant remnant of its former glory. This was a contradictory street: old stone buildings on one side, shops and restaurants with run down flats above them on the other. It was as close as I could get. The perimeter cordon and the parked liveried vehicles of the first responders made it difficult to park adjacent to the alley I needed to be in. I climbed out of my Peugeot 308 and locked it. Pocketing the keys, I approached on foot, digging my hands into my coat pockets, shoulders hunched up to my ears in an attempt to keep warm. The end of October brought a definite drop in temperature and I hated the cold. It was bloody freezing here and the wind bit at my face, snapping and sucking the living warmth out of me. As I walked towards the scene I could see the uniformed officers on point duty, preventing the ghoulish section of humanity from entering the area. It disgusted me, the horrors people wanted to see. Looking up above the shops and restaurants in front of me, my breath made a smoky pathway through the dark. Dirty grey nets and floral curtains twitched. Pasty faces of woken residents peered out at the disruption below.

My DS, Aaron Stone, came over, pulling his blue face mask down so it hung around his neck like a second chin. We walked to the Crime Scene van parked next to a flapping blue and white taped police cordon. Aaron updated me.

"The body's behind the restaurant where the industrial bins are. Girl's been dumped behind them. Naked. She's pretty bashed up. One of the workers was taking the rubbish out at the end of his shift. Poor bloke got sucker punched big time when he saw her on the ground. He's a bit of a mess. Uniform are with him at the ambulance, trying to get some details. Jack's on his way and Doug's already here with the other SOCOs." Though the new phrase for the forensic officers attending the crime scene had been Americanised to CSIs, there were some that hung on to old traditions and called them SOCOs. Aaron was particularly bad at change.

"Thanks, Aaron." I collected a sterile packaged forensic suit from the back of the van and started to pull it on, wishing I'd worn something warmer. I felt tenser by the minute. The chill in the air was biting at my fingers mercilessly. "Do we have an ETA for Jack?"

"He shouldn't be far behind you. I know he lives further out, but he drives like a newly qualified teenager with a heavy right foot." White booties, hooded suit, gloves and mask in place, we headed into the alleyway.

3

Someone had made an attempt to conceal the girl. Her arms were down by her sides and her knees bent up to her chest, jammed between the bricks of the external wall of the restaurant and the huge frigid metal containers. The bin was at an angle to the wall. She was petite and looked to be between fourteen and sixteen years of age. The area was swamped by the light of the erected crime scene lamps and I could see her skin was pale and bruised.

I held myself still, trying to stop the constrictions that pushed at my insides. A bitter taste hit the back of my throat and I swallowed against it. The alley was an occasional home to local vagrants and a piss stop for drunks. The sight of the child, along with the overwhelming stench of urine and refuse, was overpowering.

"Not pretty," said Aaron.

"No," I replied.

Doug Howell, one of the crime scene techs, gave a quick nod of acknowledgement in our direction, his face intense as he photographed the tiny framed girl, the scene around him fractured by the camera flash as he worked.

A car door slammed at the end of the alley, an exchange of voices and then Jack Kidner, the Home Office registered forensic pathologist rounded the corner into sight.

"Couldn't you get me up any earlier, young Hannah?" he shouted as he walked towards me.

"Sorry, Jack, you know how this city is. Runs by its own rules, spits out whatever it chooses, whenever it chooses, regardless of our plans for sleep."

"By Jove, you did get out the wrong side of bed this morning didn't you?" The crinkling of laughter lines around his eyes revealed a smile was hidden behind his protective mask.

"Thanks for coming, I appreciate it." I sidestepped, allowing him to see the child discarded with the rubbish.

"God help us," he muttered, crouching beside her. A medical bag that looked like it had seen better days dropped to the ground. "Doug, old chap, do stop flashing those blessed lights. I'm going to have an epileptic fit at this rate. Move the lamps in a little so I can see better, then you can flash away again before I move in closer."

Doug, whose mass of grey hair had given rise to Jack's descriptive "old chap" phrase, stopped. "It's fine, I have what I need for starters, she's all yours. I'll photograph as you work."

"Good man."

Jack stooped down and began his examination. He would take samples, test for any signs of sexual assault, do body taping and take a temperature for time of death. I gave him space and walked the alleyway with Aaron.

"You could get a vehicle down here with ease, even with the bins down the sides," I thought aloud. "The darkness would offer cover." The occasional lamp fitted above some of the buildings' rear doors gave little in the way of light. Years of grime obscured their faint yellow glow; instead they cast shadows and created darker corners. There were no CCTV cameras down here either, just discarded boxes and crates, smashed up bottles and glasses, and tired, defaced business signs, neglected and forgotten. Aaron looked at me.

"It's a shit hole," he said.

"I know, it's going to be a nightmare of a scene to process." Everyone was going to work for their money over the next few days. I stopped and rubbed the outer edges of my arms, an attempt to stave off the chills that invaded me, the papery white suit sliding over my jacket. I looked back down the alley. Jack unfurled himself from his crouched position and waved us over.

"What have we got?" I asked as he signed the labels on the swab casings.

"If you look at our girl you can see some lividity. It's not very pronounced, but I can say she's been dead longer than thirty minutes. It started on her back, but this isn't consistent with how she's laid now, so she was moved after death." He pushed the signed and sealed swabs into his bag.

"Body dump," said Aaron.

"That would be my thought. I can't see that this would be our initial crime scene and, looking at the markings on her, I'd say death did not come quickly."

"So, time of death?" I asked.

"Oh yes, as I was saying, she isn't really starting with rigor either. Putting together the facts: it's four degrees out here, she weighs approximately seventy pounds, is stripped of her clothes, and her core temperature is 34.4 degrees, I would put time of death between two and four and a half hours ago."

"That would make it between ten p.m. last night and half past midnight today," I figured. "What time do you want us for the PM?"

"Oh, I don't know, eleven a.m.? It also gives us time to process her within the scene before removal. Then I can make some sweet caramel coffee to warm back up and get organised. Sound agreeable?"

"Sounds good. I'll see you then. Thanks, Jack"

Walking out of the alley we left a large team of CSIs preparing to do a fingertip search of the area. Without knowing what is and isn't relevant, all items would be examined, photographed in situ, logged and seized, including the contents of the rather large industrial waste bins. It would be a long night with several long days ahead for them. Jack stayed with them as the correct removal of the girl from the scene was discussed and organised. I was shattered. Much as I loved my job, I hated nights like these. Nights where I'm dragged from my bed at three a.m. and sent into dark, dirty alleyways. Nights where I had to start a murder investigation of the worst kind: that of a child. From now on, I wouldn't sleep much. My head would be filled with images, of these things. Sights, sounds and smells together. I'm not just my job. I'm human and this job was a nasty one; it would take some getting through.

4

Phones were ringing off the hook and talk of a sandwich collection was at an almost raucous volume. My defrosting brain cells struggled to break through the noise.

The incident room was busy and space was tight. Coats were thrown over the backs of chairs. As well as the assigned investigating detectives, some uniformed officers had been drafted in to help with the immediate workload that faced us. I clung to the steaming mug of green tea in my hands trying to warm my fingers.

Along with my team, the investigation had the attention of the top brass. Detective Superintendent Catherine Walker, head of the Nottingham City division Major Crimes Unit, had been raised from her bed. She wore her hair in a sleek dark bob, immaculate, no matter what time of day it was. She stood tall and assured and she commanded respect. Next to Walker was my Chief Inspector Anthony Grey. He was a weasel-looking man with a narrow face, balding head and a tall frame. He was so slim any girl would be envious. As far as supervisors go he was amenable and he didn't interfere with investigations. Grey was more of a paper shuffler.

A media strategy was required, so Claire Betts from the press office was also here. I liked Claire; she was a straight talker and great at getting what she needed from the media without selling her soul. Her talkative and amiable manner hid a shrewd brain that often ran rings around the press who took her at face value. She looked up from the paperwork she was reading and caught my eye. She gave an easy smile. I pushed the corners of my mouth up in response, envious of her energy and enthusiasm.

I felt cramped and rubbed my temples with one hand whilst inhaling the rising tea vapours in an attempt to ease the tension rampaging through my head and neck.

Grey moved to the front of the room and stood quietly. His silence demanded attention. He was about to give his pep talk. Make a show of support for the officers who would work this with little to no sleep for the first few days when evidence grabbing was at its most viable. He would say the usual comments about working hard, having the support of the command team and the jolly "get on with it troops!" pat on the back.

My phone vibrated in my jeans pocket, I pulled it up enough to see the screen. *Dad*. Conversations with him often went in the same familiar circles and those circles were often about my sister Zoe. Now wasn't the time for this. I rejected the call and pushed the phone back down.

When the sandwich rumblings died down Grey spoke. "We have a dead child. We need to identify her and return her to her parents. Press attention will be high because of her age. They will be harsh and they will be critical. Keep yourselves sharp."

No one moved.

"I've spoken with Jack Kidner who will hopefully conduct the post-mortem at eleven a.m. this morning. I believe Hannah is to attend that with Sally?" He looked at me. I nodded. Sally, one of the brightest and most dependable detectives on my team, blanched. Difficult to spot with her fair complexion, but I saw it. It was unusual. "Forensics still have the scene and will be there, I imagine, for some time. What do you have, Hannah?"

I put my cup on the desk. I was up.

"We have a lot to do. We need to check our missing persons database and liaise with the National Missing Persons Bureau in case this child is from another county. I want a team to canvas the area for CCTV in local establishments. Take it wide. Detailed house to house inquiries are needed. If people aren't in when you knock, go back. I saw a lot of people peeping out of windows last night, so it's possible someone could have seen her being dumped. I want a tip line set up and for Claire to prepare press releases to include the number. Someone knows who this girl is and someone holds information that relates to her death." I had all ears.

"We need to check what time the restaurant closed and identify and locate all customers who ate there in the run up to closing. Most people pay by card in some way, shape or form nowadays, it's rare anyone pays with cash, so that should make it an easier task. Someone may have seen something but not realised its importance." My head throbbed. "The PM this morning will give us more and could help identify her. CSIs will hopefully give us something we can work with." I looked at my team, Aaron and Sally along with Martin and Ross. It was grim. It always is with a child, but I knew them and they would work their arses off. "Make sure you get some food and hot drinks down you."

The throbbing from my head hit my stomach with a nauseating roar. My next stop would be the mortuary.

5

Huge suction cups hung from the ceiling in an effort to decrease the odours of the mortuary, but I never liked the place. In the changing room I thought about what we had, or rather, at this point in time, what we didn't have. We had a dead child; no age, no name, no family. Later today we could have a cause of death. I slipped out of the jeans and trainers I still wore from my early morning call out and shoved them in the allocated locker, pulled on the usual green protective garb and entered the Queen's Medical Centre mortuary.

The room was all grey metal with white tiles that covered the floor as it sloped towards drains. What looked like medieval instruments of torture lay aligned on steel work surfaces along the two walls either side of the entrance doorways. It was large and well lit with several post-mortem tables in the centre. Already laid out on a table, prepared by the mortuary technician, Paul Marchant, was our girl. Paul was standing to the side, talking to Doug, who was here to visually record the post-mortem. Jack had agreed to this. Though the more people he had under his feet, the tetchier he got, he understood the need to do everything we could to identify the child and bring her killer to justice. And the PM being recorded was another of our tools in the investigation. Paul's persistent smoker's cough was like a staccato bass underlying the atmosphere of the clinical room.

Jack pushed his way in through the plastic swing doors followed by Sally who still sported the pallor from earlier. She refused to catch my eye as pleasantries were exchanged.

Seeing the girl's small body under such bright unforgiving light gave a fuller picture of what she had gone through. She was covered in bruises, more vivid than could be seen in the darkness of the alley. She seemed smaller and more vulnerable, and so, so alone.

A short rotund woman came into the room and took dental impressions without making conversation with anyone. Sally made sure to take her name and details, but she had such a stern face, and I wasn't in the mood for making new friends, so I left her to her business.

Jack completed a body plan diagram with each mark measured and recorded along with an appendix scar. DNA was collected for a profile and fingerprints taken. X-rays had already been done and were examined. Jack peered down his nose at the images on the light box, taking in the visual evidence.

If I didn't know better I would have thought Sally was recovering from a night on the tiles. She was quiet. Not even half a dozen words had passed between us on the drive over. This concerned me. She had been on my department for about six years and never baulked at jobs. Yet today she seemed to have some difficulty. As the exhibits officer it was important for her to be focused and in control. We couldn't take the risk that evidence would be disallowed at a later date, so she needed to log every single exhibit Jack created correctly. I paid close attention to her; watching and following Jack as he worked then writing it up. There was no clothing for her to seize as the girl had been naked. Jack was doing all the work. As far as I could see Sally was performing up to scratch, but something was off. I made a mental note to talk to her about it later.

The mood in the room was solemn as Jack progressed through the PM.

There was more than an indication of sexual abuse. She also had welts around her wrists and ankles consistent with ropes having been tied around them. There was bruising around her neck. It wasn't the twine of a rope though; it was wide and flat, with an intermittent pattern along the centre. Circles maybe. As well as these, she was covered in black, purple and yellowing bruises. Some in the process of healing. This child had suffered over a prolonged period of time.

Jack completed the PM, looked at me and snapped off his

gloves. "My preliminary report will read homicide by asphyxiation." He wiped his brow with the back of his right hand, though there were no obvious signs of sweat gathering. "Her windpipe was crushed by what looks to be some kind of belt. She was bound by rope around her ankles and wrists and she has adhesive around her mouth, indicating some kind of tape was used." His gloves went in an evidence bag. He sealed it and signed the label. "I'll send all swabs and the toxicology samples off today and let you know as soon as I get any results, but you know they can't be rushed." Jack put the pack down on the side and looked me square on, his age lines pinched. "I do hope you get this animal, Hannah."

"I won't stop until I do."

He nodded. A silent understanding.

After thanking him for his time, I told him I'd speak with him later, and went to change.

Sally had left the minute she could. It's hard to take, seeing such inhuman things first hand.

As I relieved myself of mask, footwear and gown, my phone rang.

"Han, it's me. I want to talk to you about the murdered girl."

6

Entering that mortuary, on that day, in those circumstances, Sally figured they amounted to one of the worst days of her life so far. It was inhumane what had happened to the child and it made her whole body ache. It took absolutely everything she had to keep it together in there. Today wasn't going to be the day she fell apart. She wouldn't give anyone the satisfaction of believing she wasn't fully up to it.

She had stood there. Staunch. Breathing as little as possible. Staring at places that didn't involve the girl: Jack's patterned socks under his scrubs, the huge plastic slabs for doors at the opposite end of the room, and her own feet on as many occasions as she could get away with. As well as the post-mortem there were the stark images on the light-boxes, like glowing announcements of violence. The ones visible on the child's skin not enough alone, they had to be photographed, high definition, X-rayed and analysed. The incisions were made, the girl's organs removed, weighed and measured. The slow decisive breakdown of what once used to be a child, but was now a medical evidence gathering exercise seemed to go on around her in slow motion. Her stomach pitched, watching a girl so small be taken down to the basics of what a human being was. Flesh and bones.

As it rolled heavily again, she clenched her teeth. Her mind wandered to Tom. Tom would hate this. To know she was here. She wouldn't tell him. She had to keep the difficulties down to a minimum if she was to be able to cope with the web of lies she was slowly weaving.

7

"Ethan, you can't call me at work like this."

"I'm sorry, Hannah, I thought you might have some time free by now. I waited a while before calling. How are you?"

I wasn't sure he wanted to know how I was, that he wanted to hear about the pounding head induced by red wine and lack of sleep, or that he wanted to hear I was hurt that he had, yet again, sneaked away in the night. "How do you think?"

"I think you must be knackered. Want me to bring a bottle round later, we can talk, wind down?"

His answer to any emotional problem and my downfall every time. I sighed into the handset "What do you want?" Tiredness now made it difficult to mask how I felt. A pause.

"I heard it was a tough case, so called to see how you were?"

"I'm tired, Ethan."

"I can imagine. Have you found out who she is? Who her parents are?"

"Seriously? You're asking me about my case?" I couldn't do this with him. Not now. Not standing, half out of my PM gown, with the stench of death crawling all over me. I needed to shower and clear my head. "I'll talk to you later." I ended the call. I could do with someone to talk to tonight, some comfort, but not like this, not when I didn't know who I was getting: Ethan the bloke I was sleeping with or Ethan Gale, the *Nottingham Today* reporter.

I stripped off the rest of my clothes, stepped into the shower and allowed the water to rush over me. But the brutality was more than an acrid smell. It hit far deeper than the surface clothing. I couldn't just throw it into a contaminated bin. Clothing couldn't protect from the fear, horror and harm inflicted on this girl as its truth touched me inside, crept around my heart and squeezed. Knowledge of torture so vile, it ate away at my very being. I turned my face upwards and closed my eyes as the water came.

8

Walking back into the incident room a heaviness settled over me. Sally brought up the rear. There was the beginnings of an awkward silence between us, or at least from Sally, and I didn't understand it, but time was pushed and I would have to address it when I had the chance. As of yet, there was no problem with her work to give me cause for concern.

"Give me something I can work with, Ross," I said to Ross Leavy, the newest member of the team. He was young, both in age and service and he was always eager to please. After five years' service he had gone from uniform, to CID and now here at Divisional Headquarters, Central Police Station, Major Crimes Unit. A testament to his work ethic. He pulled himself up in his chair as he started to tell me what he had.

"We're running through the Missing Persons database, checking for female teenagers between the ages of thirteen and nineteen years."

"And?"

"We have more than I expected to be honest. Too many for divisional cops to deal with seriously when they're gone for the eleventh time and it looks as though they're taking the piss."

"But they're not taking the piss are they? That girl I've seen is definitely not taking the piss," my voice rose. "She's so far from taking the piss, she's laid on the slab." Ross looked down at his desk. I had reacted on an emotional level. I took an intake of breath and tried again. "Let me have the list of the current ones, Ross, and I'll see what we've got."

He nodded. "Ma'am."

I left him printing out sheet after sheet of paper with the awful statistics of our current missing children and walked to the kettle perched on top of a fridge in the corner of the office. The statistics were bad. Front line cops were overstretched and the regular kids flew far below their radars. Children's services were pushed. We were in a constant battle with them about actions, responsibilities and who took the lead on preventing further missing episodes. Kids whom it was felt would return of their own volition were given minimal time by the cops. The attitude was that the low risk, street-wise kids, were too much trouble and time, when radios were a constant chatter in a response cop's ear with control room operators waiting to send them out to the next job. The officer doing the required return home visit would be satisfied with the fact they had seen the child home and safe, and wouldn't always push for information on where they had been, who they had been with and what they had done, especially if the child was surly and uncooperative. Their supervising officers often did limited checks, enough to tick the boxes of the computerised COMPACT system software, set up in response to some government report into a kid who didn't return and ended up on a slab like ours.

The kettle boiled and broke my thoughts. "Who's for tea, coffee?" I shouted across the rumblings of work. Several shouts of "Me!" went up and I shook my head. They had probably sat there waiting for me to get back and make the drinks. A senior officer making drinks is unheard of, but tea is a weakness and I'm always refilling my cup.

With drinks made, I sat at my desk with the missing person reports Ross had printed out.

Sixteen children missing. In our division alone. And these were the kids who had matched the wide age criteria. I knew if the child wasn't in this pile, we would have to look wider than the city centre. The reports were dismal to read. Each one was pretty basic on its own. Child's name, address, age, and date, time and circumstances last seen. Whether they had prepared by taking anything with them and also how many times they had previously been missing. I reached out for my drink as I let my eyes scan the information, but quickly focused on my cup as fingers hit scalding tea. It jettisoned across my desk and left a line of drops in its wake across the documents. "Fuck." I looked around my office, but had nothing to hand, so I pulled on the drawer of the printer in the corner of my office. I yanked out a few sheets of blank paper, but they failed to mop up the tea and simply moved the watery mess around further. I could do without this. There was so much here, so much to get my head around.

I binned the paper, sat back down and continued to read. It absorbed me. All I had wanted to do was check to see if our girl was in here, but the mess of the children's lives had caught my attention. I sat and read them all, and then cross checked other police systems to see what else was known about them and other people in their lives. It was heavy going. A pattern emerged for some of our regular missing kids. Alcohol issues, *boyfriends* over twenty-five for kids as young as thirteen years. Some kids returned home with money or clothes with no explanation, as well as jewellery and mobile phones. Secrets and lies.

Eventually I noticed the time on the computer monitor. Three hours had passed. I looked at the paper mountain on my desk, with lists and mind maps where I'd attempted to make some sense of what I'd read. Alone, in isolation, these kids looked to be unruly and insolent, railing against the rules of adults. Adults they only saw as being there to make their lives miserable, when the reality was the parents were beyond the end of their tethers, asking for help, but being stonewalled because their kids ticked the too difficult box. I needed to move forward.

I picked up the printouts I had accumulated and carried them through the major incident room, down the dreary grey carpet-tiled corridor to the office of Evie Small. Not only was Evie a brilliant researcher, she was my closest friend. She always had an ear, was energetic to the extreme and made me smile, even when I thought it was no longer possible. Today though, I needed her skills; she had the ability to search multiple databases and absorb huge amounts of information, which she would then use to produce some brilliant research packages and statistics to work with. She was the darling of our working world. As I walked through her dirty blue door, I could see she was engrossed in what she was doing, leaning over her keyboard, her hair a mass of spirals, hung around her head. She heard me enter, peered up from what she was working on, turned her head and looked over the top of her bright angular glasses, smiling a greeting at me.

"I heard you had a tough one, Hannah, how goes it?"

I dropped onto the chair next to her and sighed. "Shit, Evie. We've got little to go on and we're waiting on a lot of results from the CSU. We don't have an identification. DNA was taken at the PM but, again, it's something we have to wait on and it won't automatically give us an answer if she's not a misper or her DNA hasn't been taken. We even have to consider she may not have been reported yet." I ran my hands through my hair as I spoke. "The possibles feel limitless. I've read through some of our misper reports." I waved the mass of paper at her. "The lives of these kids are incredible, the way they survive, but I think I became a little sucked in and got disorganised when reading through them. Can you have a look and see if any of them could be our victim or if there are any potentials? There's a description of her in there somewhere that will help you. I'm not sure what I've managed to do with it, but it's in there. If you could find potential matches I'd be grateful." I looked her in the eyes. "Please?"

"Grey's got me pulling figures on the recent spate of aggravated robberies we've had in the city centre, but I can shove them to the side for this. Let me see what you've got." She held out her perfectly manicured hand, her nails were in a dark purple today, and I gave her the stack of work I had created.

"Thank you. I owe you. You know that don't you?"

"You bet you do. Next time we're out, it's mojitos all the way for me courtesy of a very grateful Hannah." She grinned. I leaned forward and wrapped my arms around her.

"Thanks, Evie."

"No worries, sweetie, I'll let you know what I get. Oh and next time you come in; fetch coffee, not just handfuls of the rainforest!"

As I left Evie's office I nearly collided with Sally who was walking with her head down and pushing the palms of her hands down her jeans as though drying them off.

"I'm sorry." She lifted one hand up to her chest as she jumped. Her face looked drawn. Pale. Worried. Something was wrong, but I couldn't put my finger on what it was. She was distracted. I needed to talk with her, so this was as good a time as any. If I talked while we walked, at least I wouldn't make any concerns obvious to the rest of the team or make her feel singled out in front of them. Being such a close team, it was difficult to keep doubts private or below the office gossip radar. Every cross word, personal call or bad mood is seen, heard and remarked on. Even well intentioned concerns voiced could make a work day hard. I understood that.

"Are you okay?" I asked as we dropped into step beside each other.

"Yes, ma'am. Why, is something wrong with my work?"

"No, not at all. I've noticed you seem a little off today." We stopped and faced each other. The office door not far away. "Not quite yourself."

She dropped her eyes to the floor and crossed her arms over her chest. There was something she didn't want to tell me. If it was something the force needed to be aware of, to protect itself and Sally, then I needed to know what it was. I also wanted to know if I could help.

"Sally?"

She seemed to consider her response before she opened her mouth to speak. I could hear the chatter of the office beyond the door.

"I'm sorry. There are a few things at home." She raised her face as she spoke, her eyes glistened. Swallowing hard and blinking, she dropped her head back down.

We all had personal lives outside work. We had to try and leave them at the door and focus on the task at hand when we come into work. "Is there anything you need from us? From me?"

"No. Work will do me good. It will keep me occupied. I thought it was."

She thought she had kept her issues hidden, she meant. "Are you okay to carry on today or do you need some time?"

"I'm good."

There was more troubling her than she wanted to let on. I would keep an eye on her.

9

After the team had identified all the child sex offenders with hands-on convictions living in a half-mile radius of the dump site we had split into teams of two and headed out. Ross and I were just off Mansfield Road. The outside of the address looked sad, uncared for. The curtains were drawn, the garden unkempt. A green wheelie-bin was dumped in front of the gate. I couldn't tell whether it was to protect the resident of the address from visitors or the rest of the street from him. I elbowed my way past it, not wanting to use my hands on the rubbish filled container. Ross wrinkled up his nose as he followed. I rapped on the top section of the door, the cold glass harsh against my bare knuckles.

"Think he's in, boss?" Ross asked.

"We'll soon see," I answered in response to a stupid question. Wishing that I had brought a pair of gloves to the office, I rubbed my hands together.

"Who is it?" A shout from behind the door.

"Police, Mr Adams. Open the door please," I shouted back. I knew he wouldn't want us on his doorstep for long, drawing attention from his neighbours. He'd asked the question though, so I was more than happy to answer him.

A key turned in the lock and a chain was dragged across its bracket before the door opened. Mr Adams stood in front of us in distressed and grubby grey jogging bottoms and a similar coloured T-shirt, frayed around the sleeves and hemline. Dark stains spread out from the neck and armpits. I made a conscious effort not to turn my nose away in disgust as the odour of stale beer and cigarettes wafted from him.

He narrowed his eyes. "What do you want? I don't have a visit organised with you."

I stepped forward, forcing him to take a step back into the hallway. "We need to ask you some routine questions, Mr Adams. I'm sure you want to help us with our inquiries and get us on our way as quickly as possible."

He looked from me to the six-foot frame of Ross and back again. "You'd better be quick or I'm going to put in a complaint of harassment." He backed further away from the doorway. A move I took as an invitation in, so I stepped over the rather dirty threshold. Nick Adams stopped moving once we were inside and the door to his neighbours' view was closed. "What do you want?" I got the feeling he didn't want us further into his home and I didn't have valid grounds at this point to push him for entry. I opted for politeness, and with great restraint I asked the questions we needed answering. As I spoke the left side of Adams top lip quivered. His mouth parted and the quivering lip turned upwards in a sneer, wet pink flesh lifting outwards. Cigarette odour leaked through his now open mouth from the depth of his body. I watched as he lifted his hand to his mouth, ran his tongue across a finger, waited a beat then placed it under his nose and breathed in. Ross stepped forward, his shoulders back, bringing his height into full effect. The sneer lingered.

"Mr Adams?"

Nick Adams' explanation of where he was the previous night held. It might not have been comfortable, but he was in the pub with people he could loosely call friends. People I would call fellow sex offenders. Certain public houses were known haunts for them. Places they felt safe. The restrictions on registered sex offenders may be in place to protect children but they didn't prevent them fraternising with fellow offenders. Offenders who built their lives around trying to fit in, to appear invisible. People knowing what they had done always made their lives difficult. Fit in or stay hidden were their only real options. This stuck in my throat like a piece of barbed wire. Sex offenders gathering, exchanging notes and suggestions, and leering at any unsuspecting young girls who didn't realise the place they had entered was such a hell hole. I didn't subscribe to the suggestion they could be rehabilitated. A bit like boxing going underground if the sport was stopped for health reasons, only more necessary for those taking part. They could no more stop their sexual interest in children than I could stop breathing. Maybe some managed to curb their actions, but I wasn't sold on that either.

Ross growled out his thanks for Adams' time, we left and moved on to the next on our list, a large five bedroom family home that belonged to a wealthy offender.

10

The contrast between Adams and Derek Habden was stark. He had a wife and a large, well-kept house in Sherwood. Where Adams had been dirty and seedy, Habden oozed class and cleanliness, though no amount of cleanliness would get Habden anywhere close to godliness with the offences he had racked up. His PNC record showed several offences for sexual assaults on teenagers, but a clever and expensive barrister had managed to convince a jury his client was not the type of man who needed to turn unwanted attention on to a teenager new to adulthood. It was, he claimed, the females who had made up the allegations after his client, a community man, respected amongst his peers and friends, had rejected their advances, advances made in an effort to progress their own social standing. The jury bought this. Habden was great at projecting the good, honest man. Why indeed, would he want females barely out of childhood? Unfortunately for Habden he was caught again, and the last time was an offence he couldn't get out of. The girl was fourteen. His defence claimed Habden could not have known she was fourteen because her dress sense and make-up indicated otherwise, her behaviour, provocative. His previous bad character was brought in to play and Habden was found guilty, given a suspended sentence, placed on the sex offenders register and ordered to complete a sex offender's programme.

The conversation was a lot more difficult than the one we'd had with Adams. He was arrogant. Ross bristled every time Habden opened his mouth.

"You understand I do not have to answer your questions, don't you, inspector?" he asked, making the word *inspector* seem dirty. I felt the movement in Ross as his shoulders went back yet again.

"I appreciate your time, Mr Habden."

"I was at home with my wife, as I am every evening."

I looked across to Lorraine Habden; her black hair hung down the sides of her narrow face, making her appear thinner, almost skeletal. She managed to look down her nose at us and nod her concession at the same time. She was a small woman, one who had stood by her husband during some pretty damning evidence and who felt vindicated by a not guilty verdict from a jury. It didn't explain her demeanour in the face of a guilty verdict a year later. I presumed she still bought his lies, it was either that, or she was afraid to go it alone without the upstanding man by her side.

"Derek has been at home since five-fifteen yesterday. I don't know why you feel the need to persecute my husband. It was all a misunderstanding."

"You're sure he was here all evening?" Ross prompted her to respond to the same question again.

"As she has already stated, constable, we were together the entire time. She is not a stupid woman and was very capable of understanding the question the first time you asked it. Unless you intend to arrest Lorraine or me, I do believe you are leaving," Habden interjected. Lorraine looked from us to him, then down to the floor.

"Thank you for your time." I nodded my assent to Ross and turned to leave. "I hope we don't need to attend again, Mrs Habden." I looked her in the eyes. I could see her hope waning. There is only so much a wife can take. I handed her my business card. I held my surprise as she took the card from me. I'd left her with more to think about.

11

She heard him before she saw him. A door somewhere past the room she was in creaked on its hinges. A sound that represented terror. She held her breath and attempted to stay quiet, be as small as she could, hoping to be invisible. She shuffled on her knees, backwards across the sticky plastic until her bare feet hit wire bars. They weren't very wide and one of the bars went between her toes. Her hand went to her mouth to stifle the sound as she cried out. He didn't like her to make a noise. It made him upset. She moved her hand down to her toes and rubbed between them. Any relief from the pain, however small, helped. She looked down at her feet as she rubbed, still trying to force herself further back, smaller. They were stained: the yellow of urine, of vivid red and purple bruises, and plain old brown shades of dirt. The small lamp plugged in on the floor in the corner offered the opportunity to see herself and her surroundings clearer. They were imprinted in her head now. Every inch of the room etched into her mind's eye. She knew where the cat came in to pee, in the corner under the old-style school desk. The girl knew the time-worn Shackleton chair with its well sunken seat, all faded flowers and leaves, the wooden legs scratched, possibly by the visiting cat.

She jumped at the sound of the metal bolt as it was dragged across the barrel. Rust and age grated together in a squealing whine. Wrapping her arms around her body, knees up to her chest, she pushed further back into the corner, eyes cast down.

"Hello, my little angel, how are you today?"

She didn't move.

"You must be hungry. I brought tomato soup, not too hot; I wouldn't want you to be ungrateful. Would you like it?"

She was hungry. She didn't want to speak to him, but she was so, so hungry and she could smell the food. The need for survival was strong. She lifted her head but fear grasped hard as he peered through the bars at her. Her head dropped. Eyes back to down to the floor.

"You need to keep your strength up, you've got to eat."

She nodded but didn't look up.

Slender fingers with filed nails fiddled with the padlock on the cage door; within a moment the plastic soup bowl and disposable spoon were set down inside.

"Eat it up; we can't have you fainting on us."

She didn't move, and she wouldn't move, until he had left. Aftershave added to the myriad of vile smells already in the enclosed space.

"Okay, I know you'll eat it. Enjoy. I'll collect it later." A smile flickered across his narrow lips.

As soon as he had left the room she allowed a real breath. It hurt, her chest hurt, breathing felt like a massive undertaking. She wondered if bones were broken. They felt broken. She felt broken.

She tried not to eat all the food she was given. She never knew what was in it. Not all the time. But she was hungry today and she shovelled the stale, mouldy chunks of bread and lukewarm soup into her mouth. When she'd finished she pushed the bowl towards the cage door and shuffled back to her corner. Her eyes began to feel heavy. The edges of her vision were hazy. She knew what was happening, she couldn't stop it. It gave relief from the pain if nothing else. She put her head on the floor, with her hands underneath to protect it, then closed her eyes and gave in.

12

I pulled the 308 into the small parking space that Central police station provided. The car park was a place we shared with the fire service in the next building and was cramped, to say the least, having space for about twenty vehicles in total. The temperature gauge in the car read five degrees. It hadn't warmed much. My jaw tightened, forcing tension further up my head. I pushed the door open as far as it would go without risk of scratching paintwork from the adjacent vehicle, breathed in and squeezed myself out. Ross grunted as he attempted to do the same on the other side, and muttered a curse as he managed to extricate himself and slam the door closed. We crossed the small patch of concrete and entered the dilapidated station through the rear door, climbing the stairs to the major incident room. I left Ross in charge of making the drinks, and checked my emails. There was one from Evie.

Going on the description I'd given her, she hadn't found a match between local missing children and the child in the mortuary. She said she would look at the recorded missing kids for the rest of the county.

In the incident room, over the round of insipid drinks made by Ross, we debriefed the interviews we'd conducted with the sex offenders. Our third interviewee had a cast-iron alibi as he had been locked up in the cells overnight for a drunk and disorderly, and the fourth had notified us about a week's holiday he planned and a follow-up phone call to the B & B lady confirmed he had gone.

"I didn't like Habden at all," Ross offered the group while he stuffed a ham salad on brown into his mouth. Mayonnaise dolloped out and onto his chin.

I sighed. "If it went on whom we liked, Ross, the cells would be full of sleaze bags."

He let out a grunt and wiped his chin with the back of his hand. I could see he wasn't happy with the situation and the type of people we had to deal with in the process of this inquiry. He needed to get his head around it though. It was necessary to get into these people, this world, if we were to find out what had happened to our girl and, more importantly, who she was.

Aaron waved his pocket book at me. "We didn't fare much better. One of them, Darren Scott, doesn't have anyone to verify he was at home all night wanking into his tissues, but there's nothing to say he wasn't either. The other three have weak alibis we would need to look into further. It feels like a complete waste of an afternoon." Sally sat and nodded her agreement as she picked bits of salad out of the small cob in her hand. Her face wrinkled in disgust at the tomato as it dropped onto the paper bag it had been held in.

"And Martin," I asked Martin Thacker, the longest serving DC on my team. "How did yours go?" He leaned back in his chair, his shirt buttons straining across his paunch, his arms crossed behind his head.

"Yeah, pretty much the same as you. They were either "in all night alone" with a "girlfriend" or in the boozer. There's room to get them firmed up, but I didn't get the feeling any of them were too worried about being tied to a body. They may have been a bit twitchy about being linked with a child generally, but not with a dead one. There's stuff to check anyway."

"Okay, so we have a few lines of inquiry to follow up, but no one gets the feeling we need to push harder on anyone, am I correct?"

Nods of agreement went around the room. It baulked them to say they didn't think these guys had done anything, but they didn't think the offenders we had spoken to had killed the girl found in the alleyway. Even if they did have a gut feeling one of them was involved, we needed more than instinct, we needed evidence. I was disappointed because we didn't have an identity for our girl and we were no closer to identifying an offender either.

"Right," I said, standing, "so the plan of attack now is to put

in the leg work and corroborate those alibis one way or another."
As I walked away I could hear the team muttering; how they
weren't happy about having to deal with child sex offenders and
how they were already feeling a layer of grime around them just
from talking to them.

My office wasn't so much of an office as a goldfish bowl
within a corner of the incident room. Shabby horizontal blinds,
lined with years of settled dust, hung on the inside of the glass to
provide privacy, should it be required. I leaned back into my chair
and looked out.

Uniform cops were milling in and out as they completed the
tasks of collecting CCTV in the area of the dump site and house to
house inquiries that had been requested of them. All information
coming in to the room would be checked and input onto HOLMES
– Home Office Large Major Enquiry System – which would keep
track of all nominals, phone numbers, vehicles, and a multitude of
other items brought up throughout the investigation and link them
to each other, as and when necessary. It would also print out
actions for officers to conduct following the input of data by an
allocated receiver for the system. Its ability to cross reference the
intelligence made it an invaluable piece of kit in an inquiry this
size, but I was always a believer in human instinct as well, and
instinct was the tool I favoured. Because of this, I sometimes

butted heads with more senior officers who thought HOLMES was the singular way to work. All too often I had seen people's instincts turn out right and I wasn't willing to quite let go of the old fashioned "nose" for a collar. The phone on my desk rang as I watched my team out beyond the glass partitions.

"Hannah, it's Catherine," Detective Superintendent Walker announced herself.

"Ma'am." I tapped the jotter pad with my pen out of an automatic frustration and a need to do something with my hands.

"How is the investigation progressing?"

I attempted not to sigh into the handset. "The post-mortem has been conducted. There was a lot of evidence of trauma over an extended period of time. She was bound at her hands and feet and also had something placed around her throat. Cause of death looks to be asphyxiation. We haven't got an ID, but I've got Evie working on it. She's already checked out divisional missing children but didn't find any matches so she's now widening the search criteria." The lack of ID wouldn't please her.

"Any idea on how long it will take to get an identification, Hannah? The press office is on my back and the command team are paying attention to this one."

The politics of the job were something I hated with a passion. I joined to catch the bad guys, but the further I progressed through the promotion boards, the more politics were involved and the less policing took place. I wouldn't go for promotion again. I wanted to police, keep my feet on the ground, investigate and get a good honest collar. "No, ma'am, I'm afraid not. We're working the case and looking at all angles. The girl isn't known to us as her fingerprints haven't brought an ID, so it's a matter of waiting for some forensic results to come in and the system searches to be completed." Doodled triangles appeared on the jotter paper in front of my keyboard.

I looked up as Ross stuck his head around the door frame.

"Keep me updated please, Hannah."

"Yes, ma'am."

I had barely got the handset back on its cradle when Ross spoke. "We've got a possible ID. In Norwich."

13

It was now dark. The roads were alive with a river of white and red lights. Well-lit interiors shone out from old and beautiful buildings, and modern and glassy architecture, making the city glow. Cars were filled with drivers impatient to get home. It took close to forty-five minutes to get through the traffic from Central.

The place I called home wasn't cosy or warm; it held little in the way of memories. It was functional and clean with glossy kitchen sides, low slung sofas, an old battered wooden coffee table bearing my laptop. A single photograph of my parents on their wedding day hung in a frame on the wall. I'd chosen to have one from way back then, as I knew those times were happy and any memories I had now were tainted and troubled. I loved them very much and I missed Mum.

The location, Park Rock on Castle Boulevard, bristled with character. It was a fairly new development, built at the base of Nottingham castle. At night-time, from the Boulevard, I could see the lit cave entrances. It was breathtaking and I could, and did, sit and look at it for hours. I loved this location, but even with its obvious beauty and surrounding history I didn't have a deep sense of connection and I wasn't sure why.

I dragged my overnight bag from under the bed and started throwing in the few items I'd need. It had already been a long day and I hoped, after speaking with the Norwich cops, we could talk to the girl's family and attempt to give them the information they needed to process their child's death. It would then be too late to drive back.

Clean clothes and underwear were thrown in the bag, together with the usual basics. This investigation was hitting me emotionally. It was always one of the more difficult parts of the job, dealing with a bereaved family, and not one I looked forward to. Conveying information to grief stricken parents was made difficult by the overwhelming loss and, sometimes, the guilt they carried. Their ability to absorb facts diminished as emotions were raw and wounds open. I struggled to wade through the obvious quagmire they created without getting myself caught up and bogged down in it. I often struggled to maintain a distance with relatives, but distance was a necessary barrier to an emotional minefield.

I tossed my mobile phone charger into the overnight bag. Walking back into the living room, I picked up the laptop from the coffee table and packed that away amongst my clean clothes in case I wanted to make notes later. I was supposed to be seeing Ethan tonight. I texted him as it was easier than making the call, letting him know where I was going, and that I would call him when I returned. There was no reply. This annoyed me. It left me swinging in the wind with no opportunity to counter or explain. It was like the thing with him always leaving before morning and more often than not, leaving as soon as I nodded off to sleep in an evening after we made love. It gave a feeling of vagueness, something I couldn't quite catch hold of, and I wasn't comfortable with that.

I pulled the zipper across the bag and dropped it on the floor near the door. As I was packed and waiting for Aaron I poured myself a quick glass of red wine. It tasted good as it slid down my throat, smooth and warm. The built-up tension that had been gathering over me like a hurricane cloud dissipated with a couple of slugs. A car horn sounded. We were off to Norwich and the dead girl's parents.

14

There was a reserved quietness about the trip. Aaron drove the works' Skoda Octavia estate. It was in pristine condition and still had that new car smell about it. He was fastidious about keeping it clean. You'd find him at the end of every week, washing and polishing in preparation for the following week. If someone had left food wrappers inside when he went to use it, he would talk incessantly about how dirty it and they were, for at least five minutes. It was rare that wrappers were left in cars now. I sat beside him as he drove.

My work bag was on the back seat. It was stuffed with note books and reports which included initial house to house inquiry results and post-mortem notes. I had the missing person report Norwich had emailed laid out across my lap. My overnight bag had been slung into the boot along with Aaron's.

"Seeing anything?" he asked of the misper report I was attempting to read.

"A lot of fuzzy lines." I squeezed my eyes together, opened them and tried again. It was no good. I hated reading in cars. "What do we have to say this Norwich girl is ours?" I asked for the third time since I'd heard she could be our victim.

"As our missing persons database didn't bring about any matches, Ross contacted the National Missing Persons Bureau, who are now a part of the Serious Organised Crime Agency. It was a bit of a long shot as their system is only as good as the forces who comply with the requirement to update them with high risk MIPSERS within forty-eight hours."

He listed off the facts I already knew, keeping his focus on the road.

"Their database brought up several potential matches in various parts of the country, on basic details such as height, ethnicity, hair colour and approximate age, but then the DNA results from the post-mortem came in and Ross submitted it to the Bureau who conducted a speculative search on their DNA database, which again has its own teething problems. Do you realise how few officers seize a toothbrush or hairbrush on the first report of a missing person, thereby slowing things down?" He was off on a tangent. I didn't know if he expected an answer. He didn't look across at me, but kept his eyes on the road and his hands in the ten, two position. "The Bureau holds a huge physical collection of body parts as well as having the massive database of missing people and unidentified dead bodies. Seriously. Body parts."

It was time for me to push him forward. "And our girl?"

"Well the DNA we submitted came back with a match."

That was it. The one sentence I wanted, but he hadn't finished. "The local cops on the missing girl must have done a great job because her DNA was on the database within required time limits, which goes to show they were serious about the investigation and graded her as high risk, so what does that mean to our case and how she got here?"

I didn't know the answer. "Our match, does she have a name?" I asked.

"Yeah. She's Rosie Green. Fifteen years old, model daughter and student until the few weeks in the run up to her going missing. First time missing, turns up murdered in our city. It's a long way from home, Hannah, how's she ended up here?"

The question bothered me. How did a child from Norwich turn from model child to a dead body, badly beaten and tortured, behind a dumpster in Nottingham, some one hundred and twenty miles away?

15

It was nearly eight p.m. when we landed at Bethel Street Police Station, Norwich. Though it was dark, I immediately liked the look of the building. It was a substantial construction made with two different sized bricks, and white, worn wooden window frames giving it an old build look. The genteel feel the place had was compounded further by the lights dotted down the street, black painted, round posts, with old fashioned glass tubes emitting the light providing a picture postcard image.

The front of the station had minimal parking outside, reserved for police vehicles. Aaron steered the Octavia into a space and we walked into the station.

DI Clive Tripps, the SIO running the investigation, met us at the front counter. We shook hands and introductions were made. Clive was a thin and wiry man. His handshake was firm, though his hands rather cool. His green eyes met mine and he smiled.

"I'm glad you managed to come down, I know the family will appreciate it. She's been missing two weeks and they need some answers." As he talked he opened internal doors by punching numbers into keypads on the walls. Green lights and a beep indicated access had been granted. We walked down the corridor until we came to some stairs on our right. We started to climb.

"I suppose the main issue for the family is they need to be told we believe we have her body and they need to identify her. What do they know about this?" I asked.

"I phoned ahead and let them know I needed to see them this evening and that I'd bring someone else involved in the investigation with me. But I haven't told them any information past that. I didn't want to end up in a difficult conversation on the phone. I thought it better to speak with you first. As you'd expect, they're in pieces."

We walked into a well lit room with an array of desks and chairs, each with its own computer terminal and, besides those, piles of folders I knew contained more jobs, more injured people and more affected lives.

"Family consists of Mum and Dad, no other children, so once they know she's gone, they're going to have to try and support themselves through this. It's all too difficult for them to take much in at the moment, but I get the feeling they're expecting to hear bad news."

We pulled a few chairs together and sat as a group around the largest desk in the centre of the room. Two detectives from Clive's team joined us. They were introduced as Nima Khan and Michael Lane, both involved in the investigation into Rosie's disappearance. Nima had a considered calm about her, a practicality and pragmatism I liked. Michael, though older, had an enthusiasm for the job I rarely saw in such a long serving detective. Between them they organised drinks and a couple of bars of chocolate. I liked the pair; they rolled off each other well. Clive Tripps had a well run team. We discussed what each force had in relation to their respective investigations before we made the house call none of us wanted to do.

"What's her family history like?" Aaron questioned.

"It's a good family home. Regular school attendance. No social services involvement. No criminal history on the parents, or Rosie. School gave glowing reports, but said she let her school work slip for the last few weeks. She became sulky and uninterested. She snubbed her friends and she became very isolated. Mum and Dad both say she continued to go out after school. She told them she was with friends, when in fact she wasn't, and her friends didn't have a clue about where she went," Nima relayed from memory.

"Can we talk to her friends again, and her teachers? Maybe in the morning before we head back?"

Nima nodded. "Of course. We'll set it up with the school as soon as they open tomorrow."

I rubbed my head again. A habit I seemed to have acquired,

but it had been a long and exhausting day. I turned to Aaron. "I think we need to go and do that knock on the parents. The sooner the better for them I think. If I go with Clive, can you stay and collate all the paperwork they have here, and make copies for us to take back?"

"Absolutely," he nodded, straightening his tie. Michael eyed him over, his own tie loose and pulled to the side. He kept any thoughts he had to himself.

Clive spoke to Nima. "Are you okay to help DS Stone with the file for Rosie and also get him the number for the school ready for tomorrow?"

"Yes, doing that now," Nima replied leaning forward and grabbing a folder from the desk in front of her.

The team ran well. I took a breath, "Okay, Clive, let's go and see Mum and Dad."

16

The Greens lived in a small terraced cottage in Lakenham, South Norwich. The wooden front door was old, with paint peeling around the edges and in the grooves of the panels. Tiny flakes of blue were scattered along the doorstep. There was a family car parked in front. With the glow of the sodium street light I couldn't make out its colour. It bore the same worn look the house had.

The door was opened by a stout man, hair thinning on top, his soft grey eyes asking a question he didn't want an answer to.

"Mr Green, thank you for seeing us. This is DI Hannah Robbins. May we come in?" asked Clive.

George Green looked dazed and uncertain. He stepped aside.

"Yes." He paused. "I'm sorry. Come in."

The house was neat, though I could see a layer of dust settled across the furniture. A sign it hadn't been cared for since Rosie had gone missing. It had the feel of a family home. Family photographs adorned the walls on faded floral wallpaper. Happier times captured and memories held in thin frames. Smiling faces, arms wrapped around each other. Three people whose lives were now shattered. I could see Rosie as she had been, not the cold grey corpse in the alley – or that lay on the steel table of Jack Kidner. This was a girl full of hopes and dreams, full of love and joy, secure in the arms of her parents. Parents who no doubt had dreamt of a future for their daughter, a future with a career, aspirations and a grandchild maybe. I looked at the woman in the chair in front of us. From the pictures I saw she had aged ten years. She looked down at her hands grasped in her lap, fingers tightly wrapped together. She didn't want to look at us. She knew why we were here and she didn't want that moment to come. George Green went over to her, crouching down as though to a small child you want to reassure. He took her shaking hands into his. She raised her head to him, eyes red and swollen. Fear vibrated off her. I took a deep breath and tried to steady myself, quell the emotion building inside me. Somehow it was possible to work with the dead and hear their stories through the eyes of a pathologist, but being so close to the emotional pain of the family was something different entirely. It latched onto me, worked at my throat and pushed up from the inside out. I had to breathe through this. This was their pain, not mine. I had to breathe.

17

Informing someone you believe their child to be dead is one of the most difficult jobs I ever have to do. Dealing with the bodies is something you can attempt to detach from. You have to, otherwise you will always be haunted by the last moments of their lives and it doesn't help anyone. You have a job to do and you need to do it well. People's lives are important. But the grief and pain of those left behind is heartbreaking. For me, it's temporarily impossible to separate myself from. The feeling is raw and tangible and I'd be more concerned by anyone who didn't feel some effect themselves. It was hard but I had to be strong for George and Anne Green. To tell them the facts as we knew them. Death is shocking in a child, but a violent death is unimaginable for a parent to face. Mr Green had clenched his body, holding it all in. Mrs Green had crumbled, falling in on herself like a pack of cards touched by the faintest of breezes. The moment Rosie's killer put his hands around her throat and squeezed the life out of her, he had done the same to her parents.

Clive started the engine and pulled away from the curb. As we went out of view of the terraced cottage, I put my head in my hands and allowed myself a moment to feel. A child was dead, her parents' lives shattered and as of yet, we were nowhere near knowing who or why.

I needed some human warmth. Strong arms and comfort. Ethan. I pushed the thought away. This wasn't the time or the place.

"It's hard, I know." Clive broke into my reverie and I remembered where I was.

Half an hour later I found myself in a small Italian restaurant, the Trattoria Rustica next to the city cathedral. Its wooden beams, brickwork, the occasional waft of warm garlic on a passing plate and the cosy atmosphere soon helped to relax my mood. Around the table sat Aaron, Clive, Nima and Michael, along with Chris Stewart, another detective from the team. In front of me was a plate of taglietelle and a glass of Southern Comfort on the rocks. The idea of food hadn't crossed my mind for most of the day and I hadn't considered I might be hungry, but now I really was. I looked around the table and saw heavy eyes within friendly faces. I needed some rest but the couple of drinks I'd had warmed me and mellowed the hardship of the day. Picking up the glass I knocked back the remainder.

Chris chewed on his food and spoke through it. "So the Greens are going to see Rosie tomorrow morning and do the official identification. I'll drive them."

"Who's the official FLO?" The FLO was a family liaison officer assigned to a family during serious investigations. They would get to know the family well.

"I am," Chris continued. "They're struggling to find reasons behind why she went missing. They blame themselves."

"Which, as we know, often happens," interjected Michael.

Chris swallowed his food and continued. "They said they tried to talk to her. Well Anne did, George doesn't find it easy to have the serious conversations; he's been more of the silent hand holding type. He left the talks to Anne. He said Rosie talked more to her mum, so he was happy for it to be that way, but it was an easy excuse for him. You can see it eating away at him now." More food went up on a fork to his mouth as he continued to talk. "Anne tried, but said Rosie would clam up. Anne thinks there was a lot of competition amongst the girls to look good and make an impression. Anne and George didn't like her wearing make-up for school and Rosie was struggling to fit in with that level of competitiveness." I watched as Chris moved his food around his mouth as he spoke, like a washing machine on a slow cycle. "She clammed up and shut down to them."

I raised my hand to attract the attention of the waiter.

"Another Southern Comfort please. Anyone else?"

"A pint please."

"Make it two."

"Three."

"Wine," requested Nima.

"So she's troubled at school, she's not talking to Mum and Dad. Who's her closest friend?" I asked.

"I talked to her friends," responded Nima. "Caroline Manders was her friend from infants, through juniors and up to the secondary school. When we interviewed Caroline she stated it was very recent, Rosie's behaviour being a bit out of kilter. When Rosie went missing, Caroline found it hard, she was absent from school a lot of the time herself. Her parents said she wasn't coping and they didn't feel they could send her in the way she was. It's hit her hard."

"Will Caroline's mother allow us to talk to her again? We could do with a chat in the morning if possible."

"They're pretty protective and Caroline appears to be quite cloistered by them, but I don't see an issue with that. Give me a minute and I'll call her mum and let her know you will be dropping by."

The drinks arrived as Nima left the table to call Caroline's parents. It was late and I wasn't sure how happy they would be with a late night call, but that was the difficulty when a murder investigation crossed county lines. We usually found we upset a few people. I hoped we could counter this tomorrow when we spoke to them. I waited until Aaron picked up his pint and took a slug of my drink, its warmth, soothing.

Nima returned. "All set up with Caroline's parents. They were a little reticent at first but said they want to do all they can to help. They asked if you could be there about eight a.m. as they will be dropping Caroline off at school about eight-thirty a.m. She's still feeling fragile after all that's happened to her friend and they want to maintain some semblance of normalcy for her."

We continued to eat our food as we talked about the case in hushed tones so as to not upset the few other diners present at nearby tables. The conversation slipped into small talk of family lives and career aspirations and I felt the weariness wash over me. It was time to go.

I drained the rest of my drink and stood. After nods and good nights all round I departed, leaving Aaron still with his drink in his hand at the table. Outside I wrapped my scarf around my neck against the bitter winds and pushed my chin down deep into it, clenching my fists up tight in my pockets, as I still had no gloves, for the short walk to the hotel on the Prince of Wales Road.

Breakfast was hot and greasy, a good enough way to start the day. Aaron's usual piercing blue eyes looked lacklustre. I'd pulled my hair back, tied it in an elastic band and attempted to cover the dark circles and dull skin with a smattering of foundation.

Though my phone had some missed calls and a couple of text messages, there had been nothing from Ethan through the night. It was possible he was busy, but I didn't like uncertainty.

By seven-thirty a.m. we were at the Bethel Street station. Chris, Nima and Michael were at their desks. I walked into Clive's office to discuss the morning's actions with him.

"Good morning." He smiled, his face friendly and open. I was finding he was a man I could work with.

"Morning, Clive. Thanks for last night."

"You're more than welcome. Did you sleep okay in the hotel?"

"Not bad." I sat in the chair opposite him, crossing my legs at my knees, work bag on the floor to the side. "Are you happy coming to see Caroline with me if Aaron and one from your team go to the school to chat to some of the other kids? If Aaron and I split the tasks we need to do we can get it done in half the time and then catch each other up later." Even though I preferred to do everything myself, I trusted Aaron and his judgment. Sometimes I wished he would think before he spoke, but he was a bloody good cop and I was glad to have him on my team.

"Absolutely. Give me five minutes and we'll head out."

"Sounds good. One other thing I want to discuss with you though."

Clive looked across at me, his eyebrows raised. "Okay, what is it?"

"How would you feel if I were to request one of my officers comes over and gives you another pair of hands to work on your side of the investigation as a liaison between the two of us? They would, of course, work under you, but I think it would be a good way of keeping the two sides cohesive." It was a big ask. Clive's team worked well. Asking to throw an unknown into the mix was a potential problem.

He relaxed back in his chair. "I see no issue with that. In fact I think it's a great idea and don't know why I didn't think of it first. Who will you send?"

"I'd not got that far," I confessed as I regarded his team through the doorway. It was something I needed to think about.

18

Caroline Manders' slim fingers were unable to stay still. She fiddled with her hair then moved to some imagined mark on the polished wood of the dining table where we were seated, until she settled on rubbing a stain I couldn't see from the hem of her school jumper. The house was old and large. There was a living area as well as the dining room we were in. From here it was impossible to see the rest of the house, but it had the feel of an old build with lots more room than modern day builds offered. It was immaculate with a minimalist feel: beige carpeting and magnolia walls. A large, overbearing framed photograph of the family adorned the main wall, taking centre stage. On the adjacent wall was a print of a Claude Monet painting and these were the only two items in the dining room other than the table and chairs. The family photo showed Donovan and Evelyn Manders, Caroline's parents, sat straight on high backed chairs, with Caroline on the floor between them. The photograph looked to have been taken by a professional, but it made me uneasy. I wondered at Caroline's place in the structure of her family as she sat on the floor at her parents' feet. It felt cold and detached and reminded me of a children are seen-but-never-heard era.

Now, Donovan Manders sat at the head of the table, straight and stiff. Barely a movement from him, other than the regular blink of his eyes. He'd been the epitome of polite and courteous when we arrived, but had said very little since.

I shifted in my seat and looked at Caroline who was sitting uneasily on the edge of the covered carver chair at the opposite end of the table to her father. She was a small girl with large owlish spectacles perched on a narrow nose, so narrow; I was unsure how she managed to keep her glasses in place without them sliding straight off her face.

Her mother fussed with an obvious uncertainty about the circumstances they found themselves in. Evelyn Manders wanted to protect her daughter and that protection looked to include a need to protect her from us. She also knew something bad had happened to Caroline's friend and had told us they wanted to help. I could see this conflict caused obvious upset for Evelyn as she flitted from the kitchen to the dining area we were seated in and back again. First came the cups of tea and then plates of biscuits and cookies, her stiff, spotless half apron bowed tightly around her back, creaseless as it hung from her waist. Her hair was pulled back tight away from her face, which gave a slight impression of a face lift. She fluttered about and smoothed every surface until I could bear it no more.

"Mrs Manders, would you like to sit down with us so we can talk to Caroline. It would be really helpful."

She brushed the velour of the chair she hadn't long vacated until all strands seemed to be laying in the same direction again, and sat back down. Caroline watched silently.

I looked at her now. "Do you know why we are here, Caroline?"

Her mouth moved but it was difficult to make out her response. "About Rosie."

I lifted my voice, hoping she would mirror me and follow suit. "Yes, she went missing didn't she?"

A faint, "Yes."

I leaned forward, resting my elbows on my knees. Clive was holding a relaxed stance on the other side of the table. "Tell us what Rosie was like the weeks before she went missing."

Caroline swallowed and looked at her father who gave a barely perceptible nod.

"She was okay. Maybe a little quieter than usual. She never told me anything."

"Did she have any other friends she did talk to?" asked Clive.

Caroline and Evelyn turned their heads toward Clive. "No. I

don't think so anyway. I never saw her with anyone."

"Did she have anything new you had never seen before, Caroline?" I asked, wondering about gifts from someone new in her life.

Another glance at her father, another nod. Of encouragement? A speck of something removed from the table by Evelyn.

"I didn't see anything and she never showed me anything." She rubbed at the invisible mark on her jumper, her fingers working at the hemline, rubbing and rubbing.

It was time to stop. "It's okay, Caroline. Thank you for talking to us."

Evelyn Manders jumped up before I had chance to move.

"Thank you for your time, Mr and Mrs Manders, we appreciate it." I stood, pulling my business card out of my pocket. "If Caroline thinks of anything else, or if you or your husband can think of anything, please do give us a call, no matter how small or insignificant you think it is."

Donovan Manders unfurled his tall frame from the chair, stepped forward and took the card proffered to his wife from my hand. He made a sharp sight in his well-cut dark grey suit. He leaned down, picking up the briefcase at the side of his chair.

"Thank you for your considerate manner, Detective Inspector. It's been a difficult time for Caroline and we were cautious about allowing further questioning, but I am happy we could help."

It sounded rather like a dismissal. I smiled. "As I said, if anything comes to mind, please call."

Evelyn Manders, removed the plate of cookies from the table and, head down, took them into the kitchen where she busied herself putting them away. Clive walked around the table, placed a hand on Caroline's shoulder and smiled.

"Give us a call if you need anything."

Donovan Manders strode out of the dining room, down the hallway, past the doorway to what I presumed was the living room and opened the front door. His look direct.

Digging into my trouser pocket I removed another work card and handed it to Caroline.

"This has my mobile number on. If you need me, call."

She nodded, putting the card in her trouser pocket, then went about cleaning the hem of her jumper. We took our cue and left the family to their business.

Before Aaron and I headed back to the city we debriefed the

meetings we'd had. Clive and I spoke about the visit with the Manders, while Aaron and Michael talked about the school visit. I voiced my concerns that Caroline could be hiding something from us. "She was pretty closed and needed consent from her father before she spoke. There seemed to be a tight rein about her this morning. It could of course be genuine concern for her well-being and the effects something like this will have on her, but I got a strange feeling from the home and the family. Her body language was edgy."

Clive nodded. "Something was definitely up with Caroline and her mum. Did you see how fast Evelyn got up to let us out? It reminded me of a jack-in-the-box I got as a kid."

"She was certainly unsettled with our presence." I pushed a loose strand of hair out of my eyes as I tried to read my notes. "We need to contact the school again and make sure she's okay and no major welfare issues come up. How about you, Aaron? Any joy with any of her other friends, enemies, school teachers etc.?"

"Pretty much the same as we've already heard. She was a good girl. Things started to go a bit awry without people understanding why, but no one took the time to find out what was happening and then next thing, she's gone. The one conversation of interest though was with the school nurse, Liz Turney. She stated Rosie had come in and asked for a contraceptive advice chat.

These can be held within school in confidence and they aren't obliged to tell parents."

"Great. Kids are being given the ability to have sex, with apparent adult consent, and it's acceptable to keep this info from the parents. Shall we ask Rosie's parents how they feel about that?" It wasn't so much a question, more of a rant. "Great confidentiality. Let's give the kids their own lives attitude and look where it leads us, picking up dead children from behind restaurant waste bins in the middle of the fucking night. Do we get to see the records from the visit or is it still confidential?"

"Liz is gathering the papers this morning and will email them over to us later today," replied Aaron, ignoring the verbal annoyance I had relieved myself of.

"I'm sorry, I get so frustrated by people who fail to see the consequences, the mess we have to pick up. And I hate it when it's kids."

Clive nodded. "I know, don't worry. We'll get statements from all the kids who were friends with her and noticed a change. Teachers too. And we'll get a medical authorisation form signed by Rosie's GP and get her notes, and again, send them over to you. I'll also get the crime scene techs to go through Rosie's bedroom and let you know if anything comes of it."

"Thanks, Clive. We need to head back; I appreciate your

help on this one and will speak with you again soon."
Straightening the papers I had been sifting through I banged the edge of the file against the table, then smoothed down my trousers as I stood. I felt as though I hadn't slept for two days and I imagined I pretty much looked that way. I needed to get home and stand under my shower for a very long time. First though, I knew I had to meet Rosie's parents following the identification and pop in to the mortuary to see if Jack was free to attend a briefing in the morning. It was always good to get everyone involved in the investigation together and see what they brought to the table. Making decisions without knowing what everyone knew down to the small details was a fool's game.

19

The drive back to Nottingham was quicker than the original drive across. It reminded me of the way childhood day trips to the coast worked. Memories of long impatient journeys with siblings sharing the backseat shifted through my mind. The sound of bickering, of who had the most sweets, who could see the most red cars on the roads and who could see the sea first. Always a competition. My younger sister Zoe felt the strain to compete, never content to be the second one to do anything. The journey out was a constant battle between us. Mum and Dad would be worn out trying to appease us, settling into a silent wait for the trip to be over and our energies to be used up on the beach.

The trip back home from the family days out were, by contrast, subdued and quiet, always faster or so it seemed, due to the lack of fighting. The quality family time had, once again, been and gone and was no more than a distant memory, even a few days afterwards. Especially for me. Memories I held on to with a mixture of love, sadness and an overall frustration. I stared out of my passenger side window, at other motorists caught up in their own worlds. Life passing by in a haze of grey asphalt. Now the childhood memories felt disjointed and contaminated and I tried to

Shallow Waters

push them to the back of my mind.

20

Aaron and I managed to find George and Anne Green in the Queen's Medical Centre with Nima and Chris. The world had now completely imploded on them. The confirmation of death would bring a closure and conclusion to the worry and fears keeping them awake at night. At least now they knew she would be returned to them. There would be a period of waiting, for test results and if an offender was likely, her body had to be held for a period of time for the possibility of a defence post-mortem. She would be going home though and they could give her a funeral and a proper goodbye. One they should never have to give, but now they could do it and Rosie would always be close by.

I had thought they looked fragile when I saw them last night, but today, every last shred of anything holding them together was gone. Shadows walked where they used to be. Fibres of people who once existed and once loved a vibrant child they had brought into the world. I took a deep breath and approached.

"Mr and Mrs Green. I'm so sorry. If there is anything you need to ask me or anything I can do for you, then please, don't hesitate to let me know." I waited. The Greens held on to each other, blending into one unit as they fought to stay upright in this cruel world. Anne Green dragged her sunken eyes across to me.

"Do you have the person who did this to our daughter, Inspector Robbins?"

My body tensed. An involuntary reflex to a question I didn't want to answer for these people. Not as things stood now. Knowing who the girl in the mortuary was hadn't helped identify the killer but had served to increase the potential suspect pool and we had no idea how she had gotten from Norwich to Nottingham. I gathered myself and spoke. "I'm sorry, Mrs Green," she stood her ground, gripping the arm of her husband, "but the investigation is new off the ground. We do have two teams working on your daughter's investigation though, one here and one back in Norwich. We're working very hard to follow all leads and we're hopeful to identify and arrest Rosie's killer." I softened my tone and put my hand on her arm. "Chris will be with you during the length of the investigation and we'll be in daily contact with him." I knew it wasn't enough. Fishing in my pocket I pulled out a business card with my contact details on and handed it to her, knowing as I did so, that I was asking for trouble, giving a grieving parent direct contact details. It was what they had Chris, their FLO, for but I couldn't help myself. Their sorrow and pain was so raw and tangible. She took the card, dark liver spots marking the back of her pale, shaking hand. It was all I could offer. It was all we had. Mrs Green sank lower into the arm of her husband, and Chris and Nima took them out of the hospital and back home, towards a life that would never be the same again. It was going to be a long and painful process for them and it left me with a heavy heart.

The incident room was a hive of activity. Extra staff had been drafted in to help with the inquiry. This was a sign the investigation was a big deal. Money wasn't thrown at an investigation unless it was something that could come back and bite the force hard. We had gained a couple of Indexers to work the HOLMES, Diane and Theresa, whom I already knew from previous jobs we had worked. They were good at what they did. Dave Morgan, a local intelligence officer, was working with us full time. Dave knew the area well and knew the people, or rather, he knew the criminals and other persons of interest who lived here. I leaned over his shoulder as I passed his desk and saw names in boxes and intelligence reports covering the monitor.

"We're keeping you busy then," I commented.

"Oh yeah, with some of the nicest people out there I see," he replied.

We had grown into a massive manhunt unit overnight and they were all under my roof.

Martin, Sally and Ross were having five minutes, huddled in

a corner with mugs in their hands, steam rising, indicating they were freshly brewed and my team hadn't been stood there all afternoon. I approached them. Sally looked tired and Ross looked nervous, as though he'd been caught with his hand in the cookie jar.

"Productive trip?" Martin asked with a relaxed ease he always had about him.

"Yes. We made contact with some of Rosie's friends, found out she was interested in contraception advice and had her identified by Mum and Dad."

"That's good then," Sally said. "Not that it's her," she added, "just we know what we are working now and her parents don't have to keep wondering."

"I knew what you meant. It is good." I looked around at them. Martin, a few years off retirement, relaxed and never fazed, still with his great people instincts and drive for the job, Sally, a great detective, always reliable, but carrying some issues I wasn't quite comfortable with and Ross, young and keen, but maybe a bit too keen sometimes. I knew who I was going to send to Norwich for a few weeks, or however long it took us to identify an offender.

"Something has come out of today we need to discuss. Shall we go and grab a few chairs in my office?"

They looked at each other then walked with me. Once seated

I got straight to the point. "We need to send someone to the Norwich side of the investigation." Sally was the one who dropped her head. An instant sign she didn't want the job. It grated my nerves a little, probably because I was tired, but she was usually the first to volunteer for something and this was important. It was unusual for her. A good job she wasn't top of my list to go. "On a short term basis," I added "to bring the two sides of the investigation together, so neither of us misses something crucial."

"Martin…" he nodded his consent before I'd even got the words out. "I'd like you to go. It shouldn't be for too long, but it gives us eyes and ears on the investigation over there and we need the smoothness of having one of our own in there with it."

"No worries. It's a nice town, so I've heard, and as long as they don't put me up in any old dump while I'm down there, it'll be fine." He smiled as he said this. I knew Martin. He'd do a good job and then he'd enjoy the social life afterwards. A few beers with the team after a long shift. His age didn't slow him down, he loved life and his job and he made the most of both.

"Thanks, Martin. Get in touch with finance and sort something out you're happy with."

He walked out of my office with an easy smile and I caught the tail end of a comment about peace from the wife. I'd met his wife and they had a good relationship. No kids but a couple of unruly Labradors. Typical of Martin to make the most of the situation, to see an upside. He was a great guy to have on the ground but his paperwork left something to be desired. I needed to make sure I got regular updates from him.

21

At her desk, Sally put her mug down, woke the monitor and logged back on. But she just stared at whatever it was that she had last been working on. She had let Hannah down. She could see it in her face. The disappointment. Disappointment. It's one of the hardest of emotions to deal with. Anger, pity, hurt, you can deal with those in some way, but disappointment means you've been held in some previously higher regard and you, no-one but you, did anything to lower that regard. And now Hannah was disappointed because she hadn't volunteered to go to Norwich. Not only had she not volunteered, but she'd made it clear she didn't want to go.

She was usually the first to volunteer for jobs no matter what they were. She knew that and she knew she wasn't being a team player right now and it grieved her that she couldn't tell them why. Would they understand if they knew? She wasn't sure, which was why she hadn't confided in anyone. Ross was sweet but he was young. Juvenile. If tested, he could feel his loyalty was to his supervisors and the right thing to do in this situation was to tell them. Martin, she could probably tell. He was Mr calm and reasonable, so he would probably advise her to talk to Hannah herself and she wasn't ready.

There was no way she could go to Norwich. How could she explain it to Tom? A normally placid guy, but he was losing patience lately and they had been butting heads. If Martin hadn't volunteered and she'd been chosen for the job she might have had to come clean and that was the last thing she wanted to do. Not yet anyway. She still had some time. Time to work things out before speaking to the bosses.

22

A couple of hours later, after answering and dealing with a
ridiculous amount of emails, sending one in particular to Evie
requesting she research the social networking sites for any sign of
Rosie, I left the office and went home.

My apartment was as I'd left it: A cup face-down on the
drainer, local papers across the small wooden coffee table along
with a book I was reading. I pulled the stopper from the bottle of
red, already opened on the kitchen worktop, and poured a generous
sized glass. In my bedroom, I stripped, pulled on my lazy jerseys
and then sat on the sofa with my knees up. The day drained away
as I relaxed. The last couple of days seemed to have merged into
one long one, but this was usual on the first few days of a murder
inquiry. I took a deep glug of red and dropped my head, resting it
on the back of the sofa. Tucking my feet under myself I lay quiet
for a while, the glass I was holding resting on the arm of the sofa.

Time slipped silently past and the tension started to ease. The
doorbell chime broke into the peace. Tinkling like broken glass.
High and tight. I took another drink of wine before putting it down
on the table and walked to the door. Ethan's head and shoulders
were pixelated in the security monitor. I buzzed him in.

"Hey." He paused before walking in. I ran a hand through my hair. I knew I looked like shit but he didn't comment, instead he took hold of me by my shoulders and pulled me towards him, his finger ends tight in my back. I couldn't help it, no matter how mad I was with him; I loved the feel of him around me and now seemed like a great time to succumb to that feeling. I allowed myself to be propelled forward and let my head rest on his chest. I breathed in his scent. Fresh and soapy. Clean. His arms were strong around me, his face touched the top of my head and I heard him breathe deep.

"Ethan, it's been rough."

His arms wrapped around my back, one hand held my head and he pulled me closer still. I felt him against me. I shifted my weight into him.

"I've missed you, Han." His voice caught in his throat as he murmured into my hair. Something stirred inside me and I turned my face up to him, his lips parting. There was a lingering taste of mint. His breath warm. I raised myself up on my toes to meet his need. I felt the soft jersey of my tee slide across my skin as it was pulled from around my waist and over my head. My hands clamoured to be free as they caught in the material. I shook with excitement. A deep need throbbing inside. I pulled at his T-shirt, desperate to remove it from him, to feel his naked flesh against mine. Our feet tripping as we side-stepped towards the bedroom, mouths locked together in a deep hunger. My breath came thick and fast. I needed to feel his warmth, his hard body with mine. I needed to fill the chasm that had opened within me, and I needed Ethan. His mouth found the curve in my neck, his kisses deep and urgent. I had never needed him more. A sound escaped from my lips. He moved and silenced me with his mouth on mine again. Reaching down for his belt, my hands worked the buckle and pulled it loose. We fell on the bed. We made love as though we had been apart for so long, desperately craving and desperately pushing for what we needed.

Resting in the crook of his arm, I turned my face towards Ethan as he lay open and relaxed. "Why are you here?" I asked.

"Why? What's wrong?"

"Us. This." I waved an armed over our tangled bodies. "I don't know..." the sentence trailed off.

"We're good together, can't we go with it?"

The needy girlfriend? Is that what I was to become. I wasn't that person. Pulling myself up and out of his arms, I got out of bed and placed bare feet onto cold wooden flooring, padded over to where I left my wine in the living room, grabbed another glass and the bottle from the kitchen and returned. I filled the fresh glass for

Ethan and passed it to him, leaving the bottle on the worn antique pine drawers near the door.

"Thanks."

I drank before speaking. "Sometimes I need to be able to reach out to you, you know." I paused. "When it's tough."

"I'm sorry about the other day, busy myself, you kind of cut me off when I did call, so I figured you wanted to get on with your case." He drank. I had cut him off. "How's it going?"

I shouldn't talk to Ethan about the cases I was working, but at times I'd seen him access more information than I had and a lot quicker. As police, we could find evidence, forensics, but with Ethan, people were willing to talk to him, people who wouldn't give a cop the time of day, so on this premise, I decided to see if we could talk about it. And try and do it without landing either of us in the shit.

"You've heard about the murdered girl?" I started.

"Of course, though your press office is being tight lipped about it."

"I know. The top brass are worried about the headlines if we don't identify and arrest an offender within a couple of days. Children are a completely different arena. People get anxious, they clamour for justice, they want to know whose fault it is, how it happened, and they worry about their kids. It's tough."

"So what *is* happening?"

Pushing myself further on the bed I rested back against the slatted headboard, knees bent. "If I talk to you about this, in return you give me what you've got before going to print?"

"You know it's how I work, I need a good angle to run a story, not just what your media liaison sees fit to share."

I nodded. He smiled and leaned closer in to me. A smile that earned trust. A smile that was practised maybe. I relented. We needed help with this and I was willing to take what I could get. No one else should have to suffer as Rosie Green had, and no parent should have to live through it as George and Anne Green were. An image of the light fading from their eyes flashed in front of me. I was right to go with this, with Ethan. I'd sort any crap that came from it later. I took a deep breath.

"Okay. We know the scene we found the girl in was a dump site, not the original crime scene. We've had the official identification today and she's a teenager from another force area. It's a strange one, Ethan, I've no idea how she ended up here, forensics won't start coming back for a couple of days and friends of the girl don't appear to know much. The info about the dump site and crime scene isn't in the public domain yet," I concluded. "Now you have to give me what you've got." I took another drink of the red as I waited on Ethan.

He sighed. "The angle is the girl herself. I'd already started to have my own suspicions about her not being local as everyone I've spoken with has drawn a blank on who it could be. We're waiting for you to release her photo so we can talk to more people. Now that group of people we need to talk to will be further afield, but she was still found here, so someone here must know who she is. When is her photograph being released?"

"Parents have been up today and identified her. Grey was sorting out the press release with Claire as I left the office. I want you to contact me if you get anything useful, Ethan." I looked at him, narrowing my eyes, letting him know I was serious. "This one, as I've already said, is sensitive, you can't go barging in and printing details we don't want releasing."

Ethan dropped his chin and raised his eyes at me. "Han?"

"Okay, but take it easy." He needed to be sensitive to our case. To my case. This was important. I worried what would happen if there was a choice between his career and mine. We weren't in what either of us would call a settled relationship; I think we'd just established that. We rarely spoke about the serious issues or about how we were feeling and I was as guilty of this as he was. It was easier to take the ride. There was a closeness though, something there, but I struggled with the issue of trust. It was something that needed to be worked through.

The last of the wine was drained and I lay back on the bed and looked at Ethan. His arms were crossed behind his head, a relaxed stance, comfortable. A body language of trust. I needed to trust him, I was starting to care. I nudged my head back into the crook of his arm and closed my eyes. Images danced in front of them. Distorted children with trash and hospital mortuaries. All blending together.

23

The incident room was quiet and still. Like an early morning pond before the wildlife wakes and creates the ripples and sound that fills their day. I'd raised myself from an empty bed again. Nothing had changed.

I searched out Grey, who kept longer hours than anyone, including me. He was sharp as far as keeping on top of things went. He'd be aware of every angle of the ongoing investigation, every progress made and every step in the planning. He was meticulous and organised. A climber.

He was at his desk, squinting, eyebrows tucked down as he read from his computer monitor.

"Morning, sir," I said from the doorway.

"Morning, Hannah." He waved a hand at the chair in front of his desk. "Come in."

I sat opposite him and watched as he finished reading. The small lines running across his forehead looked like ripples in the sand after a heavy storm. He looked up.

"What's the current status?"

My phone vibrated in my pocket. "Sorry, sir, let me just

check this." Grey nodded and went back to his work. I fished it out and checked the screen. *Caller withheld.* "Robbins."

Silence.

"Hello. DI Robbins."

Silence.

The lit screen showed that the call was still open. Grey watched. I said hello to the caller once more before hanging up and moving on.

"Rosie Green has been identified by her parents. It gives us something to work with. I'm holding a team briefing this morning and I'm going to push forensics to see where they're at."

Grey's eyes narrowed. We both knew forensic science had to be taken in context of any given situation and wasn't the be all and end all of answers. He was feeling the pressure from the top. The Chief Constable was watching the case. Any negative press on the force was always a blow in these times of accountability. It affected job security and everyone wanted to cover themselves as much as they wanted to do the right thing.

"We're putting in the hours, sir. Everyone is giving this everything they have."

Grey nodded. These things could take time and time was something the press was reluctant to give a police force in the murder investigation of a child.

"We need something positive, Hannah. Find out what happened to her."

"Now we have the definitive ID we can work on her history, her friends, family, and activities. The DI down there, Clive Tripps, has a good team and they're doing everything we ask. Add Martin to that, and we are well placed to know everything and have real time input. We're waiting on a lot of information. The trace evidence from the scene is being processed and you know that's a painful process. Being dumped in an alleyway with the rubbish isn't the easiest scene to deal with. DNA results from the semen will take a few days, as will results from under nail scrapings. Work is also being done on the bruising patterns found on her body. The investigation has everything we can throw at it." Which was a lot considering the economic climate.

Grey rubbed his forehead, but the sand ripples remained. "What else are we doing, other than waiting on people and results?"

"Plenty. There are on-going inquiries with the restaurant and banks to identify patrons where the body was found. We're following up the alibis of sex offenders, local CCTV needs to be gone through at a steady pace and all vehicles identified as well as door knocking. There's a lot of work and not enough staff as usual, but we're doing everything we can."

"Get this bastard, Hannah, and the sooner the better before the press eats us alive."

24

After updating Grey and checking through more emails that had arrived overnight, I gathered the team in the conference room, a bland rectangular space with several tables pushed together to form a larger table for users to sit around.

The inquiry team filed in. Aaron looked healthier for a night in his own bed. Sally looked happier, but still a little peaky. Ross, well he looked just like Ross. Jack sauntered in with his steaming mug, muttering under his breath about the lack of full fat milk available. I'd asked Jack, Doug Howell the crime scene tech, and Evie to attend this morning's meeting. It was best practice to get everyone together so all strands of the investigation could be discussed and nothing missed. Claire Betts walked in with her folder and a couple of pens clipped to it.

"Morning, Hannah. You going to keep me busy for a while?" she asked.

"You know me, Claire. I'm not happy unless I'm running around and overworked, so I need someone to join me." She laughed and sat in a chair, pulling it up to the table, straightening her folder. "I'd be sorry if you didn't."

Grey followed Claire in and was leaning against a wall, his frown lines well excavated. My earlier attempts to reassure him we would deal with this hadn't hit the right spot.

The local press had started asking questions of the police investigation. I'd appraised myself of the recent articles and had seen yesterday's main topic was the lack of identification. Today it would take on a whole different slant and I imagined it would also hit the national press which would put pressure on the local reporters to get in closer. It was after all, their community, plus we would be hit by hard-nosed national journalists. The media would be on a rampage only they could create, and often were unable to stop once they had started the speeding train. I thought of Ethan. He would be working this. The pressure was mounting. Having an identification meant we had somewhere to start looking from. Victimology was a better starting point for the investigation, but it was complicated by Rosie being from so far away.

I waited for the chatter to die down, then started. "Thanks for coming in. We need all heads on this." I had their attention. "The operational name has been allocated and is Operation Halyard. We'll start by looking at what information we already have, assess it and see where we go from there. We'll start with the crime scene. What did you find Doug?"

"As we've discussed, it doesn't look like it was the murder scene. The girl was naked which suggests she was dumped in the alley after being murdered elsewhere. The offender had access to the alley from two directions and no CCTV to cover it. Gives the impression of local knowledge."

I nodded.

"It was a terrible site to process. We have so much to go through back at the lab and most of it's going to be irrelevant so it would be helpful if anyone can help narrow things down. Tell us what needs to take priority and what needs testing specifically. Testing everything is going to cost." He paused. I saw Ross roll his eyes and I was glad he didn't make comment. "Also, I've brought the scene photos over with me." He pushed a brown envelope towards me. I touched it with the tips of my fingers and pulled it closer.

"Thanks, Doug. We'll give you as much information as and when it comes in."

He nodded.

"On the point of CCTV, how have the house to house inquiries gone and checks for local business CCTV recordings?" I looked at Ross and Sally.

"No-one saw anything when house to house was conducted," Sally replied. "There are some addresses that need going back to, but in the main, people are used to a lot of activity around and about there. It's a city centre. Cars and people come with the territory and the locals are used to it and sleep pretty well through noise and disturbances."

"Well, we seemed to wake them up easily." I was annoyed. It was typical around here. No-one was interested in helping, but they damn well screamed for service if they needed us. "And CCTV?" This time I directed the question to Ross.

"We're still working our way through it. A few premises have handed over their recordings, but it's going to take a while to view it all and I'm planning on taking the premises visits a bit wider than I've managed so far. It's still on-going."

"Okay. Jack?"

He put his mug down in front of him. "You have the preliminary report. Cause of death was asphyxiation. The position she was found in and the lividity present would seem to back up Doug's assumption she was indeed moved and the alley was a dump site. She was badly beaten prior to death. Some of the bruising indicates on-going abuse weeks before death, not just at the time of death."

"How long was she missing?" asked Sally.

"Two weeks," I answered.

"So what about the bruising? Does it correspond to the time frame?"

I looked at Jack for the answer. He took his glasses off and rubbed at the lenses with the hem of his stripy jumper. "She had been through the mill. She had a lot of bruising over a large portion of her body. Some bruises were recent. They were large and dark indicating they were new. Others across her body were fading and were yellowish-brown. This indicates the original bruise occurred about eight to nine days ago. There were small bruises that had all but disappeared, so yes, I'd say she was being hurt from at least two weeks ago."

"So it's a waiting game on anything further?" I asked.

"Unfortunately, yes. I'm still waiting for toxicology and results of stomach contents. They will take a while I'm afraid. I do intend to examine the body again in the coming days to check for bruises that weren't visible at the time of post-mortem."

"Thanks, Jack."

Next, Aaron talked about the school and the fact Rosie had sought out contraceptive advice. We were waiting for records from Rosie's GP and school nurse. I had nothing extra to add from the visit to the best friend's address. It was the same story. Rosie was a good girl until a few weeks before she went missing, at which point she pulled away from people and became insular.

The local sex offenders all checked out. Sally and Ross had worked hard on corroborating them yesterday while Aaron and I had been in Norwich, so they were a dead end.

Evie stated she couldn't find any trace of Rosie being on any of the social networking sites which confirms the information coming from Norwich, that Rosie was from a quiet family who wanted her to stay a child while she still was one.

We talked in circles. We couldn't find a link between Norwich and us. Between Rosie and here. Between anything.

It had been a long couple of days but I could see everyone was ready for the work we still had ahead of us. A child killer is a big incentive to get cops to pull the last drop of energy they have out of the hat and push forward.

Finally I turned to Claire. "What's the agreed strategy for the press release?"

The pen that had been swinging through her fingers had stopped and swirls had appeared on the pad in front of her. "We're going to identify her to the press. Chris Stewart from Norwich has sent us an up to date photograph of Rosie and we're going to appeal to anyone who may have seen her in and around the local area. We're expecting the nationals to pick it up today, so we will have a wider audience. Someone may be able to help."

A wider audience and a wider section of the public

demanding answers.

I left the building, feeling tired. The rest of the day had passed in a blur of files, meetings and decision making. A call to Martin had found him in good spirits and about to head into another interview with a different girl from Rosie's class. Nothing had come up we weren't already aware of.

A glass of red wine was a welcome pleasure waiting for me at home. The joy of living alone meant I could please myself and not have to worry about the sensitivities of others. I changed clothes and relaxed in front of some American science fiction drama where Earth inhabitants battled aliens. It was escapism and I sucked it all up as fast as I soaked up the half bottle of red.

A brief text message from Ethan explained he was busy and would call me the next day.

Sally was already there when I arrived at the incident room the next morning at seven a.m. She also looked more refreshed.

"Anyone else in?" I asked.

She looked around the room, "Yes, Ross is somewhere. He said something about checking the overnight incident logs."

"Okay," I mumbled as I walked away to my office. It was chilly. While I waited for my computer to boot up I hung my suit jacket up and pulled on a thick beige cardigan from the back of a chair. The monitor came to life, the force logo appeared, and then flickered as the rest of the software loaded. Eventually the computer was functioning. I brought up my email in-box. Twenty-seven emails in less than twelve hours. I scanned through them. Forensics had sent an electronic copy of the scene photos, Claire had forwarded me a copy of the press release and Jack had invited me to a murder mystery night. Just the kind of tongue in cheek event he would love. I'd need to check my diary and get back to him.

I walked back into the incident room which had filled up. Sounds of tapping keyboards and conversations. I sat on the corner of Aaron's desk and was greeted by a functional: "Morning."

"I spoke to Martin last night," I informed him. He carried on tapping at his keyboard. "Aaron?" He worked on. It was then that I noticed the discreet earplugs he sometimes wore in the office to block out the noise while he worked. I tapped him on the shoulder. He looked up, his face showing confusion at the interruption. I pointed at my own ears and he pulled out his plugs. "I spoke to Martin last night," I said again.

"Okay."

"Nothing new so far. They have a lot to get through though."

"Okay." He was not going to give me much else in the way of conversation. The door opened with a thud as Ross came in, his face serious, jaw clenched up tight. I waited for him to speak but didn't expect what came.

"Another body's been found."

25

"What the hell do you mean there's another body?" I stood from the desk corner, feeling the hairs on the back of my neck prickle, a hyper-alertness that would not benefit the situation. I had to take a step back, to be professional about this.

The rest of the room was silent. A collective breath held. The thought of another murdered child was impossible to comprehend. I looked at Ross for answers.

"I was checking the overnight incident logs for the morning briefing and, well, a child's body has been found early this morning. It's close to the previous dump site, Alfred Street, and is a similar MO." I gave him a querying look. "Just off Mansfield Road again, though further into town this time, top end of Huntingdon Street. A naked girl, suspected similar age. From initial reports it looks to be a dump site and not the initial crime scene and there are similar markings on the body." He handed me the log, his hair flopping down over his face as he looked down. He continued, "She has bruising around her wrists and neck. Rosie Green is high profile within the force, so it didn't take attending officers long to realise this was likely to be connected and the call was made to the control room. The first officers on scene have asked for our assistance and for Jack's attendance."

My head was spinning. Did this new location away from the more residential area and closer to the actual city mean anything or was he just wandering and finding somewhere to dump? "Please tell me we have an idea on identification this time? Anything on the original messages coming in?" I attempted to scan the document Ross had given me, but he could give me the highlights right now.

"She didn't have anything on her, so there is no identification we can use. I can start to pull out some of the missing persons files of similar aged girls with close and matching descriptions and come back to you."

I ran my fingers through my fringe. "Good. Thanks Ross." What was happening? Another child murder, and in our area. What did this mean and were they really connected?

Grey came into my line of vision. "I'm going to attend the scene. See what we have and report back as soon as I know anything."

He nodded, the sand ripples across his head deepened. "This could mean your team and working practices are reviewed. You need to be making inroads, Hannah, and quickly."

I snaked the car left past the clock tower of the Victoria Centre and northwards. The city was waking up. Cars were on the move and the few people out on foot had coat collars pulled up, scarves wrapped tight around necks with their focus set on getting to where they were going as quickly as they could and out of the cold. We turned onto Huntingdon Street and saw chaos. The crime scene was just off here, on Alfred Street. It would be easier to park up and walk the rest of the way. This area of the city was always grey, the buildings gradually falling into disrepair, both small industrial buildings and homes. The street was busier and a lot less organised than the last scene, or so it seemed. A frost had covered the area overnight and the morning sun was weak, doing little to dispense with it. As I parked the car I could see the police activity had created a lot of attention. These kinds of scenes were always worse in daylight hours and caused quite a stir. People wanted to see what had happened and were gathering, no doubt so they could take photographs on their mobile phones and distribute them on the social networking sites. Something to brag about. No regard given to the loss of life or its effects on remaining family. They would show an outward display of horror at what they perceived they knew, but it wouldn't stop the photographs or conveying of information, correct or otherwise.

It wore my patience, the current trend in capturing everything and splashing it all over to gain popularity. It left a bitter taste in my mouth. A child had lost her life and all people were interested in was sharing every last detail with their mates.

I picked up my pace as I strode to the crime scene cordon, taking care on the hidden patches of black ice underfoot. Tape flapped across an entryway to the scene. A baby-faced uniformed cop stood rigidly by the cordon. His job was to stop anyone who didn't need to be in there and to list those who entered. It didn't matter if the chief constable himself wanted to pass. If he didn't need to be in there messing up the scene, then he didn't get in. Some of the new probationary cops often found turning away officers of rank a difficult concept. This cop oozed crime scene anxiety. He had the look of a startled rabbit as we approached.

"DI Robbins." I raised my ID. "Major Crimes Unit."

He looked at my warrant card and lifted his notepad to register our details on the major incident log. "Ma'am," he acknowledged. His hand shook a little.

"What's your name?" I asked.

"Tony Hitchen, ma'am." He scribbled Aaron and Sally's names into the log along with mine. Loops curled up and down, but in a broken and stuttering fashion.

"Tony, this cordon needs to be a lot further out for two

reasons. One, to widen the scene so the crime scene techs have enough room to get all the evidence they need and, two, can you see all the people?" I shifted my head sideways in a nod towards the gathering crowds, keeping my hands down in my pockets for warmth. Tony looked more apprehensive. "They shouldn't be this close. Our victim needs some dignity afforded her. Do you think you can widen this scene and remove the crowds please?"

"Oh yes. Sorry, ma'am. Right away. I'm sorry."

I could see I'd made him more nervous. It wasn't my intention, but it was better coming from me than some of the more heavy handed DIs it was possible he would come up against at his next one. "It's something to remember in the future. Preserve the scene as wide as you feel it needs to go. Don't be afraid to make it over wide. Over wide we can bring in if we need to, but not wide enough makes it difficult. It means the area is contaminated. Widening our scene is about letting our teams work in a professional manner and our victim gets respect. Okay?"

"Yes, ma'am."

Just as we were pulling on the white forensic suits my phone rang.

"DI Robbins."

"Han, it's me. Heads up, I'm walking into your scene as we speak."

26

"What the hell do you mean, you're walking into my scene?" I hissed into the handset.

Sally and Aaron stared at me. Most of the time they were discreet when I was on a call, but this had caught their attention.

"I've been sent to cover it. Nothing I can do." I looked around as Ethan's voice from the phone came closer and louder. He was striding towards us, one hand pushed in his pocket, the other holding the phone to his ear.

This was difficult. I flinched. My relationship with Ethan was private. I hadn't shared it with any of my work colleagues. My love life wasn't any of their business, but the fact that he was press wasn't going to help me explain any relationship with him I might have. Journalists don't tend to be trusted, but can be helpful in some situations, especially when we need to get information out to the wider public. It means a balancing act has to be navigated. I didn't even know how to define our relationship, so having him arrive at one of the most demanding crime scenes of my career so far was not helpful. My head started to throb. I wasn't sure how he was going to play this, but I appreciated the heads up, even if it was the briefest of heads up in the history of warnings.

"DI Robbins." Ethan approached me, playing it cool, lanyard around his neck making visible his press credentials.

Aaron and Sally exchanged a quick look between them as they appeared to make a connection to the phone call.

"Ethan Gale, what can we do for you?" I didn't wait for an answer. "We are very pushed down here right now, all we can say is that there is an incident and we are dealing with it. We will, of course, make a press release when we know more."

"I know you will; thank you." He smiled. I didn't know whether I wanted to punch him for coming down here and putting me in this position or smile back. I chose the third option which was one of being professional. I looked him in the eyes.

"My editor, Patricia Hart, sent me down because we have a woman she believes to be the victim's mother at our offices. She's quite distraught, as you can imagine. Patricia asked me to come and see if you could give the woman anything either way so she can get on with grieving or continuing to hope her daughter could be alive."

Now I wanted to punch him in the face. "Why does your woman believe the person involved in our incident is her daughter and why the hell would she not call the police with what she knows and any questions she has?" The dull throb in my temples was changing from a feeling of anxiety to one of irritation.

Ethan ran his hand through his hair. "She doesn't believe she gets a fair hearing from the police." He paused as I tried to assimilate what he was telling me. "She feels discriminated against because they come from the poorer part of town. She asked us to bridge that gap for her. She heard there was a girl found here. Word travels fast and with the description doing the rounds, she feels it's Allison."

Tension ran from my head and down through my limbs as I fought to control my anger at the situation. "We haven't released a description yet."

"As you know, DI Robbins, word travels fast and uses a variety of methods. I hope you don't mind if I wait here so I can let Allison's mother know."

"You can stay outside the cordon as long as you want to, Mr Gale. We will however, be needing to talk to this woman if the child does turn out to be Allison."

A short distance away, Aaron and Sally were now sat on the edge of the crime scene van as they pulled on white forensic booties.

I lowered my voice. "How dare you do this to me; couldn't they send someone else?"

"Han, I'm sorry, Allison is my story, so they sent me down. I'll hover until you let me have something. I will try to be discreet, but this isn't looking good is it?"

At that point I knew he was talking, not just about Allison, but about the fact that this was the second child murder in the city in such a short period of time. "Keep your profile low, Ethan. I'll talk to you later."

Ethan nodded.

"What was that about?" asked Aaron, his discretion unable to hold out any longer. "A mother sitting in a press office, rather than contacting us? Seriously? We have to go to the press to speak to the potential parent of our victim? That's ridiculous."

I couldn't disagree with him. I pulled my phone back out of my trouser pocket and dialled the office. Ross answered. Updating him I requested he locate the missing persons file on a female by the name of Allison – hell, I didn't know her surname. I covered my phone with my palm and turned to where Ethan was stood, his eyes down to his phone, fingers tapping at keys. "Ethan. Surname?"

He stopped punching at the phone. "Kirk. Allison Kirk."

I resumed my conversation with Ross. "Allison Kirk. And pull up all the information we hold on both her and her mother and then go wider to extended family, associates and links that come up."

"Wow, some people, huh."

"Yeah, Ross. Thanks for the help."

"No worries, boss."

Aaron and I walked into the scene, a little more prepared for what we were about to witness, but preparation is complicated when it comes to children and violent deaths.

This time the girl was inside an industrial bin. I wondered on the significance. Maybe the offender had had more time. Time to lift her and load her into the bin rather than throwing her down. Did this mean he was disturbed last time? House to house, and knocking at commercial buildings hadn't brought anything to light, but we were still working it.

Jack was already in the bin with the child.

"Jack?"

"Ah, Hannah, just the person." Jack's voice echoed out from the depths of the bin. "I've had a preliminary look at our young girl and you're the person I need to talk to. Give me a moment and I will join you."

Sally was talking to Tony Hitchen, the first officer on the scene, getting details. He would have to write up a statement later, but for now we needed an account from him, including who had called it in and how they had come across her. Aaron was talking to Doug who was now waiting on Jack.

"Give me a hand would you, dear?" Jack attempted to get his spindly legs over the edge of the container whilst holding on to his medical bag, his spotted socks were visible under his dark trousers. I reached up and grabbed the bag handle allowing him to pitch himself up and over. The smell he was bringing up with him: rotting vegetables and meat, scorched the inside of my nose. My stomach leapt again. I clamped my mouth shut and ground my teeth together.

"What have we got, Jack?"

"It's not good, Hannah. It would appear it is the same offender as our last one." The use of the phrase *last one* wasn't Jack forgetting Rosie's name or being insensitive, the habit of not using a victim's name made it a little easier to deal with, taking the person out of the offence and dealing in the facts. "She's been dumped naked and she has multiple bruises over her body and welts around her wrists consistent with something being tied around them and then there's the same strange patterned band around her throat." He pulled off his gloves from the inside out and balled them. "She also has semen stains on her and visible signs of a vicious sexual assault. I've done the swabs, though it was far from easy in there."

"Shit. We need to be moving fast before this bastard strikes again." I was so angry. "Is it possible for you to do the PM today?"

"Of course, whatever I have tabled in already I will request be moved over for someone else to pick up. As soon as she's ready."

My phone vibrated in my pocket, I pulled it out. *Ross.*

"What have you got, Ross?"

"I've found a misper form with photograph for a girl with the name Allison Kirk. I'm going to send it to you on your phone so you can compare it with your victim there."

"Okay. What's the info on her?"

"Well, she's a regular misper, though she isn't currently recorded as missing. She comes from a broken home. Dad's serving time for a bunch of armed robberies and Mum keeps moving in new uncles for Allison to get used to." The term *uncles* had a tone of irony added to it. "The usual scenario results in domestics with divisional uniform officers in attendance after new uncle whacks Mum. Children's services are involved, but haven't deemed Allison at any particular risk and left her in the home. Allison's reaction to all this, not surprisingly, has been to go off and do her own thing on a regular basis and the missing person reports have been filed because Allison's social worker reported her missing when she failed to attend for scheduled meetings.

Mum says she always turns up, so she never worries. That's the excuse, and it also seems to depend on if she is shacked up with someone new, at which point she doesn't care where Allison is, what she's doing, or who she's doing it with. I phoned the social worker, Christine Evans, and she said Allison is a good kid who deals the hand she's been given the best way she knows how. She engages with services when she is around, but very often, she just isn't."

"She sounds like the type a predator would target. Vulnerable and insecure. Send me the photo and I'll have a look."

Less than a minute later I was looking at a photograph children's services had provided on one of the multiple occasions Allison Kirk had gone missing. Looking back at me was a slight blonde-haired girl, dark make-up around her eyes and thick foundation covering what would have been a pretty young face. She had a 'who gives a shit' look about her, but beneath was a fragile vulnerability.

I wasn't about to climb into the commercial bin, because I didn't need to. The fewer people contaminating the scene the better. I approached Doug and Aaron.

"Doug, I take it you've photographed the child before Jack climbed in there?"

Doug took a deep breath before answering. "Yes, of course."

"Would it be possible to have a look at a head shot of her? I've got a possible ID from a tenuous source and have a photograph on my phone of one of our mispers. I need to compare the photographs."

Doug was already bent over his digital camera, flicking through images. "No worries." On the small screen I saw shots of the scene as Doug had walked into it, the industrial bin and then the shots of the girl inside. When he found one with her face he handed me the camera. The girl on the screen wasn't wearing foundation; she was pale, bad teenage skin showing, her cheeks gaunt and her eyes dark and hollowed, though this time the darkness wasn't supplied by black make-up pencils. The girl with the dead eyed stare was Allison Kirk.

27

I took the passenger seat as Ethan climbed into the driver's side. Sally and Aaron had taken our car back to the incident room. Ethan looked grim.

"So it is her?" he asked, the car keys sitting limp in his hands.

"Yes, it's her." This situation wasn't comfortable. I was already finding it difficult to manoeuvre my way through the relationship I had with Ethan, without throwing in a woman who, believing her child may be dead, had turned up on the doorstep of the local paper before contacting the police. They were actions I found unfathomable. Why would she go to the press rather than contacting us? We needed to be cautious with her. She was a grieving mother, but one whose actions were at the very least, questionable.

"I didn't ask to do this, Hannah." I let him talk. "As I said, the story was already mine, so when she walked in, it came to me to follow up."

"Tell me what you know." I wanted him to tell me this would be okay. That our working worlds colliding in this way wouldn't have an effect on our somewhat precarious relationship. But he wouldn't talk about us now. It was doubtful he would even talk about us later when we were alone.

He turned to me. "It came to us in quite a convoluted way. One of Allison's friends from school was concerned about her, spoke to her own mother who happens to be the cousin of the new guy covering the entertainment section. She mentioned it at a family gathering, thinking Ted would be interested, which, to hand it to him, he was, and he passed it on to me. She had been missing a week then. Longer than is usual for her. When I showed up at her house, Natalie, her mum, was a little surprised. She wasn't concerned, after all, she said, she's fifteen now." He sighed. "Fifteen. As if that's all grown up. Natalie was happy to let me in and talk to me. She asked if she would be paid for talking to me. Seemed a little narked when I said it was a profile piece to raise awareness for Allison and the plight of missing children in the city area. I don't think I got a very honest account from her. She was more interested in what she could get out of the publicity."

I was glad Ethan had been involved with the family before the death. I hated to think he could be trying to exploit anything we had for the sake of a story. It didn't get past me that she was also the same age as Rosie Green. My phone rang again. It was a constant noise during inquiries like this. "Robbins." The line was silent for a few seconds then cleared. I pushed it back in my pocket. Whoever it was, they'd call back if it was important.

"What did she say this morning when she turned up?"

"I was buzzed by reception who told me that Natalie was here demanding to see me and something about Allison being murdered. I was shocked, couldn't quite believe it. I'd held the belief that she'd be okay in the end. I knew she was trying to escape from a crappy home life and if I'm honest, I didn't blame her. I'd been in her home. Met her mum. But this?" He paused a beat. "As I walked the stairs down to reception I could already hear Natalie wailing, but when I was face to face with her, it was strange."

"In what way?"

"For all the noise I'd heard, faced with her I didn't get the feeling the emotion she was portraying was genuine. She was making a big drama but something about her made me bristle. I took her up to the fourth floor. I wanted to get her out of the way of other visitors, and made her a drink. We sat and she recounted how she'd had a text message telling her Allison had been found in a bin. I asked her how she was doing and what could I do to help and she asked how much I'd pay her for her story."

28

Natalie Kirk was a scrawny looking woman with an instantaneously off-putting attitude. Even reminding yourself she had lost her daughter did little in the way of balancing the scales in her favour. She stood in the small interview room in *Nottingham Today's* fourth floor suite telling me how hard done by she was. Her talon-shaped red nails pointed towards me in an attempt to claw their message across, heaving breasts barely contained by the skimpy cloth passing as a T-shirt. Ethan sat in the corner in a coffee-coloured armchair. A small silver rectangular object sat on the low table at his side and I realised the conversation was being recorded.

"My baby's gone and what are you doing about it?" Natalie Kirk wailed at me.

"Mrs Kirk, I'm sorry for your loss. I have a full team of officers, seasoned detectives, working all hours in an effort to identify and arrest the offender." I paused, giving her time to take in what I'd said. I wasn't sure she was listening. Her concentration seemed limited, fractured, and not just by grief, but by other conversations she seemed to be wanting to have. Her head flicked between Ethan and her beeping phone. She'd tut as she pulled it out of her bag, but check anyway, to see if it needed responding to. The majority of time, I could see, she had the sense not to send messages as we stood there. "Please," I continued, "can we sit down?" I gestured towards the comfortable plush sofas positioned around the room. Natalie sat, crossed skinny legs in a tiny skirt, and waved four inch heels towards me. Her fingers once again went to her tired red handbag. My patience was about coming to an end. The conversation was the most stilted I'd ever attempted to hold with a parent of a murdered child. Eventually she pulled out a pack of cigarettes and a lighter. The screwed up look on her face softened. She flicked at the lighter and sucked hard on the cigarette between cherry lips.

"Natalie, you can't smoke in here. I'm sorry," Ethan said.

She eyed him, head to toe and back up again, and seemed to consider her options before she stubbed it out on a saucer in front of her.

"It may be more comfortable if we talked down at the station where we can discuss Allison and make arrangements for you to see her," I said.

"I'm not going anywhere with you. I'm staying here." She raised her voice and the barely restrained breasts were pushed forward in some kind of protest. "*Notts Today* wants my story." She glanced at Ethan for confirmation, who looked at me and recognised he needed to keep his mouth shut at this point. She continued, "Maybe I can come and see you when I've talked to them?" Her bony hands rubbed at her cheeks, where no real tears were falling.

"Mrs Kirk, this is a murder investigation and we need a formal identification of Allison. It's imperative this is done. If it's delayed, the rest of the investigation is delayed. After the ID we need a chat with you, we need to get an idea of who Allison was as a girl and where she may have been hanging out, who her friends were, what her likes and dislikes were. Just a general feel for her. That way, we can start to make inquiries, question people and find the person who did this."

Natalie jumped from her seat, heels wobbling from the ferocity of the movement. "They did this to me as well. She's my baby. It's hurting right in my heart." Her hand went dramatically to her chest. My sympathy was non-existent. I didn't feel bad about that either, Natalie Kirk wasn't feeling guilty for her lack of parenting skills. I was not surprised Allison had struggled to remain in her own home with a mother who cared so little for her. The recorder caught my attention again. Ethan evaded my silent, querying look. I stood.

"I know you're hurting, Mrs Kirk. We can contact a doctor to come out to see how you're doing and we will have an assigned detective to spend some time with you talking about Allison and also about you. How does that sound?" I had to try and show her this could be about her, that she deserved the attention the murder of her child was bringing. Her phone hadn't stopped beeping and clicking since I had walked in the room. Messages of support coming through and messages from people wanting gruesome details, of which Natalie Kirk was more than willing to share, given that she continued to respond to, rather than ignore the phone.

"I would see a doctor, for me? And a special detective to spend time with me?"

"Yes of course, it's important you are checked out and okay and you have someone around to talk to when you need it. Shall we go and deal with this?" I asked in a softer tone than I felt she deserved.

"Oh, okay. Ethan, can we do the story later after I've done the stuff with the five oh?"

Ethan looked up. "Of course, Natalie. Give me a call when you're done and I'll pick you up. I'll speak to my editor in the meantime to see what she wants out of our meeting, okay?"

Kirk was sly enough to know not to push us all at the same time, after all, it appeared, she wanted to keep us all at her beck and call as long as possible.

As Natalie went to powder her already over plastered face in the ladies room I called Sally for a car, then pulled Ethan to one side.

"What were you doing with that recorder?"

"Nothing sinister. Where you used to see reporters scribbling away in books, we now have these, it means I get to do less scribbling and my memory is terrible, I never remember what's been said. She was in here to talk to us, Han, nothing wrong with it."

I was on edge. He knew that, he stepped closer and dropped his head so his mouth was near my ear and lowered his voice. "It's okay. I'll come round tonight. It's going to be fine. Text me when you finish and I'll be there." He stepped away as Natalie tottered back in. Tissues clumped in her hand, dabbing virtually dry cheeks. My phone vibrated. Sally was outside with the car.

"Okay, Natalie, the car's here, let's go and make you a cuppa and have a chat."

She wobbled again on her shoes, mascara rubbed around her face giving her an even grimier look than she'd already had. As I pushed on the office door to exit, Natalie turned and spoke to Ethan. "I want my money. Papers pay for stories like this. You pay or I go elsewhere."

29

Leaning back into my chair I listened to the call connect and ran a hand through my hair. I'd always stuck to the rule that said personal and professional lives should never mix. I'd seen cops work eighteen hour shifts – and more – on a job and this obviously had a negative effect on family life. My own desire to succeed in the job, and in each case that came in, meant my love life had taken a back seat. And yet here I was. I thought I was safe with Ethan. He wasn't a cop, but he was a dedicated hard-working conscientious guy. Someone I could connect with in an intellectual way away from policing and not have to talk about the job, which was another disadvantage of a work relationship. It was always a topic of conversation. Now this. Now Ethan was slap bang in the middle of my investigation and in all likelihood was going to get in the way and be as difficult as I had come to expect journalists to be.

"Today, Ethan Gale." The familiar voice answered.

"Ethan, it's me."

"Hey." Warm.

I didn't know what to say next. I was so angry with him, with the situation I felt he had put me in. But hearing his voice, knowing him on such an intimate level, I couldn't bawl him out. I took a deep breath.

"Hannah, I'm sorry this is your job. That my job is a part of your job."

"I know." I tried to steel myself, to be professional, to be what the investigation needed, without trampling on Ethan and our still growing relationship.

"What is *Nottingham Today* planning on doing with Natalie Kirk when she gets back in touch?"

"I talked with my editor and she wants to run with the story, with Natalie as the poor grieving single mother, striving to bring up a child on her own in troubled times. It's a heart-breaker and it sells papers."

"Yeah and the woman would sell her own daughter if she could."

"I don't disagree, but the story's there."

"I know." My hand went through my hair again.

"I want to see the story before it goes to print and I want everything you've written up about Natalie Kirk and Allison before she was found today. Can you do that?"

Silence. I gave him a moment.

"You're going to have to give me a little time to get everything together. I wouldn't usually but if it'll help with the investigation then I can do. There may be sources of information within previous notes or articles I can't disclose, but you can have what I've got if it helps. Just give me the time will you?"

I knew he was giving what he could, but it would have helped to know any sources he was speaking to. I sighed into the mouthpiece. "Okay, Ethan, but don't take too long. I don't want this monster claiming another girl whilst we wade through the *Today's* red tape."

30

I decided to go with Sally and Natalie after the positive ID of Allison's body. The sterile viewing had been conducted through a glass partition to preserve any evidence she may have had on her. It's not easy for loved ones and the process seemed to have affected Natalie. Maybe more than I was expecting. The gaudy loud woman I was used to was subdued and compliant. We stood with her at the gates of the hospital grounds, coats buttoned up as high as they'd go, fighting off the cold wind as she smoked two cigarettes in succession before we took her away from her daughter and back home. The background sound of traffic rolled past on Derby Road at great speed, offering a stark contrast to the stillness here, right now in this moment. Lips puckered, cigarette in mouth, Natalie sucked for all she was worth, bony fingers never still and eyes downcast. The noise and demands she produced earlier had ceased and we gave her the time she needed.

Natalie Kirk's address was in the St Ann's estate, a narrow terraced house on Sketchley Street, off Blue Bell Hill Road. Several years ago the council had thrown some money at St Ann's in an attempt to regenerate the area after a serious bout of negative press due to high crime rates, in particular gun violence, where

Nottingham had managed to obtain the nickname of Shottingham. They hadn't done a bad job, but Natalie's home still looked uncared for and lacklustre.

The front door opened into a narrow hallway with woodchip paper and a yellowing ceiling. I could see the kitchen beyond as we walked into the living room to our right. I was struck by the smell; a mixture of fusty socks, cigarette smoke and rotting food. The room consisted of a shabby brown velour sofa with tassels in disarray around the bottom edges, seat cushions well-worn and indented, sinking down into the base where wire springs had long ago given up their ability to stand firm. Magazines, a litter bin overflowing onto the carpet, and DVD cases filled what little space there was of the floor. A cat litter tray was positioned on top of an old dilapidated sideboard. It looked and smelled as though it hadn't been cleaned out in a long time. The litter appeared to have been pushed out of the tray by the feline owner of the mess and was dropping onto the floor. The curtains were drawn, which had the effect of closing in the smell around you. Smothering you. The cat was nowhere to be seen and I couldn't blame it.

"Natalie, can I make you a drink?" Sally asked.

"Ooh, could you, love? A drop of whiskey with a splash of water would go down right well about now. You'll find the whiskey bottle at the side of the bread bin."

Sally looked at me and rolled her eyes. Natalie Kirk didn't notice, she was busy texting someone. Her fingers shaking now whereas they had been steady before.

I nodded at Sally and then towards the stairs indicating I planned to go up and have a look around. She nodded. I wasn't comfortable with the situation here – the lack of parenting and then lack of care when she attended the newspaper offices instead of the police station. Greed and self-service had been the tone of the whole day and it made my insides crawl. I needed to know about the woman, more about Allison and her life, both before she went missing and when she was missing. Were the two things connected? And how was Natalie going to behave in the coming days once she had processed the loss of her daughter a bit more?

Allison's was the first room at the top of the stairs. I was surprised by what I saw. An effort had been made to keep it tidy. Clothes were hung up in a small double wardrobe, with a few pairs of shoes stacked in the bottom. She had an old computer on a desk and a diary at the side of it. Coloured pens adorned the fluorescent pencil pot and a small make-up bag, covered inside by loose make-up powder, was filled with the teenage necessities: foundation, black eye-liner and lots of mascara. Several tubes filled the bag.

Her bed was made; *sleep time* embroidered on a cream bed-sheet, matching pillowcases and curtains giving the look of an organised room. Then, out of the corner of my eye I saw the air freshener, plugged into a spare socket. It explained the floral scent or at the very least, the attempt to disguise the foul odour of the rest of the house.

Though she may have been troubled, I was beginning to form the opinion Allison wanted what the rest of the girls in her school year wanted, and she was mature enough to see her home life was not that.

Sally walked in. She raised her eyebrows as she took in the tidy room.

"Natalie wants to know how long we're going to be as she wants to contact Ethan." More eye rolling. It's amazing how much non-verbal communication you can get away with when you have an opinion about a situation, and we both had an opinion about this situation.

"Not too long, I'm going to seize some items from Allison's room, then have a quick look around the rest of the house."

As I stood taking in Allison's room I got the feeling that she was a normal teenager from a difficult life. I felt a sorrow for Allison, for a life and future she had now missed, and a sorrow for the ending she had met.

We walked out of the house with a computer tower and diaries from Allison's room and a sticky, dusty laptop from the living room. I felt dirty and could smell the grime clinging to me as Sally and I loaded the boot of the car with the seized property. Natalie didn't want to talk any more, she'd said it was getting late and she needed to talk to Ethan. Sally handed Natalie her card containing contact details and told her she would be available should she want to talk. She also told her she would pop by tomorrow to see how she was doing. Natalie looked surprised that someone should offer to be there for her and a single tear had slid down her cheek without the usual drama. Maybe she had a human side after all. Maybe.

I slammed the car boot shut and climbed in the driver's seat, Sally in the passenger side. I opened my mouth, about to discuss Natalie, when a roar ripped through the air. The car was lifted rapidly from its nearside wheels. I heard a scream somewhere to my left, distant and swallowed by the huge wall of sound. My head slammed forward, air pushed out of me. The car crashed back down. I sucked for breath but there was none. Blackness.

31

The silence was deafening, covering the blackness like a shield. I pushed at my eyelids. They refused to open.

It started to break apart. Slowly. A heaviness pushed down on me and cold metal dug against my face. I couldn't make out where I was. Everything felt disjointed. Sounds began to filter through the darkness. A soft broken moaning. I concentrated on the sound, grasping for something solid, and realised it was me.

Fragments of shouting. Distant conversation. More shouting. A loud roar split through my head and senses. Flashes of orange splintered through the blackness. Too bright. A deep grinding sensation reverberating through me. It was harsh. I let the darkness protect me and gave in to it.

The noise faded in and out like an old style radio being tuned into a station it couldn't quite catch. Sounds breaking through an empty space that was sucking at me, pulling me in as I tried to find the right frequency. I could make out hammering and metal crunching. There was a pressure, a heaviness across my chest which made it near impossible to draw breath.

Hurried voices. Clawing hands. Darkness and silence.

Shallow Waters

Thoughts crumbled around me, pebbles on a beach moving with the tide.

Eventually silence.

32

She rested the side of her face on the bars, the thin metal rods cool on her skin. She wrapped her arms around her knees, pulling them up to her chest. The pain had started to lessen and she wondered about the drink she'd been given. The break from the pain gave her time to think and her thoughts turned to her friends. She wondered if they remembered her.

She let her mind wander free in this direction. Where did they think she was? Would anyone miss her? What were they doing? She fingered the bars. This wasn't an outburst. She wasn't being stroppy. All the things that used to set her off were meaningless now. Who cared who bought the latest One Direction song, pencil sharpeners or other gimmicks first, or who was most popular online. Caring about those things was stupid.

She wanted to be at home and to never leave the house again. She wished for her irritating two-year-old sister to poke her and ask for help dressing up and she'd never say no again. She'd never yell at her to go away and Mum would never have to tell her to have more patience. She wanted to tell them all how much she loved them. She had always loved them.

Why wasn't anyone coming? Didn't they care? Had she been

so bad and awful they didn't even consider looking for her? All better off without her?

She looked past the bars that confined her, out at her surroundings. She didn't like it here, she didn't want to be here. She wanted to go home.

33

"So you're in the land of the living, huh." The statement broke the silence.

The brightness bounced off the pale painted walls causing me to blink several times. Aaron stood to the side holding a brown bag like a drunk in the street. He looked as though he'd been caught stealing out of his grandmother's purse. My eyes closed against the glare.

"Unless death is carrying a gin bottle in a sun spot, I think I am."

"Um, oh yeah." He moved to the blinds and drew them across the window, darkening the room. My eyelids were heavy and a vice seemed to tighten around my head as I opened them. I raised my hand. Pain shot through my ribs and took my breath away. I winced and sucked in air. Aaron stood and watched. He shifted his feet, checked his tie with one hand, then shoved the brown paper bag at me. I imagined him on his first date and shut my eyes again.

"Grapes not your thing?"

Blinking, I took the bag. "Thanks." I dropped them on the

bed. It took a few seconds for my brain to engage. I hadn't been alone in the car. "How's Sally?" I asked.

"She's okay. You've both been battered. The doctor said you've got a concussion and a couple of fractured ribs. You took the brunt of the impact. Sally was lifted out of her seat and dumped on top of you. You've been lucky."

"Tell that to my head." I put my hand up to my forehead. The action hurt every bone and muscle. I winced.

"Docs say you'll be here a couple of days for observation. Sally will be in longer."

"What happened, Aaron?"

"Fire guys reckon it looks like a gas explosion. They're spending some time on it. You smell anything while you were in there?"

"I smelled plenty; the place was a refuse site. What happened to Natalie?"

"She survived. Looking at the house, I don't know how she managed it. It's flattened. It would seem she was in the living room at the front when the blast went up. She was knocked about and hit by flying debris, but I think she must have been protected by something to come out alive. She's pretty smashed up. She's got some burn injuries, a nasty head injury which the docs are concerned about, broken bones and internal injuries. They've induced a coma and have tubes breathing for her. She won't be talking to us any time soon."

I hadn't liked Natalie Kirk, but she didn't deserve this. She identified her daughter in the mortuary today and now she was in a hospital on life support.

Aaron stayed long enough to update me on events and then he was gone. I managed to eat a couple of grapes but nausea swept my insides and I had a serious itch to get out of there. Rosie, Allison and now Natalie. What were the connections? What were we missing? I couldn't think straight in the confines of a hospital bed. I needed to be at my desk and to read the reports as they came in. Not sat here, waiting for a doctor to assess me and tell me I was okay. I knew I was okay.

My thoughts tumbled around. Was the blast at Natalie Kirk's house a simple gas explosion or was there more to it? Why would anyone target Natalie if it wasn't accidental? My head started to spin with the questions. A wave of nausea reared up and hit me hard, I curled myself up on the bed in an attempt to ease the wretchedness I felt.

"Hannah?"

Superintendent Catherine Walker stood in the doorway. She

looked relaxed. Her feathers never seemed to be ruffled. I wondered if they ever would be. She was one of those people you hear described as born leaders. She assimilated and acted on information received in the blink of an eye, confident in the knowledge the right decision had been reached. Now I wondered what this decision was. Catherine Walker wasn't the hearts and flowers type of boss. She gave rapid sure fire answers to tough questions, but she didn't do hospital visits.

"Ma'am." I pushed with my palms on the bed and forced my elbows to lock in an attempt to get myself up. Queasiness circled inside me. I gritted my teeth.

She stepped into the room. "No. Stay still." She pulled a chair from the corner and placed it at the side of my bed, sitting herself neatly in front of me as she smoothed her trousers. "How are you, Hannah? Really."

Partially upright I collapsed back on the dozen pillows I'd been provided with and faced my superintendent side on, well aware I looked far from my best. "As you'd expect after being thrown over in a car."

The corners of her mouth turned up, but the sentiment didn't travel to her eyes. "Take as long as you need to before you come back to work. It's important you take care of yourself." She clasped her hands on her lap, never taking her eyes off me.

Oh, that's where this was headed, she was going to try and pull my job from under me.

"I'm fine, ma'am. All I need is a good night's sleep and I'll be back on the case again tomorrow."

She looked at me. I couldn't figure out what she was thinking.

"Hannah." She paused, made sure I was listening. "We need to make some progress with the investigation. The case has caught the attention of the national press. And with you laid up injured the team has no direction. I need someone to pull this in and you need time to heal." She paused a beat, her eyes never left me. "I'm sorry. Anthony is taking over as SIO for now."

I'm not sure why she bothered with the sorry sentiment. I wasn't sure she had been sorry about a decision in her life. She weighed up the options and implications and worked with what she had. "What? No! I'm fine. I know this case. I have a feel for these kids. There's a link between them. I'm learning who they were and what their lives were about and that knowledge will lead us to whoever is killing them. You can't yank me off it this way." I was more forceful than I would have been had we been in the office. I imagined the bravery came from the drugs the hospital had given me. She let it slide.

"You do know the case, Hannah, and you're the best person

for the job. I don't like to change SIOs in the middle of an investigation, but you're in no fit state to continue with it. When you come back we'll speak and assess your ability to carry on. I need someone focused on the investigation." She stood. "I also need to take care of my officers. Okay?"

I nodded. She was impossible to fight once her mind had been made up. I had to choose my battles with care. I would get this job back. It was my case and I would finish it for Rosie and Allison.

"Feel better soon, Hannah," she said as she turned on her heel.

34

The was a gentle hum of nurses going about their work behind my door, squeaky wheels of medicine carts, mellowed toned phones ringing, the chatter of soothing voices and stern commands for those not quite compliant patients. I felt comforted by these sounds as I awoke. It was dusky. The daily routine of the ward reminded me that life was on-going and I was still a part of it. It felt good. Now I needed to give my survival meaning and that meaning was to secure the arrest of the monster in our city before he had chance to strike again.

I turned to the cupboard at the side of my bed to get my phone and saw a neat little bear, and in between its paws sat a small box of chocolates. It was adorable. Not huge and overbearing like the ones you see when women have children, and massive two foot bears, balloons and little white knitted clothes take over the room, it was neat, organised and presented. A crisp white card was held in the ribbon wrapped around the chocolate box. Pain made me flinch as I reached over to pick it out. The inscription read: *Ethan x.* So Ethan had been in? Or had he sent the bear by delivery? Without knowing how long I'd been out of it, I didn't know if I had missed any visitors. It annoyed me. I was awake when Catherine Walker deemed it acceptable to remove me from my position as I lay in my hospital bed, but not when Ethan comes in. It was a fucked up day.

My musings reminded me Natalie Kirk was in this hospital somewhere. Attached to tubes, with her life supported by machinery. The woman had been through enough. I felt bad for her.

I shifted my feet, pushing them out from under clean white sheets and waited a moment, wondering if one small action would scupper me, but I was okay. I pushed round with my body until I was upright and gingerly dropped to the cold vinyl floor. The hospital gown gaped around my rear. I pulled at the ties to protect what little dignity I had. I felt weak and drained as I shuffled out of my room towards the nurses' station. It reminded me of a bee hive my father used to keep, lots of activity that looked like complete discord. It took a while for someone to notice I was there. They were busy. Ten minutes passed and after admonishments that I should be in my own bed, I was given directions to Natalie Kirk in the ICU.

She looked so doll-like. Her tiny frame was hidden by a vast expanse of starched white cotton, stamped with the hospital logo and draped across her. A ventilator chugged up and down, pumping the very breath into her. Wires and tubes snaked away from her body to monitors that were softly beeping. Natalie Kirk was alive, but only just.

35

Rain fell from the dark sky, small shallow drops. The grey flat frontage of Central police station rose ahead of me. I sheltered under the cover of the YMCA building on Shakespeare Street, watching as pedestrians walked past, uninterested in the stranger on the path, their obvious intent to move to their destination before the rain became worse.

I took a deep breath, winced with the action and steeled myself. This wouldn't be easy but I had to do it. Zipping my coat up under my chin, I pushed my hands down into my pockets. I really did need to buy some gloves. Two uniformed cops ran into the front yard of the station. No sooner was the driver in than blue lights were flashing and the vehicle was moving out of its position and turning right onto the road. Life still went on, no matter whether I was here or not. But I preferred it if I was. Everything had a different feel. There was a sense that I'd have to fight for my place, my role. The explosion had the effect of bringing more clarity. I couldn't move without wincing but I wanted to get back to work. We had a child killer to bring in. I had to fight the pain and keep going.

The nursing staff hadn't wanted to release me. It had taken a good portion of the day to get discharged. The doctor prescribed painkillers for my ribs and gave me a head injury leaflet and a list of medical issues that, should they occur, ought to bring me straight back to the ward. A nurse wrote the ward telephone number on the leaflet and told me I'd have access for the next forty-eight hours. After that I needed to go through Accident and Emergency again. I'd swallowed two pills and then left. They couldn't do anything else for me, but there was a lot I could achieve, out here on the investigation.

It was early afternoon by the time I got home by taxi. I checked my phone, which had miraculously survived the blast in my pocket. Fifteen missed calls. Evie had made four, a couple were from my dad, but the majority were withheld numbers. They were probably work calls, before the explosion. The taxi waited for me as my car was still parked here at work. A five minute shower and change and soon enough I was here. I felt in my pocket for the painkillers and relaxed when my fingers touched the plastic corner of the blister pack.

I had to go in and fight for my role as SIO. I knew more about this investigation than anyone. I had to fight for the respect of my team. I didn't want to go in and be looked at with sympathy. I had to go in there and take it over and deal with the team up front. With two children already dead and little in the way of leads, we had to work harder. I would work harder.

I walked to the rear of the building and let myself in through the secure doors where the wide, old, concrete steps wound their way up through the building. The ceilings were high and I always felt comfortable in here. Its battered but large and familiar framework gave me a sense of home. I took the two flights I needed, stopping every few steps for breath as my ribs directed their objection at me. Finally on the floor I needed I turned right instead of left to the incident room. I had a meeting with Catherine Walker scheduled. I had some red tape to cut through before heading back to my team. I wondered how receptive she'd be to having me back. She had seen an opportunity to replace me and she'd taken it, but I couldn't see a reason for her continued resistance. It would look petty and she was too shrewd to allow herself to look petty. So I would face the music and see how she would react.

"Ross, where are those witness statements I asked for an hour ago?" Aaron shouted across the incident room. I pushed the door open. The noise of a busy working office halted. All eyes turned to me.

"Glad to see you're hard at it and you've not decided to have a few days off in my absence."

Ross grinned. "Welcome back, boss." I got the impression I was a welcome distraction from Aaron whom, I imagined, had tried hard to keep the team motivated while I was gone, but didn't quite hit the right note.

"Thanks, Ross. It's good to be back." And it was. The pain I felt from my ribs was distracting to the point of overwhelming, but the hospital had provided me with some pretty good painkillers so I felt confident that I could cope.

"Thank God you're back," Aaron said, rubbing his eyes where dark shadows had now formed and taken a deep hold. A look that didn't suit him and one I didn't often see on him.

"Glad to see I've been missed. I need to see Anthony first, but then we'll have a team briefing and see where we're up to."

He nodded and leaned back heavily in his chair releasing a deep breath of air.

I flicked the switch on the kettle before going to find Grey and hoped someone would take the hint.

Grey was hunched over his desk, a frown creasing his face, shoulders tensed. A cold coffee sat neglected in front of him.

"Sir?" He looked up, bemused by the familiar but unexpected sound of my voice.

"Hannah, it's so good to see you," he gushed before he could stop himself. He stood quickly, "How are you?"

"Thank you, sir, I'm good. A bit sore, but I have all my faculties so I'm ready to go. I spoke with Catherine." Grey raised an eyebrow. "I'm to see how I get on. She's sending you an email to that effect. That you need to keep an eye on me." I grimaced at the thought I needed a babysitter during the investigation.

"I'm glad you're back." He looked desperate to let go of the case and being told to watch over me in an email with a paper trail wasn't his idea of letting go of the job. If it ended badly then the lead officer was going to be under immense scrutiny and Grey worried about his career. If this didn't go well, it would leave an ugly stain.

"The case has hit the national press as you'd imagine. They're screaming for answers. Wanting to know what actions we're taking to make sure our kids are safe. They're building up a real furore. The Chief's not happy and he's being pushed down in London. This one is being watched from the top down, Hannah."

It would be. I'd never seen murders in such quick succession, particularly ones where we had no inkling of possible offenders. Grey was feeling the pressure.

"What do we have then?" I looked down at his desk where there was an open fire investigation report.

Grey sat in his chair again. I followed suit and sat opposite.

He picked up the preliminary report and talked me through the main points. "The seat of the blast was in the kitchen, an old gas oven which, they state, had to be at least ten years old. It looks as though the ignition was created when Natalie did something to generate a spark. Like lighting a cigarette maybe." He looked up from the paper he was scanning. "Did she smoke?"

"Like a chimney."

He nodded and continued. "Or flicking a light switch or turning something on at the plug. The fire investigators are suspicious of it and have requested forensic support."

"It doesn't make sense. Why would someone kill two young girls then cause an explosion at the home of one of the child's parents?"

"Quite." He put the paperwork down. "The PM has been done on Allison."

My body tensed. It was unreasonable, but I felt remorseful that I'd somehow let her down by not being there. I tucked a stray strand of hair around my ear.

"Allison was generally fit and well. No signs of alcohol or drug abuse and she was adequately nourished. From the evidence gathered at both PM's Jack feels the deaths of Allison and Rosie Green are linked." He reviewed his notes. "The anomaly is that there were no old bruises on Allison, only new ones. It doesn't look as though she was being hurt over a period of time, but that final day, she took a real pasting." Grey looked back up at me. "The assault was furious, Hannah. There were bruises everywhere but on her face. What links the girls is that the same pattern is present on Allison's neck as was on Rosie's. It's identical. If we find the item used as a weapon, then we can match it up to the marks around the necks of both girls."

"Right, so all we need to do now is find an offender who has murdered a girl from Norwich as well as a local child and potentially set circumstances to create an explosion at the girl's house after the event."

"Not an easy job," he acknowledged. "But I have faith in you and your team."

As I left Grey's office, I wondered about the lack of conviction he put into his last words.

36

Sally looked at the dirty ceiling from her hospital bed. She'd been here since yesterday and she was fed up of staring at it. Balloons and flowers were taking over the room like an attack of triffids, no matter how much the nurses kept telling Sally's mum she couldn't bring the flowers in because of recent health and safety regulations. Her mum knew how to go over the top, especially where her children were concerned and it didn't matter how old her and Alan got, she still fussed over them like an old mother hen. Right now she was ordering her dad about, sending him to get more chairs as there weren't enough for them to get around the bed.

While she understood she had to be checked out properly she itched to get back to her home and her job. She didn't want to be away from the investigation too long. As well as wanting to be on the inquiry, she needed to prove herself a valuable member of the team. She planned to take her exams and go for promotion so she would be in a position where she would bring home a better wage, and with a child killer out there, she was determined to be a part of the team that brought him in and that brought justice for the families. A job like this would provide strong evidence in the promotion process for sergeant. Evidence of her capabilities. Promotions were tough, especially in the current economic climate with the force shrinking in size. So for everything that might go against her, she needed demonstrable investigative abilities in her favour.

She heard her dad hush her mum and then wander off in search of the chairs which apparently were stacked at the side of the visitors' toilets near the entrance to the ward. Her mum came back over to her and looked down, holding her hand. This simple gesture made her feel warm and loved. Cared for in a way she couldn't imagine was possible to feel from such a small touch. She looked up at her mum and saw her chin quivering but her jaw clenched up tight. "Oh, Mum, don't." She gave her mum's hand a gentle squeeze, "I'm okay, look." Her hand was gripped hard in return as she watched her mum try and hold on. "Mum?" A single tear escaped, saying a thousand words that her mum refused to speak. Sally gave the grip back just as hard in response. "I love you, Mum," she whispered.

The door to the room banged open as her dad pushed through it with the chair in front of him, using it as a battering ram.

"Owen!" her mum chided, still holding onto Sally.

"Sorry, love. Why bloody hospitals can't put a couple of chairs in side rooms I don't know. Anyway, here now." He dropped it to the floor at her side, clattering on the hard tiles, and parked himself in the seat. "How are you today, sweetheart? Need anything else bringing in?"

"I'm good, Dad. Thank you. And if you bring anything else in, I think we're going to have to call a removal firm just to clear me out."

He laughed. "Hey, you're right there."

The door opened again and Tom entered. He looked tired but he smiled when he saw her. Guilt needled her at the warmth of it.

"You okay?" he asked.

"Yes, fine. The doctor said rest for a couple of days then I'll be fit to go back to work. Come here." She patted the bed with her spare hand.

Tom stopped, the smile vanished, his body tensed. She didn't want this argument again. Her mum must have felt the tension in her hand.

"Come on, Owen, let's go and grab a cuppa and come back in a bit." She squeezed Sally's hand again.

"But we've just got here."

"Owen." Her tone was sharp.

"Oh. Okay." They left with smiles and promised to return after their drink.

Tom had stood waiting, his face hardening. "How many times do we need to discuss this?"

"Tom, please, let's give it a little longer, until we get a strong lead on this case. I need in, it's important to me, to my career. I won't take risks." She didn't want to beg, but she heard the pleading tone in her own ears. She needed him to understand.

He moved forward and sat on the bed taking her hand in his own. "You didn't think it was a risk getting into a work vehicle after visiting a victim's mother, but look where we are, Sally. Really look." His eyes left hers and dropped to the bed. "I love you. I love our baby." His voice softened and he gently touched the hand which stroked her stomach, where life was growing.

She knew he was right, she should tell Hannah she was pregnant, but something was stopping her. This case, the life growing inside her, gave a sense of urgency to find this killer. She couldn't tell them yet.

37

I returned to my office and read an email from Ethan. Attached were the press reports he'd written. There was nothing helpful, just background on Allison that I already knew. After a briefing with the team and talking through where we were at, I went to see to Evie. With a drink in each hand I pushed my way through her door. Hot tea and coffee sploshed over the rims of the cups as she launched herself at me and threw her arms around my neck.

"Ohmigod, Hannah! I thought I'd lost you. The report. The explosion. What happened? How are you? Why are you here? Ohmigod!"

"Evie, breathe. I'm fine, look." I pulled back out of her grasp keeping my arms wide. Tiny glass fragments had torn into my skin as easily as a knife through sun-warmed butter and the slivers of injured skin shone from my pale face. I looked dishevelled and was carrying around a couple of suitcases under my eyes. Evie looked me up and down and grunted.

"Fine, huh?"

"I know." I sighed as I stepped around her, putting the cups on her desk. "It looks worse than it is though. A few cuts and bruises is all. I'm fine."

"So what happened?"

"I don't know. I've been in with Grey who, by the way, looked worse than I do."

"Tell me about it. You should have seen the way he looked when he knew you were out of action and the job dropped in his lap; I don't think it was much to do with concern for you. He doesn't want his name on the top of an investigation this big. It's a career changer. He was shitting himself."

"I can imagine. He told me the preliminary report from the fire investigators indicates the possibility of arson with intent to endanger life."

"You mean someone wanted to blow you up?"

"It doesn't look as though it was aimed at Sally or me, but Allison Kirk's mum, Natalie. A gas leak was created and once Natalie started moving about the house something ignited and… boom. We were lucky it didn't happen while we were still in there."

"Oh, poor Sally. How is she?"

"I'm not sure; all the doctors have said is they are keeping her in a little longer for observation. I spoke with her though and she seems okay. Keen to return to work."

"I can't wait to see her. You were both so lucky. So what now?"

"Glad you asked." I smiled. "You don't think I brought tea just to get hugged did you?"

"Mmm." She sat her skinny frame down on her chair. "Let me have it."

"I need you to dig up everything we have on Natalie Kirk. Every place she's worked, if she ever has, all benefits she's claiming, all known associates; look through her financials and her social networking life. Go back as far as you can. I need to know everything there is to know about her."

"Looking for anything in particular?"

"Someone wanted her dead. It doesn't add up and I want to see what part of the picture is incomplete."

"Inspector? Inspector!" Ross was shouting.

I took a couple of strides out of Evie's office and looked down the corridor in the direction of the incident room. Ross looked exasperated. His usually preened hair was rumpled and he had a manic glint in his eye I often saw when inquiries he was working on gave him some answers.

"What is it, Ross?"

"It's the phone. For you. Forensic submissions unit."

"Put it through to my office." I strode past him. Did we have a lead? Did our killer slip up? I could almost taste the anticipation as I half ran down the corridor.

I snatched up the phone. "DI Robbins."

"Ma'am, it's Doug Howell from the forensic unit. We have something."

'Okay, don't leave me in suspense."

"We've managed to get a DNA profile from a substance recovered from the first victim, Rosie Green. Lab tests identified it as semen."

"Okay." I twisted myself around my desk and sat.

"We put the profile into the system, did a speculative search and it came up with a match."

My patience was short and my ribs were sore and disturbing my line of thought. Doug was still talking, something about percentages and matches.

"Who is it, Doug?"

"Colin Benn."

"Date of birth?" I scribbled down what Doug relayed to me.

"17th September 1965."

"And you have the completed report to send me I take it?"

The thrill of a name built inside me.

"It's coming at you via email as we speak."

My machine bleeped and an email from forensic submissions pinged into my inbox. "Okay, thanks, Doug. I appreciate the work you've done."

"No worries. Anything else you need, let us know."

The forensic submission department was backed up. With recent heavy budget cuts there was extra pressure on them to cut back, but with the expectation of no fewer detections, so I thanked him again and hung up. Now I wanted to know who Colin Benn was and how he came into contact with Rosie Green.

I wanted Benn's life tipped upside down and to see what fell out, so I input his details into the police computer systems and waited. What kind of prior did this guy have? Why wasn't he already on our radar for this? That was definitely a question Walker would ask and one the press would be asking too before long.

I pushed myself out of my chair and shouted out the door for Aaron. I hadn't had chance to talk to him about my return and his management of the team in my absence. He was a good solid guy, who knew how to work an investigation and I was lucky to have him. We needed to have that conversation but there wasn't the time right now. Results were coming back for Benn and they didn't look good.

"Shit."

"What is it?" Aaron stuck his head around the door, feet still firmly in the incident room.

"Results have come in from forensics with a DNA match on semen recovered from Rosie. A guy named Colin Benn. I'm looking at a report that identifies him as," I stared at the computer screen before I spoke again, "Natalie Kirk's current boyfriend."

38

"What? We haven't done all the background checks on Natalie yet. Where is he?" Aaron asked, standing square in my doorway now.

"I don't know. We have an address. Can you get everyone together in the incident room, see what Evie has managed to collate so far. Once everyone is together, I'll brief them and we'll find him. I've got to phone the hospital." I snatched up the handset I had just laid down and dialled. After some misdirections I was put through to the ICU ward. Natalie had a police guard but someone introducing himself as her partner would still get past. The nurse I spoke to, Joan Michaels, said that other than me, Natalie Kirk hadn't had a single visitor. I thanked her, requested no one be allowed to visit and left my mobile number asking her to let me know if anyone turned up.

We had him. The piece of shit who had viciously killed two children. This was one of those cases that made your skin crawl and made the evenings when you shut your eyes that much more difficult. But we had him. I sat at my desk and looked across all the paper I had sprawled across it; notes I had made from a couple of calls with Martin and multiple reports from various specialists, crime scene and post-mortem photographs.

Photographic reminders of what I'd seen weren't necessary. The images were etched like stone in my mind. Rosie Green and Allison Kirk would never be forgotten, or the terrible injuries inflicted on them.

Looking over my notes reminded me I needed to call Clive Tripps and update him. We needed to find out what Benn's link to Norwich and to Rosie was. So far I couldn't see a link or a motive.

Aaron gathered the team and the extra bodies we needed for the arrest and search in the incident room. It was a hive of activity and chatter. Where seating allowed, uniformed officers sat, the rest stood at the back. I looked at Sally's desk and saw a face I didn't recognise. I didn't like it but I couldn't blame the cop, it was high profile and the kind of job cops wanted in on. A job where you knew you were fetching a real bad guy in.

Sitting on the edge of a desk at the front of the incident room I reeled off the new information that identified Colin Benn as the offender. Looks passed between staff. It wasn't a name we were familiar with, but we didn't have a list of potential suspects anyway. I continued, "Benn is the current boyfriend of Natalie Kirk, mother of the second murdered child, Allison. It doesn't look like the explosion Sally and I were caught up in was an accident. It's being investigated by divisional CID as arson with intent to endanger life. We have information on Benn from a few years back. One of the many pieces of intelligence we have is that he was fired from a job a few years ago, for stealing parts from the company. He worked as a kitchen fitter which would give him enough information on how to set a gas explosion off in a house. We have three victims, including Natalie. Now we have forensic evidence linking Benn to Rosie, it means he has identifiable links to all three victims: semen on Rosie; a relationship with Natalie and in turn, a relationship, or knowledge at least, of her daughter, Allison. We need to find him and bring him in. Initially on the murder of Rosie Green, but we're looking at him hard for Allison's murder and the attempted murder of Natalie, so we still have a lot of work to do. We have no idea how Benn links to Norwich or how Rosie Green came to be found here. I need to know everything about Benn. We can't leave any stone unturned." I could see Aaron writing lists as I spoke, his head down and his hand scribbling. From past history I knew he was still listening. He had an uncanny knack of following conversations as they happened around him even if he appeared to be doing something else. A loud ringing interrupted the briefing. "Who the fuck has their phone on that loud in the middle of briefing?" I snapped. All eyes looked just to the right of me where a phone was lighting up with every ring. Shit.

"Robbins!" I was in no mood for whoever this caller was

now.

Silence. Again.

"ROBBINS."

Nothing.

I slammed the phone down hard on the desk; it bounced twice before hitting the floor. All eyes looked away. "Bollocks." I cursed again, picked it up and put it on vibrate before I set it back down a bit easier. Aaron eye-balled me, a question in his expression. I took a breath.

"Okay. The last known address for Benn is 28 Sharland Street, Basford. There is an old Y registered blue Mondeo registered to him at that address. We want the car seized as it could have been used to transport the bodies. He has some previous convictions for," I looked down at the paperwork in my hands and read from the printouts, "assault, drugs and an old USI…" USI stood for Unlawful Sexual Intercourse, "with a fourteen-year-old girl when he was eighteen."

"His taste hasn't changed with age then," Aaron commented, still writing his notes.

"It would appear not."

39

The girl was tired. Too tired to be scared. Or so she thought. The games he played with her were exhausting. She feared him and the time alone was hers. She recognised this now and was grateful for it. She rested her cheek on the cold red plastic, closed her eyes and allowed her mind to wander again.

Red was the perfect colour. It had probably been chosen on purpose. Or maybe not. She used to like red. She used to have a red woollen scarf she liked to wear when it was cold. A birthday gift from her mum. Tears gathered under her eyelids. They felt hot.

She missed her mum. She loved her. She loved her more than she loved anything in the world and wished she could take back the spiteful, hurtful words spat out in anger. The last clash they'd had, she'd said she never wanted to talk to her again. She'd said she hated her, that she'd ruined her life.

The reality was, she wanted to talk to her so very much. She wanted to feel her warmth and be held. She desperately wanted to say how much she loved her and to tell her she needed her and couldn't imagine a life without her. Did her mum hate her now? Was she enjoying the peace her absence brought?

She needed this time alone. From him. It was time where she could recover and rest, yet at the same time she felt isolated and hated it. Memories of tantrum-induced stomps to her room where she would blast out her favourite songs alone brought with it a swelling in her chest that choked her. She didn't want to be alone. She didn't want to be here.

The red plastic became damp, her cheek sticking like tacky paint as the warm tears slid down.

40

I parked the car a couple of doors down from number twenty-eight. Night time was closing in and the streetlights were on. The road was silent but for a dog barking, muted somewhere in another house. The mood felt electric. We were all wired at the prospect of an arrest. As the convoy of police cars pulled up and parked behind me, I appraised the front of Benn's address.

The house looked in a state of disrepair. Litter spilled out of an attached outhouse building onto the overgrown pathway to the front door. The whole neighbourhood had a look of open indifference. Wheelie-bins were left in the road and broken tricycles were discarded on neglected lawns.

I shifted my focus back to number twenty-eight. The Y registered Mondeo we were interested in was parked rusting on the road. The two rectangular windows in the top half of the front door of the address were dark. There were no other sign of lights from within. I wiped the palms of my hands on my trousers, damp rivulets of sweat soaking into the material.

Aaron knew what I was looking for. "He's in there. There's a faint glow in the upstairs front window, maybe a television or computer monitor."

I saw it. "Okay, listen in." I turned to the gathered search officers. "As discussed at the office, Aaron and I will enter the address at the front and Ross and..." I paused and gave a querying look to one of the uniform cops I'd forgotten the name of.

"Gavin, ma'am."

"Gavin will make sure no one exits at the rear of the property. Once Benn is secured they will take him to into custody, book him in, and leave the search teams to do their job. Is everyone happy they know why we are here and what they're doing?" A murmur of yes ma'am went around the circled group. "It looks as though he is in a first floor room, so DS Stone and I will head straight up there. Benn has markers for violence, so be careful."

We quietly moved to the address and I nodded towards the door indicating to the enforcer officer, wearing full protective gear which included face visor and gloves, to do his stuff. He held the enforcer with both hands and slammed it forward with force. Twice. The door gave with a sickening crack as it split near its locking system. I pushed on the door and ran into the house. The dimming daylight outside gave the sparsely furnished interior an eerie sepia toned feel. My feet clacked heavily on bare floorboards. The stench of rotten food and bodily fluids hit.

"Fuck." I heard Aaron at my side.

"Police!" I shouted a second time. I strained to hear a response but could only hear echoes of *Police!* as other officers entered and moved about. The stairs were straight in front of me. Holding my Maglite in my right hand, I directed the beam onto the steps so I could see where I was treading and started my ascent, shouting my identification as I went.

Moving quickly my boots sounded hollow on the steps. We needed to contain Benn and prevent any evidence being destroyed.

I went straight for the door emitting a faint line of light under the bottom and turned the handle. The sight that met me was pitiful.

Colin Benn was a slim man with a flabby belly overhanging a grubby, threadbare pair of blue and white striped boxer shorts; they left little to the imagination, with the front gaping open like the mouth of a hungry animal. He was bent over his computer, an old tower with a keyboard, mouse and monitor wires all tangled in a mess hanging down at the back of the basic desk he was seated at. His yellowing fingers tapped on the keyboard as we entered. He turned and faced us, a flash of fear registering on his face. He looked back down to the task at hand. Within a few strides across the small box room I was beside him. I took hold of his right wrist, yanked it hard away from the keyboard and wrapped the rigid metal speed cuff around his wrist. Leaning forward, I pulled his left wrist behind him, forcing his body forward, his nose almost touching the desk. Benn let out a high pitched squeal. "Colin Benn, I am arresting you for the rape and murder of Rosie Green." I locked his left wrist into the cuffs and pulled back, lifting him up and out of his chair and away from the keyboard. He let out a couple more yelps of complaint, his breath, a stench of stale cigarettes and alcohol.

"You do not have to say anything, but it may harm your defence if you do not mention when questioned..." I continued the caution as Benn spluttered, spittle flying out of his mouth. Disgusted and conscious of virus transmission I shifted my head sideways.

"I didn't do anything. You can't prove it."

His nearly naked body reacted to the stress of the situation as goosebumps appeared all over him. His legs shook. I held the rigid metal between the two cuffs with my right hand as I pulled the search warrant out of my pocket with my left.

"Colin, I'm DI Hannah Robbins and I'm in charge of this investigation. This search warrant has been signed by a magistrate and authorises us to search your house for items relevant to the offence for which you have been arrested. Do you understand what is happening?"

The shaking got worse. "You can't prove anything. I don't

know anyone called Rosie whatever her name was."

I didn't plan on discussing the facts of the case with him until I had him in a recorded interview room. "Regardless of whether you believe we can prove it or otherwise, do you understand the information I have given you?"

Benn nodded, eyes to the floor.

I handed Benn over to Ross and Gavin who had by now both entered the premises. Once Benn was out of the address in his boxers and a frayed grey blanket from one of the police vehicles, the crime scene investigators were called in.

As I stood in the small cramped bedroom, I saw a photograph of Allison on the chipped table at the side of his bed. The photograph wasn't framed but was laid face up and looked to be well fingered. It showed a smiling Allison in her school uniform. Her smile looked forced for a camera she had no interest in, by an organisation she felt wouldn't and hadn't protected her and could do little about it. The face in the image looked into the lens, saying with her eyes what she couldn't say with her words. The eyes that looked out said a big *fuck you*, yet Benn felt it appropriate to have it at the side of his bed. With my hands gloved I opened the bedside drawer under this photograph and found a box of tissues and several packets of condoms. On the floor at the side of the bed were bundles of hardened screwed up tissues.

41

Aaron and I left the search team and CSIs to go through the house. It would be a long and intense search. If Benn was our man, then his address could well be the scene of the girls' murders. I gathered everyone in the incident room to debrief the arrest and to discuss the strategy for interview. Walker had come in after hearing the arrest had been successful. She looked more relaxed than the last time I'd seen her.

As she entered the room her eyes searched me out and she gave a nod, indicating her approval at the progression of the case.

Grey on the other hand looked twitchy, his fingers worked the documents in his hand. He didn't like having to monitor how I was doing. I liked it even less, though I had to admit he was good at the paperwork, the politics and multi-agency workings, managing the press and public perception of how the job was going. I loved my job but the arse kissing wasn't what I joined up to do.

The incident room buzzed with a restrained excitement. The monster behind the death of Rosie Green and possibly Allison Kirk, and the attempted murder of Natalie Kirk, now sat in the cells waiting for his solicitor. On arrival in the custody suite he'd been booked in by the custody sergeant and searched, though, with what he was wearing, there wasn't much of a search to conduct. He was photographed, fingerprinted by the Live Scan machine and another sample of his DNA taken by mouth swab. His boxer shorts had been seized and he had been provided with a pair of royal blue, one size fits all, elasticated jogging bottoms, a plain white T-shirt and black pumps.

We still had a long way to go with the case, but the mood was upbeat.

When I'd talked to Benn at his home, he had a look of surprise but not an outrageous indignation you would expect from someone arrested for a violent murder they hadn't committed.

Forensics from Allison's crime scene and swabs and samples taken during the PM hadn't started coming in. I hadn't had chance to look over the interim PM report sent over by Jack, though Grey had given me a brief outline. With the preliminary report open in my hands I read down the initial findings.

There was a strong resemblance to the MO with Rosie

Green, particularly the binding around her neck with a circular imprint. Both girls were found discarded and naked and not thought to be at the initial murder scene. There was no information coming back from CSIs at Benn's address and I wouldn't expect anything of use to be reported any time soon.

There were so many ways this interview could go and I was concerned about the lack of real information or evidence we had to link him to crime scenes, counties, or to link him to one of the murders and attempted murder of one other. I hated to work like this but we couldn't have left him out there once we had his name. The media would have a field day if we continued to investigate all the links without making an arrest and another child was killed. Not just the media but we'd then have MPs asking very difficult questions and it spiralled from there. It would come down to me and what decisions I had made so I kept my decision log up to date, giving reasons for the implementation or otherwise of certain actions.

We had to work all the possible angles.

My arm and chest wall throbbed. Grabbing the plastic blister pack out of my pocket I snapped out two painkillers, palmed them into my mouth and washed them down with cold tea.

"Do we have the crime scene report on Allison's scene?" I asked the room.

Ross raised his arm, a blue folder in his hand. "It's a preliminary report produced by the CSU as so many results haven't come in yet, but they're aware we are on the clock now." The custody clock would restrict us with detention of an offender as we had twenty-four hours from the arrival at the police station. After that we would have to apply for extensions if we needed to. We had our guy; evidence was slow at the best of times, but when you needed it, time seemed to speed up. I flipped through the pages.

"So, we have DNA evidence that links Benn to Rosie Green, but nothing further on how they knew each other. He is linked to Allison Kirk, through her mother's relationship with him. Looking at this we have photographs of the neck injury on Allison and comparatively the same injury on Rosie. What we need is for the search team to locate the item that left the marks around their necks. Chase them up and get updates on items seized."

We had enough to ask him about while further inquiries were carried out. On the arrest of Benn I had seized his computer straight away as there was something on there he didn't want us to see, which made me all the more curious. Aaron had taken the tower to the Digital Investigation Unit. The gathering of evidence was a slow process. Time however, was a luxury I wasn't sure we had.

42

It was late by the time we got into interview with Benn. The daytime civilian staff had all left the building. Offices were closed and lights off. Booking into custody and waiting for a solicitor took time.

The duty solicitor was more than likely at home and had been disturbed in the middle of a meal by a call requesting their presence at the police station. This process and the subsequent consultation with their client could take hours again. Written disclosure was often a bone of contention between police and attending solicitors. Not revealing enough could mean the interview wouldn't run smoothly as client and solicitor broke to discuss previously unknown and not provided and consulted issues before answering further questions. The whole issue caused new officers no end of headaches. Aaron wrote ours, giving the pertinent facts of the case and reason for arrest, stating Benn would be asked about these and any items seized from the address. He was great at writing up this document without giving them our case on a plate. In this instance, we weren't presenting the DNA evidence. We wanted to see how Benn was going to play his knowledge of Rosie. I couldn't figure it out, so getting a version out of him prior to giving him our hand would be interesting.

Now, hours after his arrest, we were sat in the interview room with him. It was windowless and airless. A table, four hard plastic moulded chairs and a black box tape machine, a remnant of the eighties, were the only items in the room. Benn was seated at one side of the table with his solicitor, Ms Corinne Selby, a small blonde who looked fresh out of school. She'd taken the written disclosure from me with a tight smile.

Copious notes, reports and a couple of pens rested on the table between us.

Aaron flicked his pen against the table in an irritating rhythmic way. Corinne Selby looked at the pen, then at Aaron, lips pursed. He continued tapping to an inaudible beat.

"I'll ask you again, Colin. How did you know Rosie Green?"

"I don't know anyone by that name," Benn replied, sitting straight in his chair.

"Okay, let's start with things you do know. Tell me about your relationship with Natalie Kirk."

"What do you want to know?" This seemed to abate his anxiety. His shoulders relaxed and he shrank down in his chair in an easy slide. I was happy to let him talk about the things he was comfortable with first. If he was comfortable, I hoped he would keep talking and not notice the direction we were going in.

"How did you meet her?"

"In a bar. We hooked up a few times. She liked a good time. I like a girl that likes a good time." His lip curled up at one side. This man made my skin crawl. I took a moment, appraising him, feeling his mood.

"And Allison, how did she come into it?"

"Huh. She was her kid."

"We know that, Colin. What we want to know is: what was your relationship with her?" I picked up my cup and drank as he talked.

"I made an effort. You have to, don't you? Someone else's kid. Mind you, Nat wasn't much interested in her. Pretty much left her to her own devices, she did. All she were interested in were where her next hit was coming from."

"And you were interested in?" I put my cup back on the table and watched.

"Me? What I could get. No point in pretending otherwise is there? Nat was a whore with a drink problem. Didn't care much for anything and put out so long as she were tanked."

Aaron scribbled notes as Benn talked. The solicitor also made notes, her hand working quickly to keep up. I often wondered if these notes would match up should they ever be compared.

"What kind of effort did you put in with Allison?"

"Spent some time with her when her mum were too pissed."

"Too pissed for what?"

"Sex. Did you see her? Why else is anyone gunna be with her?"

"What happened when she was too pissed to put out?"

"I didn't get it, did I?"

"Didn't you?"

"Pissed up bitch would lay out face down on the sofa. Wouldn't have a clue what were happening around her." Benn went on, the smell of sweat and rotting feet rising up and filling the small room.

He talked for another hour. About how Natalie didn't care for her daughter, how all she wanted was her next drink. He painted a dark picture of life at home for Allison and I saw why she would want to leave it behind. It made the small space she'd fashioned for herself in her room even more poignant. Her house wasn't a place she could call a home, but she did have somewhere to go when she was inside it: her bedroom. I wondered what else she had done to keep herself away from her mother.

43

We left Benn in his cell. We'd been in interview for hours. According to his solicitor, who was not looking so fresh faced after multiple hours in a square box of a room with Colin Benn, he needed a break and some food. It was late and after review with the custody sergeant now on duty, it was decided we would leave him for the night and go again in the morning.

We didn't have a confession, but he was a talker. He liked to be the big man. To make the rules. Happy as long as his needs were met. He was comfortable discussing his relationships, seeing nothing wrong with them.

Grey looked worried as he trotted out of his office. His fingers twitched.

"Sir." I acknowledged his presence in the incident room. The team stopped and waited.

"Hannah, how's it going with Benn?"

"He hasn't given us much so far, but he's talking about his relationship with Natalie Kirk and stepping into things a little with Allison. He denies all knowledge of Rosie but we haven't put the forensics to him yet. This is his time to run and we'll see where he takes us." I couldn't tell if this response was what he wanted to hear or not. His hands fidgeted more and his eyes moved around the room. "He's down for the night, but we'll go back into interview in the morning."

"Do we have results from the computer work?"

"No, sir, they're still working on it."

"And the custody clock?"

"We're... into it. I'll have to speak with Catherine about an extension. With all the breaks and his eight hours sleep entitlement we need the time."

"Okay, okay, but we need results, Hannah. You know we're being watched on this one."

I sighed. "Yes, sir, I realise that."

44

The cage door opened.

"Come out here."

The girl shrank back. But not too far. She didn't want to annoy him. It was easy to do and when he was annoyed, things got worse.

"Come on then, out you come."

She kept her eyes down. She had to please him but knew never to look him in the eye. Eye contact was insolence and she learned about insolence very early on.

"Good girl. Stand up straight. That's it. I can see all of you now. Beautiful."

She kept her eyes down. The room felt warmer.

"Time to clean you up. Just look at you, you're filthy. How did you manage to get so dirty?"

She knew better than to answer him. He didn't want a response.

She jumped back, startled when his slender fingers grabbed her wrist. His grip tightened like a vice, locking around tiny bones and sending a deep throb through her arm.

His jaw clenched taut.

She didn't look up to his eyes.

"Now then, it's only a clean. You want to look pretty don't you?"

She nodded. Eyes down.

She saw the bowl, soapy water and a large pink bath sponge.

"Come here then, let's get you cleaned up." His grip loosened.

She tried her hardest not to flinch as he took the sponge, dipped it in the warm soapy water and started to wipe her clean. He started at the top, wiping her face, rubbing at areas, tutting at her as he rubbed hard. Areas she knew were really dirty. Or bloody. The warmth of the water felt good. It was gentle and soothing. It caressed her skin and made her feel again. She wanted to sit in this warmth, soak in the small bowl.

"Good isn't it?"

She stiffened.

He dipped the sponge again, dripping water around her neck and rubbing. The friction caused her to jump, the rubbing making her eyes water. The sponge dipped in and out of the bowl as he cleaned her from top to bottom. Dipping and rubbing until all dirt and blood was washed away.

Rebecca Bradley

"There's my good girl. Now, time for some photographs."

45

I walked three flights of stairs to the warmest room in the building: the Digital Investigation Unit. The department required special flooring so they didn't electrocute themselves, or so I was led to believe. It was like a technical Alice in Wonderland experience in here. Computer towers on every desk. Slinky double screened monitors at every workstation. Spare hard drives, discs and flash drives stacked up on shelves and the educational achievements of all the staff were displayed along the walls.

Today I wanted their professionalism to focus on the computer seized from Benn's address and, if possible, the computers from Rosie Green and Allison Kirk, though Benn's was priority. Benn had been working furiously on his computer when we arrived and I'd seen him deleting files. I wanted to know what he was so keen to get rid of.

The heat being kicked out of the servers was stifling. I removed my jacket and threw it on the back of a chair near the door. I was surprised to see someone still here. Two staff were sat at their desks; Danny Scrivens and Elizabeth Turner.

"Okay, so who's working on Benn's computer?" I asked, hopeful it had indeed been picked up as a job and wasn't sat in some queue waiting for me to come in here and explode.

"It's mine, ma'am. Over here at my workstation." Danny sat at the rear of the room. I walked over to his desk. At the side of him was a framed photograph of a woman around his age, with a child in her arms. Both looked relaxed and happy. A cloudless powder blue sky provided the pair with a beautiful background.

"Have you located anything to link him to these murders?"

Danny laughed and I gritted my teeth. After a tense day I had no sense of humour.

"What is it you think you're looking for?" he asked.

Where to start? "I need to find a link between Benn and Rosie Green."

Danny's face was serious. "Computers are complicated machines. I can't just go in and find what you think is in here. If we don't know what we're looking for we don't know where to start. Give me some kind of overview of what you think we might want to look at?"

"I don't know, Danny. Maybe contact between Benn and the victim, Rosie Green, through social networking sites, email, or other means. I need to find a link between them and if possible not just a straight forward link to her, but messages of plans to meet, etcetera."

"What I can do first if you want, is a triage of the hard drive and forensically retrieve all the images it holds. It's a good starting point as you might find something of your victims in there."

I was overwhelmed with the techy stuff, but trusted them and what they were doing, so after having an over-my-head technical discussion about the best course of action, I asked for the images to be placed on a separate hard drive so we would be able to check them out, prior to heading back into interview tomorrow. I didn't know if it would be helpful or not, but at least it was something to be going on with.

"When can the images be viewed? I wouldn't push, but he's in custody now with the clock running."

"I can have a copy hard drive full of the images on his computer within a couple of hours, how does that sound? The full-on examination is going to take days, maybe weeks to complete thoroughly."

"Sounds good. I'll ask Ross to come in and check them when they're ready. I'm thinking early doors tomorrow now?"

"Yes, it's late. I've no issue with staying on to set this running. I'm not sure we will be able to find the answers you want though, but we can look to see what he's been up to."

"Thanks, Danny." With that organised, I grabbed my discarded jacket and left.

My body ached and my mind buzzed. I'd lived through an explosion but hadn't stopped to process it. The hours of the day were blending into each other and I needed to keep a constant eye on the clock. I needed a break.

The area that used to be a canteen, before the financial cuts, was now a room filled with tables, chairs and a few vending machines for drinks, chocolate and sandwiches. A microwave and toaster were housed on one of the old kitchen counters. A half used bottle of washing up liquid and a well-worn cloth were discarded in the sink. Bread crumbs gathered around the bottom of the toaster. Cops were bad for clearing up in communal eating areas.

I fished some change out of my trouser pocket, pushed it into the slot and punched the buttons for black coffee. The machine whirred into life, dropped down a cardboard cup into metal jaws and dribbled in the coffee. I twisted my hand into the small space and wished for the time when police stations had canteens where you got your drinks in cups with handles, and a smile. I didn't drink coffee often, but it was hot, was strong enough to give me a caffeine burst, and was giving me ten minutes space.

The old canteen was empty. I sat at a table to the side, the smell of disinfectant heavy from the cleaners who wiped them all down before they left for the day.

It was dark outside and the uniformed night shift was on. Dependent on the incoming call levels, some cops would be sat catching up on paperwork created on day shifts, and a few would be out on calls. Night time left the station with a ghost ship feel about it.

I looked at my phone. One missed call. *Dad.* I hadn't got back to him after his call a couple of days ago. I knew I should call him back, but I couldn't face it. With every call I dreaded the content of the conversation, so instead of facing it head on, I avoided it. Avoided my father. It wasn't his fault, but I didn't want to deal with it. I didn't want to deal with his loss of mum as well as my own and I didn't want to deal with what he felt as a loss in my sister Zoe. I saw no loss there. Her own actions had landed her with the heavy prison sentence. A deep breath escaped from me and I put my head in my hands. I knew I needed to call him back. I promised myself I'd do it when we put Benn away.

After sending the team home and writing up the decision log it was time to head home myself. We had another early start tomorrow and I needed at least a few hours sleep. I needed to run a bath, pour a drink and sit down.

The living room had an empty, hollow feel about it. I switched the central heating on and pulled the vodka bottle from the cupboard in the kitchen. Clinking bottle on glass, I poured a heavy shot as I walked back to the living room and dropped down onto the sofa. A sharp edged pain sliced across my chest and around my back. I sucked in my breath and wished I hadn't been so thoughtless. With a more reserved movement, I lifted my feet up under myself, rested my head back and balanced the glass on the arm of the sofa. It had been a roller-coaster few days, starting with Rosie's body, then Allison's, the explosion at Natalie's and the arrest of Benn. Only now did I feel able to let out a slow breath. It felt like I hadn't taken one in days. But now we had Benn and we had a good case against him. I slugged back half the drink then remembered the painkillers I'd been taking through the day. It crossed my mind I shouldn't be drinking. I took another drink. I wondered how Sally was doing but knew it was too late to call her now. She'd be asleep and after what she'd been through she needed her rest.

Thoughts of Natalie stirred guilt in me. I hadn't checked on her before leaving work. A point in time when I could have called Sally. But I could do something about my error over Natalie. I finished my drink then dialled the hospital. I was put through to the ward sister who sounded like hers had also been a long day.

"There's still no change, but she's stable, Detective Inspector."

"She's had no visitors?"

"No, and there has been a police officer by her all the time. Is there anything else I can help you with?"

She wanted me off the phone. She had things to do. I understood. "No thank you. I appreciate your time."

"Good night, Inspector."

I ended the call. Natalie was safe. I hoped in the next couple of days I could tell her we had her daughter's killer.

My phone vibrated in my hand. I checked the caller display expecting it to be work related, with a request to go back in, but instead the caller ID showed *Ethan*. Thumbing the green accept key, I answered.

"It seems an age since we spoke," Ethan said.

"It does." I was happy to hear his voice. I picked up the vodka bottle and poured another drink.

"You need someone to lean on."

"And where would I find someone like that?"

"Right outside your door."

I pulled the phone away from my ear and stared at it for a couple of seconds before Ethan's distant voice reminded me he was still there.

"Hannah?"

I opened the door, phone still in hand, the back-light still showing Ethan on the call. He stood in the hallway of my apartment building, his back resting against the wall opposite. Dressed in jeans and a shirt open at the neck, his hair slightly damp, he was staring intently at me.

"Ethan?"

He stepped through the door and his hand went up to my face. I remembered how I must look.

"I needed to see you, Hannah." His thumb traced one of the small red cuts caused by the impact of the blast, before he leaned down and kissed me.

He took my breath away. His body leaned in to me and with one foot he kicked back and closed the door. I pushed my phone onto the table at the side of the door and ignored the crash as it dropped to the floor.

"I was worried. You didn't return my call." He broke away, a look on his face I didn't recognise.

"I'm sorry. It's been so busy. We have someone in custody. It's been hectic. I meant to call," I rambled.

Ethan cupped my face with his right hand, his eyes connected with mine. I didn't move. I could feel the heat rising in my cheeks. His left hand wrapped around my waist. Something shifted inside me. The weariness I was feeling had changed and now I felt alert, alive.

I managed to find my voice. "Ethan, what are you doing here?"

"This." His mouth found mine again, his lips warm, the odour of freshly washed skin filled my nostrils. My mouth parted, my brain function slowed. I wrapped my arms around his neck and winced as my ribs resisted. I pulled my arms down and rested my hands on his chest. "Hey." He noticed. "Easy." He took my hand from his chest and led me from the doorway we still stood in, through the living room and into the bedroom. We stood there a second, just looking. "It hurts?"

"Yeah." I took a deep breath. Admission is a killer. "It hurts." His eyes narrowed and he cupped my face in his hands, leant forward and kissed my lips, so softly I barely realised he was there. I pushed my hand up under his shirt to his chest and felt his heart thudding under my palm. His fingers took my shirt buttons and, one by one, he unfastened them, never taking his eyes from my face. I couldn't move. I didn't want to move. I didn't want to be anywhere but here. I leaned into him and kissed him. Deep within me there was an ache that just needed to be met. As I pushed forward and up to meet him, I also felt the pain of my ribs wrap itself around my chest; it blended into everything my body was now feeling. Ethan held my shoulders, slowed me down and dropped the shirt from me as the last button yielded. My skin felt alive. His mouth came down and found the curve in my neck. I dropped my head back, he held me secure, one arm wrapped around the small of my back and the other holding my head. His mouth was hot but his movement slow and easy. A groan escaped my lips. Ethan stopped.

"Here." He held out his hand and pulled me gently over to the bed, lifted me up and on to it before lying down at the side of me.

"God, you know how to make a man come running don't you? Just get blown up!" He laughed, but it was forced, his voice raspy. It was my turn to show sensitivity. I kissed him. I had never wanted him so much.

46

The room was still dark. I could smell coffee. Though I rarely drank it the aroma was wafting through the apartment into my bedroom where I now lay, naked and holding a memory of something that should be covering me with a blush. I groaned and pulled the sheets over my head.

Thoughts of the previous night were interrupted by soft footfalls coming through the door.

It was five a.m.

"Morning, sleepy." Ethan walked in holding a large white cup and saucer in each hand, the smell of coffee stronger as he neared the bed. He handed me one of the cups as I shuffled into a more upright position.

"I know you need to get to work, so I thought we could do the morning thing early, rather than miss it out altogether."

"I don't know what to say. I'm surprised you're the make coffee in the morning type of guy. Thank you."

He eased himself down onto the bed and pulled at the sheets while balancing coffee in a hand. "What time do you have to leave?" An innocent question but filled with a meaning I could clearly see.

I rolled my eyes as I retrieved memories of what was waiting for me. I needed to be in early. I needed to check in with DIU, view the images on Benn's computer and plan another interview around what was in the partial report. We then needed to push all the evidence we had on him, give him no place to twist. The only place left for him would be the straight truth. That was the plan anyway. How many times it ever went to plan I'm not sure. When you deal with humans things are never predictable. Fight or flight mode kicks in. Criminals get grand ideas of how they can get away with crimes, even heinous crimes like murder. If we planned this right, though, we'd have our guy.

"So?" Ethan interjected.

"Sorry... I need to leave in about forty-five minutes. I have so much to do; this job isn't in the bag yet. We can't be too confident and lose track of what we're doing."

He stroked my hair away from my eyes. "Isn't he cooperating?" The movement was soft, sensitive and distracting.

"He likes to talk; we need to get him to talk a bit more honestly."

"What's he saying?"

I flicked my free hand up and pushed Ethan's away from my

face. I felt uncomfortable.

"You know I can't tell you, Ethan. Is that the reason you're here? To find out what's happening on a case?" I pushed the cup onto the bedside table, frustration scratching away at me.

"Of course it's not the reason I'm here, Han. I'm here to spend time with you, to see you. The timing's not great, but don't think I only see you as an information source." His voice hardened and the coldness of the day crept into the room. I wanted the warmth of the night to come back. I rubbed at my eyes with the heels of my hands.

"You have to go, Ethan. I need to get into work."

The cup rattled in the saucer as he put it down. "Okay, okay, but if Natalie wakes, she's only talking to you through the paper, so you're going to have to work with me. This..." he said as he waved his arm across the bed sheets, "last night, was something else." He sat on the edge of the bed, pulled on his jeans and, picking up his shirt, slipped into his pumps. He walked towards the door.

"Last night was great, Han. Don't let it go."

And he was gone.

47

After a quick shower, I drove to the office. The place was quiet and still. Paperwork was everywhere. The team were working different angles, creating mounds of information, not just on the murders, but on all the people involved. Histories and backgrounds on Rosie, Allison, Natalie, and Colin. We needed to know their lives as well as they knew them and more. I filled the kettle, flicked the switch on and picked a green teabag out of the box. The team would start to arrive soon. Plans for the day ran through my head.

The click as the kettle boiled brought me back from my reverie. We had a big hole in our investigation and we needed to find some answers. Time was working against us.

I phoned down to the custody suite and spoke with the sergeant on duty. Benn had had his eight hours and was awake and about to eat the microwaved cardboard that passed for breakfast down there. As soon as he'd eaten we were free to go back into interview with him. I needed to see what was on his computer beforehand. I pulled myself up the stairs, using the banister rail as a lever, every step an effort. Danny Scrivens was the only person in.

"Morning, ma'am."

"Morning, Danny. What've you got?"

"I thought you'd ask, that's why I brought my lazy arse in early. I'm loading the results up."

I leaned in to look at the monitor. "I appreciate it," I said as I watched him scroll through different drives until he found the one he wanted, opened it and clicked through the parameters he wanted to set for the images to be viewed. The screen loaded with a wave of thumbnails.

"These are all the images he has on his computer including deleted files. There's a lot on here, it could take some time to go through. Do you have someone who can view these for you?" Danny asked.

"Yes, I can get someone to come up and do that. Can I have a quick look through to see what kind of images he has stored on here?" I grabbed the back of a chair, wheeled it over to where we were and sat down in front of the monitor.

"Yep. You know the drill. Use the arrows to scroll through. Whoever does the full viewing can categorise any illegal images."

"Thanks, Danny." I started to look through the page of thumbnails facing me. There was a lot of pornography. The usual stuff was present as well as more extreme images involving props and weapons. Pins pushed through the breasts of women as they were strung up in chains being held from the ceiling, and others whose breasts were bound so tightly in rope they were turning purple. Faces of pain and agony did not deter the dominant males inflicting the evils in the name of sexual arousal. This bloke's tastes were hardcore, a sexual predator who couldn't fulfil his sexual needs after gratifying them in a specific way for a period time. So he craved something a little harder, a little more extreme until that then failed to raise his interest as it had originally done and the cycle continued. I knew these images would get worse. I closed the window down. I had no need to see these. My career had brought me into contact with sexual predators many times. Their *collections* were disturbing, and the effects of viewing detrimental. It always gave me a sense of achievement when a child predator was sentenced at court. What I needed to know from this computer today was if there was any link on here with Rosie, anything we could use in interview. I'd ask Ross to view the images. He had his work cut out for him, though, with the volume Benn had stored on here. He needed to be alert to be able to identify if the girls were on here at all.

"Thanks. I appreciate the early morning support. I'll send Ross up to do the viewing if that's okay?"

"It's fine. Ready when he is."

The incident room had started to fill. Grey was in and hovering, casting his eye over proceedings. Even though we had Benn in the cells, he wouldn't look any more settled until we had him charged and locked up in a prison somewhere. Grey was a seasoned detective and he knew we still had a long way to go before this was in the bag and Benn was in front of a judge. He was skimming the room like a good host does at a party, checking in with everyone, making sure they were up to speed with their actions. He wanted the team tight, and we had that. I trusted them. As I stood inside the doorway watching him work, he looked over and saw me.

"Hannah. Good morning. Great to see everyone here so early. Can we have a moment in your office please?"

"Yes, sir."

As we walked I stopped and asked Ross to go upstairs to view the images on Benn's computer. "Take a photo of Rosie and Allison with you, Ross, to make sure."

He walked over to one of the desks and collected the photos before leaving.

"Shall we?" asked Grey as he walked into my office and sat behind my desk. "Okay, Hannah. What does today have in store for us?"

I bristled as he questioned me on the investigation from my chair. As he wrote his notes, his blue hard-backed notebook began to shift my paperwork from its given place.

"Other than the DNA evidence from Rosie Green, what do we have to link Benn to the murder and attempted murder of Allison and Natalie Kirk?" he asked.

I took a deep breath before I answered and attempted to keep my face from showing any signs of annoyance. "Following on from what I said last night, we're still awaiting forensic results from the dump sites, post-mortem and his address. The quickest result we will get from his address will be fingerprints, but he's not denying being in a relationship with Natalie so there's every reason to expect her prints and potentially Allison's to be there. CSIs are still working at his address. As long as we can get a charge on Rosie's murder we can keep him locked up and that gives us time to continue processing the evidence from the other scenes."

He paused, seemed to think, then scribbled in his notebook again.

"Have Rosie's parents been updated?"

"Yes. I spoke with Martin yesterday, after we arrested Benn. He was going to see them with Chris, the FLO over there, and let them know. I'll call him again today and see how the visit went and find out other lines of inquiry he may have."

"Okay. Good. What about neighbours of Benn, what do they have to say?"

"We're a bit thin on the ground with Sally off and Martin in Norwich so I'm going to borrow a couple of uniform today and get them to do more door knocking."

Grey nodded. My response seemed to appease him. He closed his notebook with an over exaggerated snap and walked out my office. "Keep me updated, Hannah."

I let go of my annoyance with a deep sigh, walked around my desk and sat down, claiming the space as my own again.

I updated my officer's log, signed through overtime forms and re-read the notes from yesterday's interview before Ross came through the door.

"You need to see this, boss."

48

She was hungry and her stomach moved like rolling thunder. It seemed so long since anyone had come in to feed her. So long since anyone had been in to see her. She scratched at the dried brown mark on her knee, her nail bending as she pressed it down to scrape the skin. It was light; didn't that mean it was morning? She tried to remember when she had last seen him and couldn't. The mark split in two as the substance concertinaed under the feeble nail.

It was quiet. She flicked underneath the bending nail with another weak nail to remove the grime and strained to hear. It was so often quiet. The darkness made the quiet much more tangible, like she could reach out and touch the silence.

Dust danced in the streams of light shining through the narrow gap where the dirty curtains hung, not quite drawn together, over the window at the top of the wall. She continued to scratch at the mark on her knee long after it had gone. She scraped the bending nail on the plastic beneath her, just to hear the sound. Why didn't anyone come? She'd been good. She'd done as she was told and she'd even stopped crying now. It was quiet, apart from the scratching of her nail on plastic. She didn't like the quiet.

She was a good girl. She was trying.

49

The eyes of Rosie and Allison stared back at me from the desk where I'd put their photographs. Absently I flicked the bottom corner of Rosie's picture. I felt as though I was about to violate them again, even if they were now a world away.

I shifted the mouse, bringing the screen back from sleep with a vicious start, from the quietly moving unobtrusive screen saver badge of Nottinghamshire police to a page of thumbnails. My eyes flicked across from the screen back to the photographs with a sense of sorrow. You never get used to these things. Maybe slightly removed, compartmentalised, but never used to.

The sound of shifting feet behind me pulled me back to the task in hand. No one wanted to speak. I could feel the collective breath holding of Danny, Ross and Grey.

"You're sure?" I asked of Ross, looking down at the photographs, not wanting to see it for myself.

"Yes."

Nothing else was needed. Grey shifted into my peripheral vision, the movement alone telling me he wanted to know.

I turned back to the screen, leaving my thumb resting on the photograph. I double tapped the mouse over the first image in the line. The screen changed. A single image of a female child filled the screen. She looked to be between about seven and nine years of age. The child was wearing pants in front of a backdrop that looked to be a cheap white sheet. She was smiling for the camera. Ross leaned over my shoulder and pointed towards the monitor. "There's one on the top row, third one in, and the second one in on the second to bottom row is also relevant."

I ground my teeth together to prevent myself bawling him out. It wasn't him I was angry with. I closed the window and moved the cursor across the tiny images. I could see what they all were. Skin tones melding into one disgusting story. Eventually I steadied the cursor enough to click on the image Ross had indicated. As it opened, my teeth ground harder together, the force pushed up to my temples. I looked down at the photograph of Rosie I was touching, then looked back at the screen.

"Filthy, fucking, dirty bastard."

Danny leaned over my shoulder and deftly moved around in the software. "It's the whole file these images are stored in that you need to be looking at. It'll give you a wider picture." His fingers moved quickly and soon, two folders were on the monitor, waiting to be viewed in their entirety. Photographs of both Rosie and Allison were saved in named folders on the hard drive. One folder contained pictures of Rosie. It had been given the name *Rosie Shared*.

I recognised the locations in the photos, recalling the dark blue flat weave of the carpet and the paper falling from the walls. I saw in the background the very same computer the photographs were now stored in. The photographs of Rosie had been taken in Benn's dingy two bedroom terrace house.

Not for the first time since picking up this case I found myself fighting to contain a stomach lurching sickness as I worked my way through the folder with Ross; Grey and Danny apparently doing the same if their silence was anything to go by. Benn couldn't deny knowledge of Rosie now, but I still didn't get the link. She was so far away.

I moved through the images in the *Rosie Shared* file, taking in how Benn had started photographing her dressed in a dirty white vest and pink pants. They didn't look like they had been washed in a long time. Where were her clothes? What had happened to her? I knew I needed to check back on the original missing report to see what she'd been wearing when last seen. The look on her face told me all I needed to know about how she felt. She was utterly terrified. There was no colour to her skin, and her mouth, though attempting a smile, wavered at the sides, cracking in fear, cheeks forced out, eyes registering every feeling she was pretending didn't exist.

The collection of images changed and Rosie's two items of clothing made their way to the floor as she was further posed and she became more distressed. Her body looked thin, the way I had seen her. The forced smile so difficult to keep in place now, her mouth a straight line across her ashen face. Then Benn joined her and the still images made way for videos, the camera placed in such a way it captured everything. A picture of violation and horror unfolded in front of us. No one spoke. Then just when you think you can't be shocked in this job, the next video started. All the evidence of Rosie's wrist welts and bruises were played out for us in full colour and with sound. At the end of the film, the marks around her neck were explained as the silent office watched Benn pull the belt from around his jeans. As I watched him pulling at it, it dawned on me what I was about to witness.

No one said a word.

50

Today she wasn't as sore. She had no idea how long she had been here. Though days and nights were different, there had been times when she hadn't cared what day it was, she just wanted the pain to stop, the fear to subside and for her mum to hold her.

Today was a better day but she was hungry. She heard the grinding sound of the metal bolt as it was dragged across the door and the key turn in the lock. She sat upright as she hoped it was food. There was a semblance of routine that she was getting used to and she was hungry.

"Good morning, little angel," he said, carrying a small plastic tray. She could see the rim of the pink plastic plate he always used.

She twitched her nose in an attempt to figure out what he was carrying.

"So you're not speaking to me today?" he asked.

"Yes, sorry," she apologised, staring hard at the approaching utensils.

"Hungry?"

"Yes."

"Are you going to be a good girl today?"

"Yes. Yes, I'll be good," she answered on her knees trying to look up.

He crouched down. His face appeared close to the bars. She stumbled back landing on her bottom. "S... s... sorry."

"You want your breakfast, little angel?"

"Yes please."

He placed the tray on the floor while he unlocked the small padlock that secured the cage door. She could see the food now. A slice of burnt toast with little sign of butter. She was hungry and desperate for it. She pulled her feet up to her bottom, raised herself from the floor into a crouch, waiting for the plate but keeping some distance between them. She saw his smile. Her reaction to him always delighted him.

He put the plastic plate through the open doorway and down on the cage base in front of her. He then closed the door and padlocked.

"Tammy?"

"Thank you," she answered as she moved the toast towards her mouth. She ate ravenously. He sat in the chair and watched her. His presence no longer putting her off as she ate to sustain herself.

51

With a heavy feeling I exported the photographs of Rosie onto an HTML file and burned a disc for use in interview with Benn. I leaned back in my chair hard, pushed my fingers together on top of my head and released a sigh of complete mental exhaustion.

Grey shifted on his feet. "I don't think I need to see any more to know we're interviewing the right man. I'll phone the search team and let them know we need to seize all belts at the address and I'll have a chat with Catherine to update her and discuss how much information we put out to the press. There is no need to tell them we have footage. It will come out at court, but it's too much now."

I'd had enough of listening to him after *I don't think I need to see any more*, but he continued to talk. "We'll let the public know we are still questioning a male suspect in custody in relation to the murders and we are working hard to bring this to a conclusion for everyone involved. Hannah, do you have a minute?"

It wasn't a question. I tried not to sigh out loud as I stood and went for what I knew would be yet another case discussion.

In the corridor, Grey spoke again. "I know you've had a tough spell," he picked at a finger, "I need to know you're okay to do this, to finish the job?" I stared at him as his finger picking distraction continued. What answer did he expect? He didn't want to run this case. He wanted to be as far away as possible without giving Catherine Walker the impression he couldn't handle the task. His eyes flicked from his hand, down the corridor, checking the open doorways, before bringing his attention back to me.

"I'm fine, sir. I can't pretend it's an easy case to work."

His eyes shifted back to his fingers.

"But we have him now," I continued. "We're close to answers. I've no intention of letting go."

It was what he wanted to hear. His eyes made contact with mine. A look of relief flooded his face. "That's great, Hannah, you're doing a good job. Let me know if you need anything." And without saying another word, he walked away.

There were two folders containing photographs of Allison. One was titled *Allie private* and the other *Allie sharing*. The photographs were different to those in Rosie's folders. It hadn't seemed to matter where they were, Benn had deemed it a perfect place to take what he wanted and photograph it for posterity.

There were shots taken inside Allison's bedroom, living room and bathroom. There were shots taken outside. Places that seemed familiar but I couldn't put my finger on. Then there were photographs taken in Benn's house. Danny explained what he was reading from the images as we went through them.

"The images all had a creation date. There's a date created when the images were put onto the computer hard drive at the point of transference from the camera, but there's also a date the photograph was taken."

"You mean we have an electronic trail? A time line?" I asked in disbelief.

Danny smiled. "Yes. He's created a recorded time line for us."

I looked back at the photographs. I could see from the uncertainty in Allison's face on the first photographs taken, in her school uniform, she wasn't sure why it was happening, why her mother's boyfriend was focusing on her. She had a gentle smile, a tentative need to please and Benn preyed on this. The move to indecency was slow with Allison. He had a free space with her in which he could build a relationship while Natalie chose alcohol over life, over her daughter. The uncertainty in Allison's face changed to one of resignation. The smile had gone. It hadn't been exchanged for fear though. It was as though inside her had died.

The last set of created images made my insides curl up and I felt myself shaking. I clenched my jaw hard. I was the team leader, I had to deal with this professionally and be strong and supportive for the team.

The thing that stood out about these images, taken in Natalie Kirk's kitchen, other than the obvious, was Benn's face. The camera was set up on a table or kitchen side so he could watch himself back. His eyes were wide in his face as if terrified, but he was far from the feeling of terror; he was on another level, maybe horrified, but unable to stop.

I had moved the girl's photographs from the desk after I had spoken with Grey. My fingers drummed an anxious beat at the side of the keyboard as I desperately fought the urge to slam the keyboard into the monitor.

The last movie went silent. Danny pushed a nearby chair hard into a work station as he walked out of the room. I swivelled to look at Ross. His face was ashen, his stance rigid.

"It's okay," I said to him. He turned and walked out.

Feeling drained, I sat completely still, like every living, functioning cell within me had decided to desert me. Any sane thought process escaped my grasp as I sat and looked at the screen with the blank black box of a watched movie staring back at me. I took the moment of quiet and let myself wind down until a feeling of relative normality settled again. Then I'd attempt to gather my rambling thoughts, emotions and fears and fit them back into their compartments in my head and restart my function as the DI on this case.

In my years in this job, kids are what get to me the most. Innocence and trust shattered at the whim of adults on a self-obsessed driven track. Rosie and Allison had no chance against a man like Benn. A man who confessed he was driven by his own needs at the expense of anyone else. A man who created relationships with beat down with life, alcoholic women just to get close to their child. A man who not only satisfied his own dark and dangerous needs but laid it out for the sordid satisfaction of others. That's what the sharing folders were. Images of wrong shared with others.

I had a long day ahead of me. I now had to go into interview with Benn after watching these sordid images. I had to discuss them and put the evidence to him. I then had to give him his own opportunity to answer for what was there. Give a reason if he could. A reason I had no interest in, but would give him time for. I dropped my head towards the back of the chair and closed my eyes. Closed out the world. There was a sudden flash across the inside of my eyelids. Flesh tones and small featured children moved across in front of me. My eyelids flew open and I bolted upright. My mind was going to work against me now and I would be replaying these images internally for a couple of days to come. This was a product of the role, of dealing with men like this who *collected* images. We were left with imprints in our brains, always filed away but recoverable should they be discussed or a similar job triggers their release. A nasty side of life people should never have to see. Catching the bad guys and locking them up made up for the time we were haunted by their offences. It was hard, but I was ready for it. I was ready for Benn.

52

Benn sat across from me looking like he'd spent the night in the cells. His hair had taken on a coarse unkemptness and his skin looked pallid. He had a sour feet smell about him. Despite these unpleasant things, he still had an air of arrogance. He slouched on his black plastic chair, feet pushed out in front of him crossed at the ankles, his head cocked to the side in an uninterested stance. His solicitor, however, was in stark contrast. A perfect night's sleep, it appeared, had been had by the newly qualified solicitor. She looked as though she had spent a week at a spa. Her hair bounced around her face and a slick of gloss was slashed across her mouth. Her legs crossed at the knees where she held a notebook and tapped a pen lightly against the lined paper. Her mobile phone was off and laid on the table in front of her. Her leather bag leant against the leg of her chair.

I sat and waited for Aaron. I'd shown him the images and we had discussed and planned the interview strategy. It was a quiet office when we'd left. Silence seemed to be a precursor for this job. We were scraping up the very slime of the gene pool with this case and it was having an effect on everyone.

Aaron pushed the interview door open with his shoulder,

carrying three steaming cups in his hands. A mug from the office filled with green tea for myself and two Maxpax cups filled with powdered milk and cheap coffee for Benn and the solicitor. She eyed me over her thin hot cup and smiled. Aaron didn't like to drink when interviewing, but I found it gave me a few seconds break when the going got heavy.

The interview tapes were turned on and I ran through the introductions and caution before summarising the previous day's interview.

I went over his relationship with Natalie. It had seemed like a good idea at the time, but he soon found out how much of a drunk she was. So, instead of walking out on her, he chose to spend some time with her daughter.

"It were the right thing to do," whimpered Benn. "I couldn't walk away could I? The kid needed me. Her mother were a waste of space and I kind of liked being around them."

"Today we are going to move away from asking about Natalie and Allison for the moment, and talk about Rosie," I said.

Benn looked at me.

"Tell me about Rosie Green, Colin," I continued.

"I don't know nothing about no Rosie Green. I told you this yesterday."

"You do realise the forensic guys are going through your place with a fine tooth comb, don't you?"

"Yeah. They won't find anything."

He was confident.

"Okay, let's talk computers."

"What about them?"

"When we entered your house, you were working on your computer. We seized it. Tell us what you use it for?"

"You know. Internet stuff."

"What kind of 'internet stuff'?"

We ran through his computer basics. His computer use. Make and model, when bought, who lived at his address, what websites he visited and what sites turned him on sexually. There were no unusual answers and he was getting more and more comfortable with the interview. He hadn't noticed the laptop plugged into the wall on the floor behind me. He was, once again, open with us, his legs apart and a bored sounding tapping coming from one of his feet on the floor. He admitted to having quite a large collection of pornography with some extreme and hardcore images.

"I think they go a little past hardcore," Aaron commented, barely shifting a muscle.

"It's just another taste though, innit?" Benn replied, more as a statement of fact than an answer. He lounged back on his chair, his confidence in his ability to cover up his crime oozing from him. The interview tapes in the machine were about to come to an end so now was a good time to collect more drinks.

I leaned from my chair, reaching down to the laptop. "Can we get you another drink, Colin, before we move onto the next part of the interview?"

"Yeah, why not? It tastes like crap but I could drink another one."

I put the laptop on the table between us. Benn's smile faltered.

I closed the interview and sealed up the tapes. Aaron left to get more coffee. Corinne Selby looked bored and sat foot tapping the air with her perfectly styled pointed shoe. The computer questions seemingly held scant interest and had little relevance to the murder investigation her client was being interviewed about.

Aaron returned to the interview room, the silence broken as he dropped another cup in front of Benn. Sitting down he opened another set of tapes and started them running. This time Aaron took the lead and focused on Rosie. His tone was straightforward with no hint of what he was thinking or where the questions could possibly go. His analytical mind moved deftly forward. Benn kept up his denial of ever having come into contact with Rosie. He seemed to be distracted, his attention continually moving to the laptop on the table, considering its relevance to the questions. Miss bouncy raised one of her contoured brows at me at one point, to which I shrugged in response. She made no comment. The coffee sat untouched on the table.

"We have your DNA, Colin. It was taken when you were booked into custody yesterday," Aaron said.

"Yeah, I know. What of it?"

"During the post-mortem of Rosie Green, DNA evidence was recovered and profiled."

I watched as Benn began to twitch.

"Yeah?"

"Yes. The DNA profile was run as a speculative search against the DNA database to search for any matches." He didn't go further. Benn started fingering the Maxpax cup. Selby looked at Benn. Benn refused to return her look.

"And?" he asked.

"The DNA found on the body of Rosie Green was matched against DNA held on the database, taken from you on a previous detention with us." He stopped, giving it time to sink in.

Benn now turned to his solicitor, panic clearly starting to

rise. The laptop was forgotten. DNA typing and matching was now forefront in his mind. "I... I... I don't understand."

"It's simple, Mr Benn. Rosie Green was brutally murdered after being sexually violated. Semen recovered matches your DNA. You raped and murdered Rosie Green."

"I want this to stop. It's my right. Stop this. I want to speak to my solicitor. Stop. Stop it now."

The interview was stopped.

53

The consultation with his solicitor could take some time. There would be the need for a serious conversation and, depending on how talkative he was, the outcome of the subsequent interview would be determined. I walked with Aaron up the stairs towards the incident room.

"Thoughts, Aaron?"

"We have a good case, regardless of what he does or doesn't say in the next interview."

"I know that, but how do you think he's going to go now?"

"It doesn't matter, Hannah. We don't need a confession. We have his DNA and we have the photographs and videos on his computer. He's told us it's his computer. We have a strong case to put to CPS for a charging decision." It was like pulling teeth with him sometimes. I ran my hands through my hair; the action pulled on my ribs. I felt in my pocket for the painkillers. Aaron went with the facts. He didn't see the point in guessing what direction offenders were going. He asked the questions, anticipated some of the answers and wove his way through his interview plan, pulling in all the potential loose ends until, by the time the important questions were out, they had nowhere else to go. He was cool and calm and never let his emotions lead him on an investigation, or at any other point I could think of, and he bounced off my emotional, occasionally hot-headed approach well.

"I know. But this guy's scum and I want him locked up. Sometimes I can't stand the dance we do with them. And with the solicitors."

He shrugged. "We get there, Hannah. There's nothing else you can do."

I pushed the door to the incident room and everyone stopped talking.

"What's going on?" The quiet unnerved me. It was never a good sign when cops ran out of things to say. Grey was stood at the front with Danny who didn't look at all happy to be in front of this crowd. He looked up at me like a startled rabbit caught in the headlights. No one spoke.

"Danny?" Aaron asked from behind me.

Grey took hold of Danny by his arm and pulled him towards me. I sidestepped the oncoming duo. Danny shook free his arm and followed Grey through the doors and into my office. Aaron and I followed suit.

"Shut the door, shut the door," Grey stammered as I followed them into my small office space, which looked even more inadequate with the four of us stood in front of my desk. Aaron pushed the door to and looked at Grey stonily. He didn't do drama well. I wasn't sure I'd ever seen Grey look more panicked than he did now, and that included when he'd heard about the second murdered girl, Allison Kirk.

"What is going on, Anthony?" I asked, standing in front of him with crossed arms.

Grey turned away from me, looked through the window out to the secure custody yard below, then drew back his shoulders and turned to face me, tense and pale. Danny looked at the floor. "Danny's been looking at the photographs in Benn's computer and located the last photograph Benn was sent. He thinks it's something we should know."

I sat down on the edge of my desk, knocking a precariously positioned pile of paperwork down to the floor.

"Crap." I bent to retrieve them. "What is it, Anthony?"

"Danny went through the photographs Ross categorised and he found a photograph that hadn't been placed in any folder, but was in the downloaded file." He looked to Danny for confirmation. "Right so far?"

Danny nodded.

My skin started to crawl. I didn't like the way this conversation was going. "What was the photograph?" I held my breath for the answer.

"It's another girl, Hannah."

I let out my breath. "But he has several collections of images. We know about them. What's different?"

"Danny has checked the image and can tell the date the photograph was taken. It was two days ago. The child in the photograph was in a cage, Hannah, with something around her neck and she was there two days ago." He looked hard at me.

"Oh my God." I stood up, adrenalin coursing through me.

"She could still be alive. There's a girl out there, held in a cage, who could be alive and Benn is our link to her. He could tell us who has her."

54

I sat on what I knew while Benn revealed details. I'm not sure what happened with his solicitor but he talked, and he talked a lot. The laptop had been placed back on the floor so it wouldn't distract him from what he wanted to say now. He got through three cups of coffee, barely stopping for breath. It was as though coffee was his cigarettes. His lifeline to some semblance of calm in a rapidly disintegrating world. He talked about his needs. His lust. His pathetically desperate attempts to control his behaviour. I could barely contain a snarl as he spoke of it, his self-pity evident. He wanted acceptance and understanding. He wanted to know we thought he tried hard. He wanted us to accept his pleas of just how difficult it had been for him.

He started with an explanation of the dynamics with Natalie and Allison, and in greater detail than his previous interview. We let him run with it. It's never a good idea to interrupt the flow. Then he told us it was Natalie's fault. She didn't put out for him often enough, she neglected him and she loved her booze more. She had a daughter. She had a daughter who was there for him. Who listened to him and spent time with him, who laughed at his jokes and was a friend to him. It was Natalie who had thrust

Allison on him with her neglectful behaviour.

As he talked I listened with disbelief that he could say these things and hear it in his own ears, but not hear it as it was.

The relationship had a slow start. Their friendship blossomed but their becoming closer was a slow burner and Benn had worked hard to gain her trust. Talking, intimate chats, smiles and knowing looks. She had laughed as he started to take photos. He'd told her they were memories for her mum. He played on her vulnerabilities and her need to be loved. He said the photographs would be there when her mum was ready to look at them so no matter what she missed in her drunken stupors, she would always have the memories because he, Colin Benn, was there to give her this gift. She enjoyed her time with him, she was comfortable with the photographs and one thing led to another and the natural progression was the removal of clothes for the photographs. She was beautiful. She recognised this and she revelled in it. She loved the attention he gave her. They complemented each other. He was kind to her and gentle and in return she gave herself to him. He began to love her. He didn't feel bad for Natalie. Natalie brought it all on herself. She didn't deserve him and she didn't deserve a beautiful daughter like Allison.

Benn was animated when he spoke of his relationship with Allison. He believed it had grown into a full relationship. But when it started to break down, he turned to the internet. He needed someone to talk to. We understood didn't we? He needed to talk and he knew people wouldn't understand, they would judge and be critical, so he searched for people who would understand and would help him rebuild the failing relationship. He said it took a few false starts. There were a lot of nasty people online. He wanted to talk about his love and his relationship. Some people wanted to exploit it and poison it, they wanted to meet him and for him to bring Allison. He was disgusted. Allison was his.

Eventually he found someone who understood it for what it was and introduced him to a group of like-minded people. He felt validated. Relieved. At home.

The next part of the interview didn't prove to be any easier. Even Corinne Selby appeared to flag. Aaron, on the other hand, looked as though he'd just arrived at work. His tie was still neat, unlike most of the team who couldn't even tie them correctly in a morning, never mind all this way into a long shift.

Benn went on to disclose conversations with his new friends that had gone on long into the nights. Many days and weeks passed, with interests shared and thoughts explored. Eventually, one of his new-found friends broached the subject of bondage and how it brought an extra thrill to relationships. If done properly it would benefit both concerned. The friend shared his own photographs and Benn nearly exploded right there in the interview room as he talked. I wanted to punch him. And hard. Him and his prissy little solicitor. But at this point even she had gone an odd shade of yellow. I fidgeted with my cup, banging it on the table as I moved it around. Benn was so caught up in his own story he didn't notice and his solicitor looked pleased for the distraction.

The small interview room felt smaller, looked dingier and smelled sourer.

After the first photographs were shared others in the group shared and soon Benn found himself desperate to join in but reticent to involve Allison. This was when it was suggested he be provided with someone. As long as he gave the group what they needed, he could take what he wanted from the girl. He was encouraged, the sharing of the images the nightly norm.

He had to drive to collect her. They met in a park in the early hours when there would be little chance of anyone being about. Even the local cops would be sat in their nice warm stations, too cosy with their TVs and takeaways to monitor a children's park, so he was told. There, a girl was passed to him, from one trunk of a car to his. She wore only underwear and was wrapped in a blanket. Her hands were bound in front of her with rope you'd find in a garage. She was floppy and mumbled incoherently as she was handled. He made it back before it began to get light and transferred her to his house, making sure he kept her wrapped in the blanket. Once in the house he kept the bindings on so he wouldn't lose her and put a strip of silver electrical tape over her mouth. He didn't want her to start screaming and alert the neighbours. The walls were pretty thin, but she didn't seem capable of making such a noise, she seemed so out of it. He then tied her wrists to the bottom of the radiator and got some sleep. It had been a long night for him.

The interview felt never ending. We took another break; I spoke with Catherine Walker and obtained the extension we needed to keep questioning him. Grey and I then discussed the updated press release. My body hurt and I was tired. I called Ethan. He picked up on the first ring.

"Detective Inspector Hannah Robbins, what can I do for you?"

"Come round to mine later when I get off work?"

"I can do that. How are things?"

"Pretty grim and I need some relief from it."

"Relief I can do, and very well."

I felt myself blush. I wasn't usually so forward with wanting time with Ethan, afraid of rejection, but I was feeling reckless. "It's going to be a late one here, is that okay with you?"

Ethan didn't have a key. The relationship was far too new, which meant he had to sit and wait for my call before he came over.

"It's fine. I'm all yours, no matter what time it is."

"Great. Fetch a bottle of wine?"

"And my toothbrush?"

"Yes, and your toothbrush." I propped my head in my hands, feeling heavy. I needed to finish this and go home. "I'll see you later."

With my evening planned I walked through to see Evie, who was turning off her lights and heading out the door.

"Hey. How's it going?" she asked.

"Disturbing," I replied.

She flicked the switch and the office space lit back up. "You obviously need to talk to me. What can I do?"

"Thanks, Evie." I pulled at a chair and sat down. "An image has been located on Benn's computer that DIU are saying is only a couple of days old."

"Right. What's the image?"

"Another girl. In a cage."

She didn't say a word; she just continued to look at me. The strip lighting glinted off her lenses, making it difficult to see the thoughts play across her eyes.

"I need you to work with DIU and the National Missing Persons Bureau to see if we can identify her and get to her before we end up with another death. I'm still in with Benn. It's taking some time. He may give us what we need, but if he doesn't, I'll take all the help I can get. She's so small, Evie. We need to get to her."

Evie nodded. Not a word passed her lips.

55

A sense of horror was unfolding within me and in front of me as Benn told the final part of his involvement with Rosie and Allison. His solicitor now looked sick and completely out of her comfort zone. Her smart appearance took on a look of exhausted dishevelment without a crease having appeared on her immaculately pressed suit. Her hands had obviously been busy, both running through her hair, and rubbing her face. Her eyes looked less sharp and outlined, and all her pouty lip glossiness had disappeared. Her curls had less bounce and were now pushed behind her ears. Everything in the room had a feeling like nothing really mattered any more, other than the atrocities being spun by Benn. He continued.

When he woke he had felt lost and confused when he saw the girl. The girl who had been delivered like a local Chinese takeaway. He knew he had to keep Allison out of the house until he figured out what to do with her. He texted her, as was usual, and wished her a good day at school and said he couldn't see her until the next day. Then he turned his attention to the girl tied to his radiator.

He hadn't looked at her properly the previous night, but now in the cold light of the morning he could see she had already been used up by whoever had given her to him. She was bruised and thin. She carried a look he didn't recognise. A tired fear. He tried to be nice to her. She needed someone to love her now, didn't she? So he released her wrists and loved her, then left her tied to the radiator again as he took a walk to clear his head.

When he talked to his new friends, photographs were demanded. Payment for the delivery. He felt cornered. What else was he supposed to do? He had this girl, she was tired and injured, and they knew what he looked like, knew his car details. They could turn on him and turn him in. He had to do as they asked, didn't he? He was out of choices. That night he did the things they wanted and photographed them. The girl was weak and already hurt. She couldn't take the belt for long. She left him. Just died there on his floor as his camera sent the images to the group waiting for them. He felt shocked, but something within him shook and bucked and he also felt more alive than he ever had. He knew he had to dispose of her and get rid of the evidence. The photographs weren't evidence though, so he could keep them. No one would stumble on them. It was a group of friends sharing an interest. He needed them. They helped make him feel alive. Keeping the images without the girl was okay. The girl would get him into trouble. He wasn't stupid, he had to get rid of her. So in the darkness he took her out and after driving around attempting to think of what to do, he stopped at the next alleyway he passed and left her there. The shadows unnerved him and made him feel watched so he pushed on the bin to cover her and he left. He didn't know how far he'd driven or if he'd driven around in circles. He just wanted her out of his car and out of his life.

Allison was an accident. Loving gone that step too far. The thrill of what had happened with the girl still vivid and alive in his veins. He hadn't wanted it to happen. He wasn't a monster. He loved Allison. We had to believe him. He was jittery about Natalie, and about what she would be able to see in him, so he decided to visit her. The house was quiet. Allison was upstairs with the door unlocked. He let himself in. Everything felt strange. Disturbed. A hyper awareness was steamrollering through him and the smells and colours in the house were overbearing. He shouted for Allison. She came down the stairs and stood in front of him, arms by her sides, hair loose around her shoulders. She never said a word. Now he didn't know how to talk to her. Not after the girl the night before had given up on him. Stupid girl. It felt tainted with Allison. No longer pure and sweet. She looked him in the eye. He was losing her. She was slipping away from him. So, with the memory of the thrill from the previous night, he decided he was going to take Allison to that special place. Take her to the edge and watch her come alive again. Rebirth their relationship. Right there in the kitchen. He asked where her mum was and was told she was in the pub. This was his time. He had to take it now. He could feel the house around him and he wanted Allison there with him. He got to work as she watched, bringing in from the car his tow rope and camera. She still never said a word. He hooked up his camera and set it on the worktop. Then he set to work, to bring life back to his relationship.

She resisted, like she'd resisted nothing else in her life. He didn't understand it. She was fighting as he was coming alive. He bound her wrists with rope from the car to keep her still. He felt the electricity of life flowing through him. The hard edge of the world was fading and narrowing. He was growing and growing. Allison fading. The fight started to ebb and the feeling of euphoria with it. He pulled harder on the belt, pulling to save his life. The camera in the corner forgotten, the energy of life his aim. He pulled and pulled, harder and harder. It was euphoric.

She was gone.

56

The toilet bowl smelled pretty much as you'd expect a toilet to smell after a day of workers had passed through. My insides heaved hard against themselves. Great big angry spasms. I clung to the edge of the bowl and dropped to my knees as my energy seeped away. The hair I'd tied back fell forward and rested on my cheek.

I knew we had him now. We'd taken an evil from the streets, but was this job taking something from me? Why did I choose to put myself down here with the pit of humanity? Who exactly was I saving? The kids? We would never be able to work hard enough to remove this scourge. No matter what we did they would always exist to prey on the young and vulnerable. The internet had created a perfect space for a predator's playground. A place to both meet the vulnerable and to meet others to share the filth. There was no way we could get on top of it. Did I really make a difference or was this all just to bolster my own flailing self-esteem? An honest question that shook me down even further and I slipped from my knees, down to my bottom as the heaving subsided. I rested back on to the wall of the toilet stall, tears from retching drying on my cheeks. I didn't have an answer, just a feeling of weariness. A feeling that it was all a pointless exercise and I wasn't able to help anyone. As my head dropped down towards my knees I closed my eyes. An image flashed before me. The girl in the cage, eyes downcast. A reason. A reason to drag myself from the toilet floor and keep going. A child locked in a cage and we were close to getting answers, to finding her and recovering her from a living hell. Whatever the reason I or any cop puts themselves through this, there is a definite purpose. I picked myself up.

The interview continued. I'd splashed freezing water from the tap over my face and armed myself with a fresh cup of green tea. Aaron sat steadfastly unperturbed, his tie and his back straight. Benn's solicitor looked as tired as I felt. She'd made no attempt to stop his free flowing verbal account. She sat in silence as he let it all go.

When he dried up I plugged the laptop into the socket in the wall. Benn's eyes widened and his body pushed back into his chair. An automatic response of flight without the ability to go anywhere. He had thought he understood what we'd found but I doubted he wanted to be confronted with it. His solicitor gave me a tired questioning look I interpreted as *"what, more?"* I pressed the power button and the screen loaded. Inputting the password I turned the screen so Benn and Miss Selby could see it. Then I opened the file on the desktop. It loaded with the image of the girl in the cage.

"Who is this?" I asked.

Finally he understood. The realisation that we wanted to know who his fellow offenders were, dawned. I watched several emotions play out across his face as he looked from the image to Aaron and me, then to his solicitor. She looked back at him with no answers and nowhere to go. "I don't know. Really I don't." The pleading tone again. The need for us to believe him, as though it would make the process easier for him.

"Where is she, Colin?" I wasn't about to let him escape this one.

He wriggled in his seat. His face flushed. "I don't know. They never tell me anything. I swear to God they don't."

Something in me believed him but I needed to know. We needed to progress this. "The photograph was taken two days ago. This child was alive two days ago. You expect me to believe you don't know where she is?"

"If I knew I'd tell you. I've told you everything else haven't I?" he whined.

I pushed him further and harder. He refused to give up his instant messaging username or those of the others in his group. He held his ground and then he wept for Allison.

57

Sally perched on the end of the bed absently crinkling the fabric of the duvet cover between her fingers. She had been released from the hospital a day earlier than expected but nerves were eating at her. Tom paced like a tiger stalking his prey. The confines of the room in their suburban semi restricted his strides and made the pacing erratic. It made her anxious. She understood his reasons. She even knew he was right. But she felt driven to return to work on full duties and that meant keeping the pregnancy a secret.

She'd received a call from Ross earlier in the day. He'd phoned to tell her they'd made an arrest. He was ecstatic and thought Sally would be pleased. Instead she was hurt and angry. He'd remembered to ask how she was and Sally told him she was fine and couldn't wait to be back. It was true, she couldn't wait, but she had wanted to be there when they brought him in. She had wanted to look in his face when he knew he'd been caught. She had wanted the buzz of the incident room and to have had a part to play in such a large and now, it would seem, successful operation. The difficulty was getting Tom to understand any of this. He wasn't a cop. He didn't understand the drive to bring serious offenders in. He thought he understood the horror of the offences, but she knew she would never be able to convey the emotion involved. Tonight she had to try. She had to convince him she knew what she was doing. Enough for him to acquiesce to her return to work with his blessing, and return with full duties. Just until this job was finalised.

"Tom?"

"What do you want me to say, Sally? That it's okay to go back to work and not tell a soul you're pregnant? To be around disgusting, filthy paedophile bastards with my baby, and it be okay?"

Sally sighed quietly to herself.

"It's only short term, Tom. Until this job is finished. He's not going anywhere and I won't be alone with him."

"But I worry about you, don't you get it? I worry about you, both of you. You should be taking some time off after the explosion."

"The doctor said I was fine. We got thrown about, but the baby is fine. You heard him say so yourself. He's fine."

"He?" The pacing faltered.

"Well I hate the word, it, and we're not far enough along to know. He just feels like a he."

She smiled. Tom looked at her. From her eyes to her still flat belly where her hand rested. He sat beside her, took her hand from where it rested and replaced it with his. Hope swelled inside her. She needed him to understand.

"Sally, I don't want you to go to work, full stop, never mind full duties, with no one knowing you need to be protected. Why can't you see that?"

She stood quickly; his hand dropped away. "I would never do anything to hurt our baby. Trust me. The investigation is based in the bloody building, for God's sake." She couldn't help but raise her voice. "What do you think is going to happen in there? You're being ridiculous!" Anger and frustration pushed forward words she knew they would both regret tomorrow. She gulped hard and continued. "I'm going back to work, Tom. You're not my keeper; I don't need your permission. It's my body and I'm the one carrying the baby. It's safe. I'm not stupid. Just give it a rest."

Tom rose just as rapidly. "All you care about is that fucking job. You're a reckless idiot. What about us? Your family? Me and the baby?"

"It's not about me. I love you. I love our baby. I want to be in at the end of this job and then that's it. Grounded to the nick, making people tea and shuffling sodding paperwork around."

"Do as you please, but do not come to me if something goes

wrong," Tom hissed before he walked out the door. She was wound up and frustrated. She wouldn't be able to sleep tonight and she was going back to work in the morning.

58

Colin Benn was charged with the rape and murder of Rosie Green and Allison Kirk, and the attempted murder of Natalie Kirk by arson at eleven-twelve p.m. It had taken no time at all to get a CPS lawyer to sign off on the charges. There was still a considerable amount of work to do but with Benn charged, we could keep him off the streets while we continued to gather and process the evidence from crime scenes. He had nothing to say when charged. His solicitor was long gone as there was nothing further she could do at this point. He would need his legal representation again in the morning when he would be put before a court with a remand application, but for tonight, we were done. He looked at the floor, his shoulders sagging. The weight may have lifted from him in the telling, but now he had to face a future very different to the one he had imagined for himself. His future now held court rooms, uniformed guards, handcuffs and isolation from prison inmates due to his crimes.

I drove home barely taking in the red lights or junctions I came across. I was glad the day was over. The sense of joy and pride usually associated with charging an offender was marred by the real loss of two young girls whom I had never met.

I'd put a call into Martin, who was in the pub getting a round of drinks in when his phone rang. We talked for a while, the light-hearted banter of a local public house in the background, until it became too distracting and Martin stepped outside. He said he would visit the Green family with Chris in the morning and update them. A family already torn apart by the death of a child, now to be told of the circumstances of her death. It couldn't be avoided. It would all come out in court. They had to be told.

I thought of Natalie. Of how I couldn't inform her of events. The hospital had said there was no change when I called. She would never win a mother of the year award. She gave the impression all she cared about was the money, but I'd seen a hint of something more. A deep rooted remorse for the knowledge she'd let her child down. She may have even known, on some level, what was happening with Benn and her way of dealing with it was to hide even deeper within the bottle.

I heard screeching and car horns as I failed to notice another red light in time. I could do with a drink myself.

The wine slid down easily. I poured myself another, carried it into the bathroom and turned the shower on. I discarded my clothes, downed the contents of the glass and stepped in, turning the heat up as far as I could bear it. Then a little bit further.

Benn had failed to tell us who the others were in the group. He clammed up and wouldn't answer any further questions. His solicitor informed us her client had said enough for us to charge him and he would not be providing any further information. I'm not sure I've hated anyone quite as vehemently as I did his solicitor at that point. Benn and other scum like him were nasty, evil beings who deserved anything and everything that came to them, but her, she was, debatably, a hard-working normal functioning member of society, yet here she was defending this bastard. After hearing all he had done and what he had been involved with, she had stood up for his right not to answer questions, questions that could help identify and save another child. I lifted my face to the water and closed my eyes. Hot shards pricked at my skin, still swollen and tender from the blast. The water stripped the entire day away from me. I stood and allowed it to cleanse me.

Eventually I stepped out, dragged the towel from the rail and wrapped it around myself before taking my empty glass back into the kitchen and pouring another.

I remembered Dad had called me a couple of days ago. I took my phone from my coat pocket and sank down to the floor in front of the sofa to dial his number. He picked it up on the third ring. I took a gulp of wine before speaking. "Dad. It's me."

"Hannah?" he mumbled, and I realised how late it was.

"Yeah, Dad. Sorry. I didn't mean to wake you."

"Are you okay?"

"I'm fine," I lied. "I missed your call a couple of days ago. I'm sorry." Why was I always apologising when I spoke with him?

"Oh. Okay. I was up early and saw the news about the girl and presumed you'd be there and up so I thought I'd call." A pause. I waited. "Zoe sent a VO for you, I've got..."

"No, Dad." I snapped. "I won't visit her in prison. She made her choices." A wave of guilt washed over me. He'd been lost since Mum died. Then with Zoe.

"I just wish..."

"I know. It confuses things with my job, you know."

"She's your sister."

"Yeah."

Silence. I could hear him breathing down the phone. I drank from the glass again. An awkward silence. Unspoken thoughts running simultaneously through our minds.

"Why don't you come over on Sunday, I'll cook you dinner?"

I took another long drink, emptying the glass. "I'll probably be at work Sunday. It's a big case."

"Your next day off then? Sunday roast, mid-week. I can do that."

"Of course. I'll let you know when it is. I'm sorry if I woke you." The glass chinked on the floor as I put it down a little too hard.

"It's okay. I like to hear from you," he murmured, his mind following other conversations from times gone past.

"Goodnight, Dad."

"Goodnight, Hannah." The buzz in my ear confirmed he had gone. I sighed and dropped my head back onto the seat of the sofa. I missed Mum, but even she would have problems trying to resolve the issues created by my sister.

59

I was at the hospital by seven a.m. I'd had six missed calls from Ethan through the night and one withheld number. Another mental to-do was created. The hospital smelled of floor antiseptic, whatever it is they wash the bedding and gowns in, and sick people. Sick people have an awful smell about them, like the illness is seeping out of their pores. I felt rough but I'd made a conscious effort with my appearance that morning; concealer and foundation attempting to cover narrow pink cuts.

Natalie was still in the same room, but this time it was a different uniform outside her door. I flashed my warrant card and walked in. Clear plastic tubes ran over her body, keeping her alive. Her face was relaxed and the harshness she portrayed when she talked money and her missing child was gone. Her hands, pale with age spots, rested above the cream weave of the hospital blanket. The severe red nail varnish she wore had been removed and her hands looked sallow. She looked pathetic. Weak and pathetic. I sat myself in a chair at the side of her bed and let her know I was there. She didn't flinch. I took her hand in mine. "Natalie? We have him, Natalie. We have the man who hurt Allison." I stared long and hard at her. Waiting. She could hear me couldn't she? They say hearing is the last sense to go and she wasn't about to go anywhere. I waited some more, her hand limp in mine, her finger ends curling downwards towards the blanket as I held her.

"Natalie, it was Colin. I'm sorry." I willed her to hear me. To react. "We have him. He admitted everything. Hurting Allison and setting the hob on the gas oven open. He wanted to destroy evidence and wasn't concerned if you got caught up in it." I studied her hard. There was no movement. Nothing to suggest she had heard. "He was scared you knew what had been happening and would link things together. He tried to protect his measly little life. He thought a gas leak wouldn't be identified as arson. We have him though; he's going to prison and for a very long time."

Silence.

60

Sally walked into the incident room, shrugged off her jacket and threw it across the back of her chair as Grey entered.

"Sally, how are you?" Grey approached, a smile widening his usually thin face. He shook her hand. Her cheeks changed from a pale shade to rosy pink dots. Crap, she would to have to attempt to control these bodily signs that were trying to give her away.

"I'm well thank you, sir. I needed a couple of days rest. I'm now fit and can't wait to help put this case together on Benn." Ross had told her the offender's name, along with a lot of other information. There wasn't a lot Ross hadn't told her. He was so giddy with the size of the job, and the pressure that came from on high only served to increase his eagerness.

"That's good. We've a strong team who work well, but all hands on deck is what we like." Grey paused, pushing back a silver strand of loose hair, "So long as both you and your doctors are happy that you're fit to be here. I know we all want this, but we don't want to push so hard we injure one of our own, do we now?" His brow furrowed in a questioning look.

"Sir, I'm fine. The hospital released me."

"Happy to hear it."

Sally sat at her desk and brought the computer to life. Her life felt uncertain. Tom wasn't talking to her this morning. Deceiving her friends and co-workers like this wasn't in her nature, but once she'd finished this job there would be no more secrets just a happy news announcement. Everyone would be pleased, and Tom would be happy. Her role would change at work while she was pregnant but afterwards, well, people did manage to juggle full time jobs and have a baby, so she didn't see why it couldn't work. It would be hard. She'd be tired, exhausted, but she could do it.

61

After the hospital I had to attend court for Benn's remand application. All went according to plan and a steady drive of ten minutes from the magistrates' court to Central police station found me back at the office in no time at all. It would have taken half that, but traffic was heavy and slow. The visit to Natalie had hardened my resolve to do what could be done to locate the unknown girl. There was another family out there suffering. Parents wondering where their daughter was and a girl held in a cage with who knew how little time before she became another statistic to be counted in government figures. We had little to work on, with no specifics on the girl, which made it close to impossible to search the National Missing Persons Bureau database. The investigation into her identity had the feel of an impenetrable brick wall. We were completing the case against Benn, getting justice for Rosie and Allison, yet unable to make a real start on the girl in the photograph.

The kettle roared its way to boiling point, breaking into my thoughts. I emptied its contents into the line-up of mugs on top of the refrigerator, shouted for everyone to collect their own and to listen up for the debrief on the case so far. I turned with hot mug in hand and looked at the team. It had been a good job done by all.

At this point I saw Sally in her chair. Because I hadn't expected to see her and hadn't noticed her when I first walked in it was a jolt. She had her head down and looked busy. I'd expected to speak to her before her return, to be informed. Or maybe I felt ashamed. I hadn't made that call to see how she was. After all we were in a car together when the world went bang. She was either refusing to look at me or she really was engrossed in what she was doing. I suspected the former, though I was unsure why.

Ross looked relaxed and happy and Aaron looked calm in his neat tie, tapping at his keyboard. Once drinks were collected and the chatter had died down I thanked everyone for their hard work, let them know we couldn't slack off or let our guard down and we had to finish the investigation properly by tying everything up neatly with the paperwork. It was an exercise in team management. It was necessary and required; they knew the drill. In the middle of the debrief I took another call on my phone. *Withheld number*. Again silence greeted me. It was starting to become a bit too regular for my liking. There was no way to identify where the call came from and with the amount of people that had my work number, there was, at this point, more to lose and nothing to gain from changing the number. I just couldn't figure out who would call but not speak.

I continued with the debrief. "The digital investigation unit are working on identifying markers in the photograph of the unknown girl. There is little we can do at this moment in time. What we have to focus on is getting the file prepared and in order for the Crown Prosecutor. Once we have something to go on from the photo we will deal with it. I know you are desperate to find her and the people behind this. As soon as the DIU come back to me you will be the first to know." It was little comfort but it was all we had. Knowing the girl was out there, held in a cage, was frustrating, painful and personal. Aaron nodded, taking it in his stride, acknowledging the boundaries in which we worked. Ross verbalised his frustrations.

"Bastard fucking paedos. I'd like to put them in a cage and then leave them in an open prison, see how they like it."

"Or we could get the evidence against them and put them away for a very long time," I responded, not in annoyance, but in practical terms. They needed to stay grounded and not too emotionally invested. It wouldn't do them any good, but I realised they needed an outlet, a place to vent and I had no issues with that in the safety of our working environment.

"Yeah, that," answered Ross. A pulse flicked in his jaw.

I looked over at Sally. She had dropped her head at Ross's outburst. She felt it, but didn't have the same level of comfort at verbalising it as Ross did. I understood that. I compartmentalised, closed it off, shut it down. It was how I could see the things I see and not internally combust.

I took a black coffee into Grey, placed it in front of him and sat down. "Morning, sir."

"Morning, Hannah. Good job well done with Benn. How did it go at court?" He smiled with a natural easy smile. One that illustrated his relief at an expeditious conclusion to a nasty high profile investigation. The media hadn't been informed of the photograph. There was no need for them to know, *"not in the public interest"* was the term coined. Grey would give an interview and everyone would be happy. The families would be forgotten by the public and life would move on until the next big media sensation.

"It went well," I answered. "The remand application went through and he hopefully won't see the light of day on the outside of those particular walls again." I placed my cup on his desk. "He didn't say anything in court other than to offer his name and address."

"Good job. I'll let Claire know and we can reassure the public we have the right man off the streets and the girls can now be put to rest."

The remainder of the day went by in a blur of paperwork,

meetings and calls with various agencies. The prosecution file was being put together; the forensic evidence from the crime scenes, dump sites, bodies and computers was coming in slowly but steadily. Several belts had been recovered from Benn's address and forwarded to Jack to consider for weapon match. A blanket had been found in the boot of his car along with a plastic sheet. A pair of children's pants and vest were seized from under his pillow. These were all processed by the Forensic Science Service. Benn hadn't had a lot of time to plan for his crimes and was sloppy with evidence. I didn't know how his fellow offenders were thinking and what preventative measures they were taking.

The image of the girl in the photograph wouldn't leave my mind. It was on an endless loop. She was looking out of the cage waiting for me to come and save her. How long would they keep her alive and would we ever find her body should we not get to her in time? The Digital Investigation Unit were working hard on it, I'd reassured my team they were, but it was leaving me with a very uncomfortable and strung out feeling. The image had been taken recently so I was holding on to hope she was still alive, but I couldn't bank on it, not with the speed Benn had killed Rosie and Allison. I had to address the issue of how quickly these offenders progressed from torture to murder. The child looked so small, and afraid. I needed to know who she was.

I looked up from the decision log I was working on and spotted Sally making her way from the photocopier to her desk. I took the opportunity to call her in to my office.

"Sally, do you have a minute?" I asked through the doorway. She nearly dropped the pile of paperwork in her hands when I spoke. Her knees sank a little as she tried to keep hold of them, paper fluttering like a pack of butterflies trying to take off, but she managed to keep it under control. I knew she had been in the same car I had and she had every reason to be on edge and not quite as sharp as usual, but this uneasy feeling I had about her had begun before the blast. There was something wrong and it was lax of me to let it slide because we were having a busy few shifts. I liked to think of myself as approachable and fair, but Sally wasn't forthcoming and I didn't like it. Did I need to be worried?

"Yes, boss." She stood in the doorway, shuffling the paperwork in her hands, her eyes downcast.

"Come in, sit down."

She sat in the chair opposite my desk, holding herself tightly. She tapped the sides of the papers on her knees to straighten the edges, then turned them to another edge and repeated the action.

"How are you?" I asked her, giving her my full attention.

"I'm good, ma'am."

"Don't give me that; you've just got out of hospital. I'm certainly not expecting a good. Maybe an okay, but not a good."

She looked relieved as though I had given her some magic answer.

"I have to admit, I feel a little shook up. It was hard coming back in to work, but I feel passionate about this job and wanted to be here." She relaxed.

"Do you think you came back too soon? I know I'm feeling the strain, so I understand. Do you need to call it a day for today?"

"Maybe. Soon. I need to finish what I'm doing. I don't want to slack off with this." She genuinely cared about the case. Maybe I had it wrong. She had been through an ordeal. We both had.

"Finish that, then knock off for the day. If we don't see you tomorrow, we don't see you."

She practically jumped out of the chair.

"Oh, I will be in tomorrow. I'm fine. I'm tired. I will be here tomorrow and won't leave until I've finished this."

I leaned back and smiled at her.

"Great. That's good to hear."

62

Sally breathed a sigh of relief as she walked out of Hannah's office. She had just photocopied documents to be sent to the CPS when Hannah had called her in. For a minute she'd considered her boss already knew about the pregnancy, so she'd jumped on the excuse Hannah had handed her in mentioning the blast.

The blast wasn't the distraction, though indirectly, it hadn't helped matters. It had fuelled Tom's need for her to disclose the pregnancy at work. It was better if Hannah continued to believe any distraction was a result of the explosion they'd been involved in. Should her DI become aware of the pregnancy then Sally had no doubt she would ground her and potentially remove her from the case. She felt connected to this case, seeing what the girl went through when Jack did the PM on Rosie. Maybe it was her parental instincts kicking in, or the hormones, but she had a need to close this for Rosie and see it through to the end and she was not going to risk that by disclosing the pregnancy, especially if there was no chance of harm coming to the baby.

Sally walked back to her desk, happy she was still on the case and pleased she could, for a short time at least, juggle the job, the deception, and Tom.

63

After talking with Sally I decided to catch up with Evie. She was still going through the intelligence work I had given her the previous day and didn't have any useful information. It frustrated the hell out of me.

The last thing I did before I left work relatively early, was to text Ethan to see if he was free to meet up, and to apologise for not calling the night before. Texting was a coward's way out, but the ease of a message without having to deal with any kind of conversation appealed to me most of the time, so it was the default option when I was feeling in the wrong. I expected him to be annoyed or at least ambivalent to my request after standing him up, but he answered straight away and we made arrangements to meet in the local Antibo Italian restaurant on Lower Parliament Street, half an hour later.

The lighting was low and gentle music created an ambiance. Dark wooden tables and chairs, against the white tiled floor gave the restaurant a comfortable feel I could easily relax in. I lifted the bottle of Pinot Noir and topped up our glasses. The restaurant was quiet; evening diners hadn't started to fill up the tables. Other than ours, three others were taken. A young couple chatted over pasta, their faces lighting up as they spoke in hushed voices. A middle-aged couple with two small children, and what looked to be a working dinner: five people in suits and heels on the women. I had no idea how the women walked in their killer heels for five minutes, never mind a whole working day that extended into the evening. How were Ethan and I perceived? Did we look like a couple out for a quiet, close dinner, or two strangers with nothing to say to each other? I studied Ethan over my glass as I drank. His face looked drawn and heavy, but his eyes found mine and it felt as though they were searching my soul. The one thing I wasn't sure I still possessed at this point in time. I felt violated by the case, like the dregs of humanity were permeating my very being. I looked away and allowed myself to succumb to the safety of the glass in my hand.

"Do you want to talk about it, Hannah?"

I placed my glass back on the table and looked at him. "I don't know. There's something else to this case the media don't know and it's eating away at me."

Ethan didn't move a muscle; he just continued to look at me. "And you don't want to talk to me about it because you're worried about what I will do with the information."

A statement rather than a question. I didn't know how to talk to anyone about the things I saw, never mind a journalist I was in some kind of relationship with. "It's difficult."

He nodded.

"It's not that I don't want to talk to you." I took a breath. "It's the case itself. It's nasty and words don't seem enough." I raised the glass to my lips again. An easy transparent barrier.

"I won't probe. I want you to know that you and work are two different things. If you want to talk then I'm here, but for now, let's eat." He gave me an easy smile, the tension in his face broken by a softer, gentler look. I exhaled, not realising I had been holding my breath and leaned in to the table. I was happy to see where the evening took us.

I hadn't been at my desk long the following morning when Evie walked in with a stack of paper and her laptop tucked under her arm.

"Hey," I looked at her, "since when do you make house calls?" Evie rarely left her office.

She plopped herself down in the chair opposite my desk and threw her papers on it before putting down the laptop. "I'm hoping the biscuits also have a home here and not just in my office." She opened up her computer. "Otherwise I might have to take my sexy, intelligent ass, and its computer accompaniments, back to civilisation."

I smiled at her. "I'm sure I can find some. But will it be worth my while?"

She looked up from her tapping, feigning shock. "Since when is anything I give you not worth your while, missy?"

I acquiesced and pulled open my drawer, placing the chocolate biscuits on top of my overflowing desk.

"You ever clean your desk?" Evie asked, fingers tapping away at the keyboard as report boxes popped up all over the screen.

I grabbed some papers and dropped them onto the chair at the other corner. "I know where everything is," I replied. The chair failed to hold everything I had just dumped on it and we watched as half the contents slid to the floor.

She raised her eyebrows in question.

"Okay, most of the time I do." I stuck my nose back into my mug and eyed my best friend over the rim of it. "Stop moaning. You have biscuits. Now, what do you have for me?"

Evie grinned, perfect teeth on show. "Remember all those background inquiries you set me a few days back?"

I remembered. It felt like a bottomless pit of a task when I handed it over to her and I wasn't sure whether I had expected results from it. But Evie was bolt upright in front of me, her body language very much saying otherwise.

"Stop gloating and let me have what you've got."

She shoved half a biscuit into her mouth and started to speak. "I found a link between our cases with Rosie and Allison and another misper in another force area. And if we have a link like this, we may find a lead on the girl in the photograph, right?" She coughed a little as she forced the dry crumbs down her throat and reached for my mug. Taking a slug, she then looked at me in disgust as she realised it was cold.

I liked her logic but realised it didn't necessarily mean that it would lead to the girl we needed to find. However, it was a step we currently didn't have. "Okay, tell me about it."

64

Sally answered the phone on the fifth ring as she pulled at the towel rack in the ladies toilets.

"Sally?"

"Yes. Yes, it's me." She wondered how they had coped before the invention of mobile phones. If you wanted to avoid someone, all you had to do was get out of their way. Walk out of the house and go to work. Now though, now was different. She knew he was worried. But not giving her time and space was not going to make their situation any easier.

"How are you? How's things?" he asked.

"I'm okay. It's busy. We're under deadlines from the Crown Prosecutors and waiting for the Digital Investigation Unit to give us something to identify another girl. There's no need to be concerned about me here today."

"You shouldn't even be there." He was annoyed. "You've just got out of hospital and you wonder why I'm worried and checking up on you?"

"I won't be late home." She tried to placate him, give him something back, to show she understood where he was coming from and was taking care of herself and the baby.

"If I have to come to the station and collect you, I will. I don't care what she says."

"She won't say anything. She won't need to. I'll be home. She's not making me do this, Tom. You didn't see the girl." She knew he couldn't even imagine. How could you explain to someone the horror of a child's violent death? She had now also seen the images retrieved from Benn's computer and she was angry. There was no way she could describe those. No way at all. She couldn't get her own head around it never mind asking a loved one to comprehend. "I'll be home and we'll talk. I'll get a takeaway on the way. I love you, Tom."

"I love you too, Sally. So much. I don't want this to drive such a wedge between us, I just worry. I nearly lost my mind when they came to pick me up from work when you were involved in that car blast. I have never been so scared in my entire life. I thought I'd lost you. It's my role to protect you, you're my wife and maybe that's why I'm finding this so difficult." Sally looked in the mirror at her pale face. Her husband was scared. She owed him more.

"I'm going to make an appointment at my doctors' and set up my antenatal appointments. Trust me. I will keep this baby safe."

She ended the call, pushed the phone back into her pocket

and walked back to the incident room with a feeling of dread.

65

"Well," Evie went on, stuffing another half biscuit into her mouth. It made me wonder how she kept so trim. "You gave me a pretty hefty task of searching through the national database of missing children of a certain age. Do you know how many there are at any one time?" she asked, not really expecting an answer. "A bloody lot, I can tell you. Around 200,000 children under sixteen years of age go missing in a year and up to 500 are missing at any one time."

"Go on." I was disheartened by the facts and figures Evie was reeling off.

"Well, as I worked with Danny in DIU, I was able to narrow down a general location to help with my searches, due to some specific markers in the photograph of the girl you want identified. I narrowed it down as much as I could, then took into consideration which of them had the potential to be sexually exploited." She knew her stuff. "And while I was doing this I came across a linked file." She looked at me as though this should mean something. I returned her look with a blank one. I knew my way around the basics of the missing persons software but it had been a long time since I had used it so the terminology was going over my head a little.

"Oh, Han," she said, swallowing hard. "A missing person report has links on it. People – friends, family or associates – where the person could or has turned up before, or know in some way. It's so investigating cops have somewhere to start checking." This I remembered and I could tell Evie was leading somewhere. "One of the regular missing children in Peterborough has a linked file with…" she paused for effect.

"Yes?"

"Rosie Green."

66

"In what way is this girl connected to Rosie Green and why don't we already know about it?" I snapped.

"Hey." Evie stopped me with a stare. She was well aware this case had got to me, but she still wouldn't give any ground to take it out on her. "She was a tenuous link. It wasn't picked up. Rosie lived in Norfolk while Izzy lived in Cambridgeshire."

"Izzy? The missing girl?" I asked, trying to catch up.

"Yes. Isabelle Thomas. Fourteen years of age. A problem child for her parents, the education authority, and with a knock on effect for local police for a couple of years. Always going missing, drinking, seen hanging around with older boys. Inappropriate relationships."

"And the link to Rosie?" I didn't get it. The information on Rosie was that she was a good child with none of these behavioural problems. This wasn't the life Rosie had been living and they lived so far away, so why the link.

"Isabelle's list of friends, contacts and associates is huge. She was often found in different counties because she'd get into cars with anyone that offered her money and alcohol. They'd use her up then leave her stranded wherever they'd taken her, so she got to know people in the areas she found herself."

"How does Rosie come into it?"

"Her name was added to the list of associates one night by a conscientious neighbourhood policing officer in Norwich, where it seems Izzy found herself once or twice. It looks as though they spent a couple of evenings hanging out in the same inappropriate places with older boys that were no good. Police attended outside some shop fronts, removed alcohol bottles from the teenagers, took some details and moved them all on. Not long after that incident Isabelle went missing for good."

"What happened to her?" There had to be a reason this had come to my office, biscuits or not.

"She was found dead a week later. Beaten. Post-mortem results show asphyxiation by strangulation." She stopped looking so happy with life now. Inputting and collating information was what Evie did and she did it well. She hadn't paid attention to what any of it meant. It was easier for her that way. This was a stark reminder of the shitty side of life out there, beyond the comfort of the walls she was used to.

"How long ago was this? I need details. Where was it and who was the SIO?" My mind was running several steps ahead.

"Just a minute." Her fingers worked the keyboard. "Three weeks ago. The offender was arrested and charged."

"They have an identified offender?"

"It says they do here. The SIO of the investigation was DI Shaun Harris and the body was found just outside of Peterborough."

67

She didn't know why she hadn't told Hannah about the pregnancy. Something was stopping her. Tom believed she had told Hannah. It happened when Benn was charged. It had been what she promised and Tom had taken her at her word and never thought to ask the question. She knew she was in the wrong, but she never corrected him. She let him believe it.

She didn't feel pregnant. There was no growth around her middle. And the nausea was bearable. There hadn't been any great heaving, vomiting down the toilet every morning. Neither had she craved strange combinations such as gherkins and ice cream, or anything else equally as odd. There was nothing to stop her telling Hannah, but something held her back. Something she couldn't put her finger on. What harm could there be in doing the file for trial?

"Ross, have you got a copy of all property seized please?" Sally looked up and asked as she typed. His desk faced hers, his face was screwed up in a mask of concentration as his fingers worked through more paper they'd created, pen in hand, scribbling notes in his blue pad as he went.

Ross, easily distracted, looked up and grinned as though she had just asked him if he wanted to go out for a pint. He was frustrating. Reminded her of her younger brother, Alan. "Electronically or do you want me to stand at the printer for an hour?" he answered, reminding her even more of Alan and their constant sibling spats which usually ended up with Alan taking a punch in the arm and him buying her a drink down the pub.

She glared and Ross put his head down. "Email will be fine," she said, knowing the problem was her mood and not Ross. "Thanks."

Her inbox beeped as the list arrived. She opened it. There were pages and pages of items. She needed to list the ones to be used as evidence on the MG9 exhibits form. The rest would be logged as unused material. She began the onerous task.

"Tea?"

She lifted her head. Caught up in bodily fluids, computers and components, she didn't see him coming. Ross stood at the side of her, a sincere look on his face.

"Fancy a cuppa?" he asked again.

She felt ashamed and cornered. "Thanks, Ross. Tea would be great."

68

I picked up the handset and dialled. After several frustrating re-directions, I was put through to the correct homicide unit at Bayard Place, Broadway, Peterborough, and the DI in charge of the investigation into the murder of Isabelle Thomas, Shaun Harris.

I needed information in relation to their investigation, to find out what linked these girls and these very different locations. If we could find the link, we had some chance of finding the girl photographed in the cage.

Harris was personable and helpful. Due to the intense press attention, he was aware of the Rosie Green and Allison Kirk case, but he hadn't connected it to his investigation. As soon as he was aware of what we had found on Benn's computer he was more than happy to share what he knew. He talked me through the sequence of events that led up to Isabelle's murder, the stuff we already knew from her missing persons report, then went on to the murder investigation and where that had taken them. The picture painted of Isabelle was a now familiar one. There had been issues at home, a failure to attend school which had not been addressed by her parents and when she did attend she was surly and uncooperative with regular missing episodes. There was a rapid and now obvious decline, and one that was not picked up by any agency: the police service, children's services, education or health. All agencies failed to engage with each other sufficiently to make a difference. There was now a Serious Case Review running. These are conducted when a child dies and a factor of that death is abuse or neglect, though reviews are also conducted under various other scenarios but ones based on harm to children. The review is not created to allocate blame, as culpability is looked at by coroners or criminal investigations. It's a means to identify shortfalls and to learn lessons and to see what could have been done differently by the various organisations involved with that child before and after death.

As well as the behavioural similarities between Isabelle and Allison prior to death, the MO drew us another parallel. During Isabelle's post-mortem, ligature marks around her wrists and marks indicative of a belt around her neck had been recorded. A vicious sexual assault and weeks of recorded missing episodes prior to death also screamed out this was more than a coincidence. The problem was, this case was already detected and not attributed to Benn and because of the detection, the further, more obscure links on Isabelle's missing persons record hadn't been fully investigated as viable lines of inquiry.

The differences and yet the similarities between the girls and the offences gave me a bad feeling. I pulled at my fringe as I went through the information with Harris, explaining the account Benn had given of a group of organised offenders. I needed to go to Peterborough and look into this further. If this was going the way I thought it was, then our case just got a whole lot bigger and the offender charged with the rape and murder of Isabelle Thomas could be the one lead we had on tracking down other offenders to enable us to identify and locate the girl in the photograph. I caught the team before they left for the day. I'd already updated Catherine Walker and Grey, and both were on side for our team to continue the investigation into the unidentified girl, and to take the lead within a cooperative cross force investigation. I updated Martin and asked him to check if there was any mention of Isabelle Thomas within the Norwich investigation. Walker had spent the day in conference calls to various heads of departments, along with the relevant command teams on each force. Eventually agreement was reached. Aaron and I were to travel to Cambridgeshire in an early morning start and meet with Shaun Harris. It was a messy affair by all accounts. The command teams in the various force areas didn't like the idea of an organised crime group involved in a case that was under such scrutiny from the press crossing their borders. On top of that, having another force come in and take the lead was hard to swallow, but Walker had sold me as being most knowledgeable on this group and their MO. It didn't say a lot about the state of the investigation in total as I was just getting my head around it. Crossing county borders had made connecting offences difficult, but a picture was being built.

Aaron's desk was uncluttered. I parked myself on the corner of it and talked through what we knew with everyone. I briefed them on Isabelle Thomas and the connections that had been made. I could see the same consideration for the girl in the photo cross their minds as I watched them look at each other.

"We don't have anything positive, but it's a good lead. Aaron and I are driving over tomorrow and will take a copy of the photograph with us. I'd like you two to finish up the Benn file here and talk to the Digital Investigation Unit to see where we are with it."

Ross looked disappointed not to be going. He was always so eager to be involved.

Sally, on the other hand, touched her hand to her stomach. The whole case made my insides turn as well.

69

It was getting close to that time of day when she knew she would be let out of the cramped space. There was having structure to her days. A routine. Details about her past home life felt vague and distant as she focused on what was important here. When she was due to be fed. A survival mechanism. She took the food from him. Sometimes it was good and she shovelled it into her mouth. Other times the food wasn't so good and after eating, she felt weak and dizzy and she'd lie down, her cheek warm on the cool plastic base. She couldn't recognise the bad food until she'd already eaten it, but she'd learned to take comfort in the release from the fear it gave her as her eyelids dragged closed and the cage blurred and softened around her.

Another thing she had learned was if she waited long enough, she didn't have to sleep in her own urine. She worked out toilet break times. Occasionally the routine was a little off, but when they remembered, they let her out twice a day.

A few days she was washed and if she behaved she got her hair brushed. Right now it was knotty and wild. She always tried to be good for the photographs, staying as still as it's possible to stay and taking her thoughts down a different path to the one she's being physically taken down. It was getting harder and harder to hold on to her memories as they seeped out of her mind like water from a pot with the smallest of cracks, invisible to the eye, but there nonetheless. She tried to cling on to memories of her mum, craving the feeling of safety they brought. It was getting harder but she tried.

She holds on to routine. If she's good it may get better. Her body screams in the cramped space and she sits and waits for the time she will be let out.

70

Sally heard the click of the kettle as she closed the front door behind her. Tom was already home. She didn't remove her coat, she wanted to see him. Be near him. He was the one person who could make this all right for her. He always knew the right words to say, or the right spot to massage to relax her. He was always her protector. She might be in a strong role at work, but at home she needed her husband and she really needed him tonight. She walked into the kitchen as he put two mugs down on the worktop. He turned to look at her.

"What's wrong?"

"There's been another child killed." She sank on to one of the chairs around the table, dropping her bag on the floor. Her phone slid out through the open zipper and clattered as it hit the tiles but she ignored it. She was done in.

"Where?" Tom believed she was on restricted duties at the station now. He'd understood her reluctance to talk about the conversation with Hannah. He'd told her he was proud of her, that he knew it was hard for her to do it and he would give her the space she needed to adjust. He trusted her.

"Peterborough."

"So you're not dealing with it?"

She looked at him, a mixture of sadness and something else. "No. I'm not dealing with it. Hannah and Aaron are travelling over tomorrow. Martin is in Norwich still and Ross and I are dealing with what we can from here."

Worry flashed across his face. He turned away, took a breath before looking at her again. "But you're not going out to deal with anyone are you?"

Sally stood, the chair legs scraping on the floor as she pushed back. She couldn't stop herself. She was angry. "I'm safe. Safe as houses. Does that make you happy? Someone's child is in the ground. Someone's baby. But I'm safe. Okay?" She didn't have the energy to explain the child's death had occurred several weeks ago and it was mostly a paper exercise. She was so tired. The girl still had no life, no future. It had still been violently stripped away from her.

She walked out of the kitchen, her bag and contents lying where she had dropped them, Tom rubbing his face with his hands. The kettle whistled into the air.

71

He was annoyed with me. I could tell. His silence spoke volumes. I handed him a glass. "Wine?" He took it and knocked half of it down. He still hadn't said a word. He was waiting for me. "I know I didn't call when I said I would," I paused. He waited. "It's been hectic." He finished what was in his glass. I followed suit. "Ethan?"

"Tell me about it?" His face softened and he leaned back into the sofa. I was so unsure of this relationship but something about it, about Ethan, pulled me in. We sat together on the sofa, cradling our glasses as though they were fragile. The press release had gone out and the promised first call to Ethan to give him the heads up had not happened. I wanted to explain. We'd met the day Benn was charged but I presumed he had given me breathing space because my face still showed such visible injuries, it had obviously been eating away at him and it seemed he couldn't put it off any longer. I pulled my feet up under me.

"There's been another death."

A pause. "A child?"

"Yes."

"How can they be connected if Colin Benn is locked up?"

"We just think they are at this point."

Ethan looked at me. Where to take this now? I didn't know how to handle the uncertainty that came with a relationship with him. I'd called him in a moment of weakness when what I wanted was to feel his arms around me, his warmth, his masculinity to envelope me and to hold me in tight. Instead I sat waiting, wondering. I sighed, frustrated with my inability to say anything more. Ethan leaned in towards me. I felt his closeness and my breathing deepened.

"Talk to me, Han." So close. "Don't push me out."

I felt confused. I leaned past him and for want of anything else to say, I picked up the bottle from the floor and topped up our glasses. "You can't print this."

"I don't want to print it. I want to talk. I want us to be able to talk."

I took another gulp. "The MO is very similar. I've got an early start tomorrow. I'm heading out to talk to the team who have been dealing with it to see what we have." I couldn't tell him about the girl in the cage. Something was stopping me. Not just my integrity, the knowledge I shouldn't, but a feeling, an uneasiness. I was treading on dangerous ground and it felt unsteady beneath my feet.

"Keep in touch with me while you're there." He leaned closer and kissed me, I wound my arm, still holding the glass, around his neck.

72

It didn't take long to get to Peterborough. We beat the satnav by some fifteen minutes or so. Aaron could have a heavy right foot when necessary. I'd endured multiple questions on the silent phone calls I'd been receiving. Aaron wanted to know if there had been any threats or suspicious activity around work or even my home address. He asked because he cared, but as I told him, they were just phone calls. Nothing had happened elsewhere. I'd had no mail, no strange unannounced visits, no gifts left for me, or threats made. They were just silent phone calls from an unknown number. I wasn't worried.

"But keep your eyes peeled, Hannah. Don't become too comfortable with it. It is a little strange, you have to admit. And it doesn't sit right with me."

Large steel gates groaned as they closed behind us in the secure yard at our destination. Aaron parked the car in a vacant space. "I will. It could be anyone though. I give my number out to a lot of people." I knew Aaron was capable of taking measures a little far if he thought he needed to protect one of his own and he'd be submitting authority requests for who knew what if I didn't go out of my way to reassure him.

"Yeah. Too many. I'm not surprised you've got some nutter calling you."

As we got out the car we were met by a portly man. An obvious desk jockey with an amenable smile.

"DI Robbins?" he asked as he held out his hand. "It's Hannah." I shook his hand.

"Shaun Harris."

"Shaun, this is my DS, Aaron Stone." They shook and Harris walked us into the building, up a couple of flights of stairs to their incident room. Though smaller than ours, I could see they were organised.

We'd brought case files with us and we dropped these down on to the table Harris had cleared for us. We'd also brought records of the taped interviews with Benn.

The murder of Isabelle Thomas had already been detected. A man, Karl Howard, was inside a prison on remand, awaiting pre-sentence reports and sentencing. Everything that led to the detection was now in this room and we were going to cross reference all we had and go over both cases again with both investigation teams present. We would talk to witnesses again, go over post-mortem results. We would turn this inside out until we knew what the link was. If we were doing this, we were doing it properly. We needed to find the girl in the photograph.

Once we had everything out and everyone was there, I spoke to the room – Harris, Aaron and a small team of three young looking DCs introduced as Rob, Dave and Nick.

"We believe there is a group involved in the abduction, abuse and murder of these young girls and it seems likely Isabelle is a part of that."

Harris raised his eyebrows. "You're talking about an organised group operating around the country?"

"It does appear to be that way, which is why we need to check both our investigations against each other."

"Okay. Where do you want to start?" Harris asked. The office was quiet as everyone took in what we could be dealing with.

"What did the PM find?" I asked him. He stood and walked to another desk where Nick held out a brown folder. Taking the folder he scanned the material inside.

"Welts around her wrists and a similar one around her throat. Significant visible proof of a rape. There were no defensive marks. The welts appear to have been made by something like electrical wiring. Cause of death was asphyxiation. Tox screens have gone off, as have stomach contents. It will take a while to get those results back, though we've put a rush on them." Harris went on skimming the report which I knew would contain a much more detailed account of injuries. "The pathologist was more than happy to put the tests through as urgent. He was quite sickened by the case. Just had his first grandchild. A girl. He wasn't happy."

Harris spoke to his team. "Let's work through this and see if there is any way we can make some links and identify this girl. Alive." he said, with more conviction than I'd previously heard from him.

73

Sally was bored. The paperwork was tedious, time intensive and far from stimulating. Ross, on the other hand, approached each action like it was the most important task in the world. He was like a big puppy, eager to please, and it annoyed her. It never used to, but she couldn't keep her emotions in check at the minute and it frustrated the hell out of her and made all other tasks, objects and people all the more frustrating. Annoying. She wished she was the old Sally. The old Sally, but with the future Sally outcome.

She turned her attention back to Ross and the job in hand. The amount of follow up inquiries and paperwork created following an arrest and charge were ridiculous. You could never rely on the admission alone. Some offenders could admit the crime during interview then plead not guilty at court, so if you were unprepared it could throw everything up in the air. The investigation continued on as though no admission had been made. With Benn, there was a hell of a lot of extra work to do. On a basic murder inquiry you needed to know about the relationships of both the offender and the victim and interview everyone involved in a detailed fashion. Background inquiries often gave you information you wouldn't have previously considered and doing a proper job was supposed to counter any new defences the offender may come up with at the last minute. Sally felt the need to speak with people rather than spend the entire day sat at her desk listening to the enthusiasm ooze out of Ross. It wasn't Ross, it was these bloody hormones, but they were driving her insane and she felt so over-sensitive to everything and she might be able to bear him if they were out and about talking to other people. Even if it wasn't his fault, the work needed doing and now was as good a time as any to get it done.

"Come on, Ross, let's go and knock on a few doors. We can do the addresses where there was no reply to knocking first time around on Benn's street, then chase up some of the customers identified as being at the restaurant the night Rosie was dumped."

Ross looked at his desk, then at Sally and stood up with a grin across his face. It didn't take much to persuade him. Sally wasn't sure he had a life outside of work.

"What about the file?" he asked of the CPS paperwork.

"It can wait until we get back," she replied, conscious of how much time she spent at work and how Tom was feeling. But if they worked together it would help speed things up so she could get home at a reasonable hour. She put her hand to her stomach again. She wasn't showing, but she knew it wouldn't last forever.

74

We spent hours comparing notes on Rosie, Allison and Isabelle. The similarities with the injuries and lifestyles of the girls were significant. The way they had all been reported as missing at one point or another and a marked change in behaviour stood out. Signs, though not picked up at the time, pointed to the potential for sexual exploitation and, going on Benn's recent admissions in interview, it was likely this was the same group operating around the country. The weakness in our theory was the man, Karl Howard, locked up in Lincoln prison for the rape and murder of Isabelle. He didn't give a very strong account of how he had taken Isabelle. There had been no mention of networking on the internet or talking with others who had the same interest in children as Benn had talked about. On review of the interview transcripts it was obvious the initial admission on the abduction of Isabelle was vague, but the murder detailed. There was no way Shaun Harris could have known this was a network of people working together and the interview was taken at face value because of the admission of murder. It was now he could see the importance. He removed his spectacles and placed them on the table in front of him. The glass inside the frames looked as tired as he did, with smears and fingerprints covering them.

"So we go back and interview him again. We find out who he's been talking to, who's behind this and how they organise themselves." Harris looked over at me. I could see his guilt at not identifying the issue in the first place weighing him down. "I take it you would like to interview him, DI Robbins." More of a statement than a question.

"Please call me Hannah." I corrected him again. "And yes, if it's feasible, I'd like to be in on the interview. Having already interviewed one of the offenders, I have a pretty good feeling for the case and knowing more than he thinks we know will be an advantage when interviewing him."

"We'll set it up for this evening. Considering the very high possibility there's a child being held whose life is in danger, I can't see the prison being difficult about it; we have a pretty good relationship with them." He looked across at Rob. "Would you mind setting it up please, Rob? Three visitors for Howard."

"Three?" I queried. Interviews were usually set up with pairs of interviewers.

"Yes. I believe the interview will run better and be more productive with two new interviewers, yourself and Aaron. I'll be about if you need any information in relation to the Isabelle Thomas case." He surprised me. My experience of police officers, not just in other force areas but in other units in our own force, was that they liked to keep a tight rein on their own investigations and someone else coming in resulted in some massive brick walls being built. Harris was another thing altogether. He wanted this girl found and he recognised the best way to do that was with Aaron and me going in. I didn't think he'd messed up as much as he felt he had. They had the murderer of Isabelle Thomas locked up tight. I was grateful to have come across such a dedicated detective.

"Thank you, Shaun. Let's hope Howard talks before time runs out." If it hasn't already, I thought to myself.

Prisons are always grim. They make me feel on edge. The level of security and suspicion on entry automates a guilty reflex in me. Dealing with offenders in a police station custody suite is one thing, but prisons are another thing altogether. Harris manoeuvred the car into a parking bay. I could feel Aaron's natural calm behind me. I wasn't sure if anything unnerved him. It was another reason I liked working with him so much.

As we entered the building, the hairs on the back of my neck started to rise. The reception area was shielded behind thick glass and a uniformed member of staff eyed us over his oval shaped glasses. Harris informed him who we were and why we were there.

After a couple of minutes, a prison intelligence officer came through the doorway, introduced himself as Alex Foster and led us through the doors. His keys and chain clinked as he walked.

"It's a late one for you today then," he stated. The doors locked behind us.

"It's one of those days," Harris replied as we waited for the next set to unlock.

"You know the drill. All property in the trays and lockers. Only paper and pens allowed through." This guy enjoyed his job too much I mused as I emptied my pockets. Once our property was secured we were wanded and told to sit in the boss chair. You have to love a chair whose sole purpose is to see if you have items secreted inside your body cavities. It's a plastic moulded chair, high backed with arms, that acts as a metal detector. It lets staff know if you've inserted anything metal inside your anus or vagina.

Once all the security protocols had been passed, Foster showed Aaron and me into a single interview room and Harris into the communal interview room where he would wait until we might need him.

I'm not sure what I expected when I met Howard but he caught me off guard. Benn was a permanent loser, the type of person I've come across on a daily basis since I first joined the job. Howard, however, looked previously well groomed and cared for, though it was obvious time inside, albeit short, had had its effect. A significant weight loss was evident around his neckline as the T-shirt he wore hung loose around him. He had a decent haircut which was now growing out and was curling around the bottom of his ears; his nails were clean and not bitten down to the quick. They looked neater than mine and I pushed my hands into my pockets. Howard's stubble seemed to be something he was not used to as he continually rubbed at it with one hand. He looked, to all intents and purposes, to be a blue collar worker, in here for a crime of the financial kind rather than the horrific abuse and murder of a child.

My own surprise was reflected back at me as he looked at us. I imagined he would be used to being interviewed by the local team who arrested him and then probation officers and those inside the prison, but he obviously hadn't expected to see anyone different, especially at this time of the evening, long after visitors were allowed in.

"DI Hannah Robbins." I held out my hand as I introduced myself. "And this is DS Aaron Stone." Aaron kept his hands in his pockets but nodded his greeting. A puzzled look crossed Howard's face and I could see the informality and first name terms were causing confusion. In here, he would be used to disdain and disgust on a daily basis and would be expected to call the prison officers either miss or sir. For someone to enter this environment, use first name terms and shake his hand would be disconcerting. It was meant to be.

75

The interview went at a steady pace and every word was being recorded. Howard was unsure of us and it took some time to settle him and put him at ease. He couldn't keep still on his chair, crossing and uncrossing his legs. He made the same admissions to us that he had made to Harris's team. He took Isabelle to a lock-up he owned and raped and murdered her there. The crime scene techs had confirmed evidence of this.

"Where did you meet Isabelle?" I asked.

Howard's eyes widened. "Erm… I… I... met her in a park."

"You met her in the park. How did you strike up a conversation with her?" I could feel the tension rise and knew this was the same scenario Benn had described. This was part of a bigger picture. We were about to break into a well organised ring. If we could get Howard to talk.

"I… erm… she, we talked. I liked her. We connected. You know. You know all this. You know what happened. Why are you going over it again?" The tone of his voice rose.

"We need to know *how* it happened, Karl, not just what happened. How did she get to your lock-up?"

"She liked me. She wanted to keep talking. It happened." He gulped down the water in front of him. His hands shook so much I was surprised any of it made it into his mouth.

"I don't believe you, Karl. We know it didn't happen like that. Tell me what happened." I looked at him. I could practically see his nerves fraying. He twitched in his seat again.

"I told you how it was. I told you already. Please."

Aaron looked up from the notes he was taking. "Tell us about the online meetings and how the arrangements were made."

Shock registered on his face. He'd got this far without much in the way of questioning about the abduction. A simple explanation had been taken at face value. Being confronted with the reality someone else had been involved and he wasn't in this alone seemed to shake his already fragile demeanour. Howard crumbled in front of us. He wept as he told us of the online meetings. Of the arrangements to provide a child with the condition that everything was recorded and shared with the group. What we previously didn't know was that money was exchanged. Howard paid to do the things he did. Sadistic sexual gratification at a price. He told us he couldn't control himself and it was a need deep within him. As much a part of him as being heterosexual or homosexual was to those who were born that way. We listened to the excuses and weepings of a depraved man who paid for and murdered a child for his own selfish ends. I was seething inside. Moments of silence came and went while I gritted my teeth before going forward with the interview. Aaron's analytical mind worked wonders, running rings around Howard. Finally he gave us the email address of the person in charge of the whole group. The main man who organised the sale of children and demanded photographs and video evidence of the violent sexual acts committed against young children. The email address didn't consist of a name, it was a random phrase made with an attempt to keep his identity secret. Shallow waters. Howard didn't know who the man was. The arrangement had been the same as Benn described. A meeting in a quiet place where the girl was handed over from the boot of a car. It was dark. Howard was more interested in the girl, his excitement and thrill of the situation blinkered his attention to his surroundings. All he remembered was a saloon shaped car, dark in colour and a man in a baseball cap, wearing jeans and trainers handing him the child. That was it. As nondescript as that. A baseball cap, jeans and trainer-wearing driver of a dark coloured saloon.

My pleasant demeanour ebbed and all that was left was a empty void. The room seemed to shrink and the pitiful face of Karl Howard filled my vision. He repulsed me. We left him rubbing his chin with a dejected look. There was no shaking of hands or words of thanks. I steered Aaron towards the door as his usual calm looked in danger of being lost when he took a step towards Howard with his fist clenched by his side as Howard apologised to us again. It had been another long day and I could see Aaron's five o'clock shadow starting to form. We were a step closer to the girl in the image but I didn't know if it was enough.

76

It was dark and late when we returned to the station, the wind picking up dead leaves from the ground, scattering them about with force. No matter the lateness of the hour, we still had work to do. We had to work as though this girl was, as far as we were concerned, still alive. Knocking off before that work was done wasn't an option. Harris parked the car and didn't move. I turned in my seat to look at him.

"Shaun?"

Aaron sat in the rear, silent.

"I'm sorry we didn't pick this up earlier. We could have saved you a lot of trouble and a lot of time. I have no excuses. We will do all we can to help. Our resources are your resources."

While I appreciated the sentiment, he couldn't just hand over his force resources like that, but his team could give us a dig out while we were here. "You couldn't have known it would turn out like this." I tried to relieve some of his guilt. The rear door opened and I heard Aaron climb out.

"Really, Shaun, give us what you can now and we will find her. Nothing is final." There was silence for a moment. I didn't want to break it. I knew how I would feel if this had happened on my area.

Harris sighed. "Okay then, let's get on with this. Identify the account user?"

"Absolutely."

I love police stations when it's late. There is a quiet lull. The nine to fivers have all gone home. The only people left in the building were the custody staff, the night shift uniformed cops and the odd late-nighters like ourselves. The automatic ecological lighting had the place in near darkness. There were lights on at the far side of the building, where I imagined someone on nights would be filling in paperwork. We walked to the major incident room, the lights in the hallway illuminating our path as we moved. The quiet around us broken only by our own footfalls and the clicking sound of lights switching on as we walked.

I pushed on the doors of the incident room and watched it light up like a silent fairground. Harris walked to his desk and switched on his computer terminal. Aaron turned around and walked out of the room without comment. At times I couldn't read him and this was one of those times. His words were often quick and factual, but his silences were like gaping chasms. It was better to leave him. No matter what was happening inside his head, he would always work through it and I could rely on him.

I turned my attention back to Harris, who was now loading the documentation we needed to obtain details of an email registrant. It was a long-winded, bureaucratic pain in the arse to complete, but Harris tapped his way through it diligently, considering things like this are usually completed by a constable rather than the inspector of the unit. Once the required details were in he submitted the document and made a call to the control room inspector so that the request would get immediate attention. It was marked 'urgent life at risk', but turnaround still couldn't be quantified. I thanked Harris and found Aaron on his phone in the hallway. He hung up his call on seeing me.

"We done for the day?"

I nodded. "We're done."

77

Sally lay awake, Tom snoring at her side. It made her ability to think all the more difficult. He slept soundly. How she envied him that. The streetlights illuminated enough to make out his profile, the softness that came with sleep, the man she had promised her life to and who had promised his in return. She raised her hand to touch his cheek but stopped short. Her fingers hovered over the shadow on his chin, feeling his breath with each exhale. Warm and strong. Then let it rest on the pillow at the side of his face and watched him.

Her deception of Tom, friends and colleagues was wearing, but on top of that she worried about the longer term issues the pregnancy brought and those fears were carried alone, in the night, when darkness fell, that it all became too much. There was a thin line when withholding the information from the organisation. The contents of the health and safety policy form for pregnant officers had sent her spiralling into a panic. So much change and so much to consider. Could she continue with full time work and stay in the unit? How would her life change and what would this pregnancy do to her? The enormity of what was happening to her physically and to her relationships scared her. The future was now completely mapped out. There would be no more spontaneity, working over as much as needed, boozy nights, late mornings or random episodes of sex around the house when the mood took both her and Tom.

There were massive changes occurring in her body, even at this very point in time. Though it wasn't visible, the baby was growing and her body was accommodating it. Tom would fuss and make more of an issue of the work thing, wanting to know what Hannah had said about the impending happy event.

She felt far from happy. Hormones raged around her body, taking control, leaving her with none and her mood in the gutter. Would she love this little being growing inside her? It was a part of her, after all. A child she was keeping warm and safe becoming a perfect little human.

Her mind was drawn to the girl on the mortuary table. Rosie Green. The image of the girl in the cage. She couldn't give up on the investigation while she was still out there. Everyone was working this case hard and she was not going to be the exception.

78

The email address results would take some time and I worried it was time we didn't have. The first girl we were visiting was Samantha Bryant, a friend of Isabelle Thomas. We knocked early so we could catch her before school. Her mum was anxious throughout the interview. She sat on the very edge of the sofa checking every couple of minutes with Samantha that she was okay, rubbing her knee constantly as though the very act of contact would secure Samantha from a world we now wanted to ask her about. Every time her mum asked, Samantha confirmed she was fine.

After several minutes of reassuring her mum, she told us of the drinking sessions she would engage in with her friends. She spoke to the floor, directly at the dirty grey trainers she wore. She talked about how they would get together and drink anything they could get their hands on. She then went on to tell us about Jesse. Jesse was wonderful.

"He took care of us you see. He stopped us getting into trouble. Looked out for us. If Mr Timmins in the shop got annoyed with us, Jesse would walk us somewhere else, make sure we didn't get into trouble. He was a good guy."

Mrs Bryant looked hard at her daughter, hearing for the first time, I suspected, about just how bad things had got with her youngest child. Samantha, for her part, kept her eyes focused on her shoes.

"How old was Jesse, Samantha?" I asked.

"It's Sam."

"Okay, sorry, Sam. How old was he?" I could see how difficult this was for her, not just our interest in her lost friend, but upsetting her mum. I kept my voice low and casual, not letting on how potentially critical her information was.

"He said he was twenty-one." Her head flicked up from its downward stance, eyeing me. "But he was cool, you know. Didn't seem old." Mrs Bryant's lips parted. She wanted to say something, to chide her daughter for her stupidity. She looked at me before she said what was on her mind; I shook my head. Samantha would clam up if she felt upset, anger or criticism from her mum.

"What was his last name, Sam?" Aaron asked.

"Erm, Davids. Jesse Davids. He had a flat somewhere and a car. We thought it was so cool that he had a car. And he didn't look twenty-one."

I felt an excitement beginning. We had a name, something to go on. But he was only twenty-one. Was he capable of setting up arrangements of this size and complexity? He had a car and he had access to girls. One of the murdered girls in particular. We were closing in. I could feel it.

"We were jealous." Tears filled Samantha's eyes.

"Jealous?"

"Yeah, Jesse chose Isabelle and we were jealous of her."

"What do you mean, he chose her?"

"The last night we saw her he gave her a gift, a chain. It was pretty. Then they left. I was jealous." Her eyes filled as the pain came through. Mrs Bryant softened and she leaned in towards her daughter, wrapping a protective arm around her that said, *It's okay, I'm here, you're safe, you're okay. Oh god I'm so glad you're okay.* Samantha collapsed into her mum and we left them to their grief and relief.

79

It didn't take long to come up with an address for Jesse Davids. He was recorded on our systems with a string of petty theft offences to his name.

"How does an offender go from theft to child abduction, rape and murder?" I asked the open office.

Harris rubbed his face. "I don't know. It's a big leap. Maybe he's not in it alone. We seem to be up against that a lot."

"I agree. What's he doing with them once he has them then?"

"He's taking the girls directly off the street after building some sort of relationship with them. That takes time. And he's taking them away from close friends without anyone batting an eye. That takes trust. He's putting a lot of effort into this, so he has to be getting something out of it. I'd imagine he's getting a lot out of it. When he was stealing, it was to feed whatever habit he needed money for, but there's a lot more risk with the girls, so the pay-off has to be considerably higher." Aaron analysed the situation out loud and it made a lot of sense.

"You think he's being paid?"

"Maybe. He could be providing the girls for the buyers.

Trafficking young girls is a big market, there's a lot to be made from it, especially when you get people like Benn and Howard who want the girls, but are afraid to make any moves themselves," he continued.

"Well let's go and find out." I rose from my chair. "Let's bring this piece of shit in and hope the girl is still with him." I didn't want to think about the consequences of her having been moved on already. It made my head hurt.

My nerves were on edge as we pushed through the front door of Jesse Davids' flat. It was on the top floor of a three-storey complex. It was dirty and smelled worse than my kitchen bin after a few long shifts where I'd forgotten to empty it. It was dark and dingy. Davids was laid out on a sagging sofa, his eyes rolled deep into his head. I informed him why we were there and Harris and Rob searched the tiny three-room flat.

I reached down to Davids, impatient with the slurred response to my demands for him to stand. I grabbed his once white T-shirt by the neck and pulled hard. His head jerked wildly on his thin neck. "Get your fucking arse up. Where is she?"

He tried to focus, his face centimetres from mine spewed out an odour that made me sick. It infused my anger and frustration and I pushed my gripped fist into his shoulder harder, then pulled back towards me, making his head rock precariously on his shoulders. "I said, where is she?"

"Who?" he managed to slur in my general direction. He was high on something.

"The girl you're keeping in a cage. Where?" I demanded.

"Ma'am." Rob interjected waving a baggy in the air. "Smack. On the floor at the side of his bed. It's an expensive habit to keep."

"Yeah, and where's he getting the money from?" I shot back as I pushed hard on Davids' shoulder, letting go of his shirt as I did so. He fell into a heap on the sofa I had just pulled him up from. My frustrations cascaded down in a fury at him. He'd sell his grandmother to get a hit so I imagined children wouldn't be too much of a leap for him.

"You mindless piece of shit. Where is she? You tell us where she is or I swear I will bring hell down on you, more than you can imagine," I shouted, my face again too close to his rotten mouth. Rob backed away and returned to the bedroom where Harris was still going through Davids' few material possessions.

Aaron stepped closer. "Hannah. Back up." The three of us stood so close. "It won't help. We'll figure it out. Let's take him in. Let him come down, then we can question him."

I turned to face him, defeat pushing away at the anger. "It's taking too long."

"I know. It's all we can do, though. Come on. We can tear this place apart and then talk to him when we get him back to custody."

He was right. I looked down at the jumble of clothes and bones that was Davids and let out a sigh. Were we going to find the girl? We didn't even know her name. A nameless child, held in a cage and we still had no idea where. "Bastard." I hissed through clenched teeth. He never heard me. His mind was back wherever it was when we first entered.

80

She lifted her head as she strained to hear the noise again. The action pulled on her neck and she winced, putting her hand to the spot under her hairline and pressing down to ease the cramping pain. She tilted her head a little, lifting her ear higher. Every noise made her anxious. She had distinguished a few sounds as some level of normal, considering the circumstances, and others made her hyper aware and brought out the clawing animals inside her. This sound was giving her such a feeling now. It was unusual. Different to the sounds she had already categorised as *normal*. It was very quiet down here, so sound had to be close or particularly loud to travel to her, she had figured that much out. The silence she lived in could be deafening and invasive. She strained harder, she knew she had heard something.

Then it was there again. Her neck twitched more as she leaned in to listen. Her narrow fingers pushed in, pleading with the muscles to stop their complaint. She thought she heard voices. She never heard voices or conversations. The voices became raised. She shuffled backwards and put her head down. She didn't understand. Why the shouting? Was it to do with her? She had done as she had been told. She hadn't argued and after the first couple of times, she had learned to not complain. She may have cried, but even the tears had dried up, too scared to make an appearance. They angered him, made him hurt her more. Why the shouting? She pleaded in her head for it to stop.

81

We came away from the flat with Davids and a few items of property consisting of a mobile phone, the little bit of his expensive smack habit he had and some recordable DVDs. He didn't possess a computer. We'd torn the place upside down looking for one but he just didn't have one. Not there anyway. We'd searched his car, an old Ford Orion, parked in a covered area at the bottom of the flats reserved for residents. It was rusted with mismatched coloured doors and bodywork. We found nothing but empty bottles of alcopops, junk food wrappers and a couple of unpaid parking tickets. Harris contacted the control room and requested a forensic recovery of the vehicle.

It took several hours before Davids was fit to be interviewed, and my impatience to get to him pushed the local custody sergeant to his limit. Eventually he let us in before Davids was fit for interview. I didn't care. I took the photograph of the girl into the interview room along with a hot tea for myself. We didn't bother to offer Davids a drink. The custody sergeant would have looked after his needs. I had no interest.

He sat there with a coarse grey blanket around him. His feet looked ridiculous in a pair of too-large black elasticated pumps, provided by the custody sergeant because we'd seized his clothing and footwear for forensic examination. His skinny frame was barely able to sit upright in the chair. He was rattling, his body in need of another fix. I pushed him hard knowing he would want the interview to be finished. He wouldn't be able to take sitting here, still, for very long.

"We know you took Isabelle Thomas, Jesse, we have a witness. What we want to know now is where is the other girl?"

He smirked. I straightened up in my chair. "Which one?" he asked.

Aaron spoke to counter my rising temper. "We want to know about the girl held in the dog cage. She looks to be about ten to twelve years of age and has shoulder-length brown hair. Where is she?" His tone was even and calm. I took a drink from my cup and silently thanked him.

"I don't own no cage, man."

"Do you recognise the description I gave you?" Aaron continued.

"Huh. Urm." He shook in his blanket. "Maybe. I can't remember. I don't. When?"

I took the photograph from the folder and pushed it across the table towards him. He pulled the corners of the blanket closer under his chin and leaned over it to peer at the image. His eyelids dragged shut in his forward leaning position, then his body vibrated and he sat upright again. "I don't remember who she is."

"But you remember her?" I asked. Hopeful.

"Yeah. Kind of. Alls I do is get the girls, drop 'em a bit of smack and pass them on. Whatever happens to them after that ain't none of my doing."

A chink of light appeared in my mind. "Who do you pass them on to, Jesse?"

" I... er... dunno, some bloke. He pays me good. All I have to do is get the girls interested, give 'em a bit of sommat, then hand them over wherever he tells me and job's done. I get paid."

"How do you organise this with him?"

"By phone, he gave me a phone. I contact him with me phone."

82

The Cambridgeshire Mobile Phone Investigations Unit was small and restrictive, like it had been a last minute thought. Three men and one woman were working in the enclosed space. Computers and other technical looking equipment filled the few available worktops, with adapters and chargers for every conceivable make of mobile phone hanging from hooks on the walls. Mobile phones were an ever-expanding area of business for police forces. As technology advanced, so did the crimes and the need for units just like this one.

We walked to the corner desk and Harris introduced me to Terry Black. Terry shook my hand then went back to what he was working on when we came in. We gave him a couple of minutes then I watched as he clicked *save* and closed down the window on his computer. "What can I help you with?" he asked as he swivelled back to face us.

Harris dropped a secured evidence bag containing Davids' phone onto the desk in front of Black. "We want the listed number for the person registered under the name 'Shallow Waters'."

"Shallow Waters?" Terry laughed. "They think because they give themselves some fancy fake names, we're not going to find them. Jerks."

I watched as Terry did his thing, extricating the seized mobile phone from the evidence bag, photographing it then plugging it into a large computer to access the phone's information. After a few minutes he handed me the number listed for Shallow Waters and told me the full report would be available within the hour.

I thanked him and offered a smile to Harris. We were another step closer.

As we were out of our force area I didn't have access to any of the systems here so Harris completed another subscriber request, this time for the registered user of the phone number we had recovered. This would supply a result a lot quicker than the email address request would. Email addresses are notably more difficult and dependant on what part of the world the email provider was, the result could take more time.

We caught back up with Aaron, Rob, and the others in the incident room. I found myself a chair. It was then I realised how drained and exhausted I was and how this had been a growing feeling since the start of the investigation. I had let relationships slide. My father was upset at me, even if he didn't say so. His good natured calls were always a reminder of the darkness within our family and his constant effort to pull it all together and right it.

I had neglected Ethan. I hadn't the time to give him. I didn't know how I felt about us. As a cop, having a relationship with a reporter is difficult, and it's probably why I had shied away from making a conscious decision, one way or another. So I stuck my head in the sand. I knew I needed to talk to him, but it would have to wait until this investigation had been completed.

As my thoughts roamed I became aware of a ringing and jumped. Harris answered the phone on his desk. I listened to the one side of the conversation I could hear.

"Yes. Right. Okay. Thanks."

I sat in my chair, picking at the corner of my eyes where make-up was starting to gather from constant eye rubbing.

Harris dropped the handset into its cradle, stood, stretched and waited a moment before meeting my eyes. "It's a pay as you go number. We don't have anything on this guy."

83

Davids had been sat in his cell festering for how long, I didn't care. The only clock I was running to now was the clock against the girl in the cage and I didn't even know her name. My frustration level was rising. How the fuck could we be so close, and yet so far away? We had a phone number but the bastard had used a pay as you go phone and everything was up in the air again. I was raging and wanted to get Davids back into an interview room, but he was seriously rattling and was being seen by the force doctor in the custody suite surgery room.

I paced in front of the custody desk, which was raised so that offenders could not jump over and assault the custody staff. For fairly short stature officers, like myself, it caused another irritation as we were forced to raise ourselves on to our toes just to talk to the damn custody sergeant. I was starting to feel emotional and this wouldn't be good. I needed to keep focused. Not just for the girl, but to keep the respect of all officers, so the investigation could stay on track and she could be found sooner rather than later. There was an increasing chance she would end up on one of Jack's tables.

"Drink, ma'am?"

"What?!" I spun and saw a petite female in uniform smiling at me. I looked back at the custody desk for signs of her being told to get the mad woman out of their hair, but no one was taking ownership. I looked again at the officer in front of me.

"Can I get you a drink? You look as though you could do with one," she reiterated.

"Green tea?" I said, more to be obtuse than anything else.

"Coming right up." She turned on her heel and out of a blue door to her right, before appearing a couple of minutes later with two mugs with actual handles, rather than polystyrene containers, which indeed, contained green tea.

"Thank you." I took the chipped white mug from her and lifted it to my face. I inhaled. The smell of the tea smoothed away some of the irritation and brought with it my more level head. "Where did you get this from?" I asked.

"I bring it in. I like either this one or chamomile. You need something to unwind with after some shifts." She had a real calm air to her as she held her own cup in her hands.

I slurped on the hot tea. "What's your name?"

"Chris Maitland, ma'am. I'm on attachment to custody for a couple of weeks. You do see all sorts down here. And that's not just the offenders they fetch in."

Was this young probationer cheeky enough to be referring to me? At this moment in time I didn't mind. She had put me on an even keel momentarily while we waited for the go ahead to take Davids back in to interview and the tea was going down well. "Custody does get some real interesting people through its gates." At that point, I saw the force medical doctor exit her surgery with Davids. "And thanks for the tea, Chris. It was a perfectly timed pit stop." I absently handed back my half-empty cup. Now we would find out if we could interview Davids again and if it would provide us with any more detail.

The custody sergeant turned to me. "Inspector."

I straightened my fringe out and walked over.

"You're good to go again." He tapped at the keyboard in front of him. I waited. There was nothing else coming. His head was down, his pate shone through threads of hair still clinging for life atop his head, the fluorescent lighting easily picking out the bare patches like an old worn rug. His fingers worked rapidly as he input details I presumed belonged to Davids following the meeting with the doctor. I had no time for precious sergeants and do-good doctors right now.

Ten minutes later Aaron and I were, again, sat opposite Davids. He didn't look good. I didn't care.

"I told you everything, miss," he snivelled. Miss. A word that instantly told me he'd done time in prison. The grey blanket was still wrapped around his shoulders. Shoulders that were shaking and shaking hard. I waited. Not a word. Nothing. Aaron tapped rhythmically. No words.

Davids' knees bounced, the balls of his feet like small trampolines. There was nothing about him that was still. "You've got his number. I gave it you. It's in me phone. Just look. You've got it. You took it off me. You have it."

I waited another beat. Aaron tapped.

"Tell me about your meetings with him, Jesse," I said.

His knees bounced harder.

"I dunno. Yunno. It were dark."

I leaned forward. "Jesse, you either cooperate with this investigation or you don't. If this girl we're looking for dies before we find her, you're looking at a lot more time inside than you can imagine right now." I leaned back again, giving it room to sink in. Aaron turned and looked at me. He wasn't going anywhere for a long time anyway. He was wrapped up in the murder of Isabelle. We couldn't lie to him about evidence we had, but this wasn't lying. He was too dumb to realise how much trouble he was in. His body seemed to relax, his forearms rested on the edge of the table, his head dropped forward. The shaking continued but I could practically see the cogs turning. I breathed in and held. The tapping continued. Just as I could hold my breath no more, Davids pulled himself up, his grey face looking more drained than I thought possible. His mouth pinched, lips cracking.

"I want me solicitor."

84

I paced the incident room. Davids' solicitor was going to take an age to arrive and we couldn't say another word to him without the solicitor being there. He was with another client mid interview, at a station twenty miles away. No one else from the firm was available and Davids was insisting on having a named solicitor. Charlie Marr. I wanted to scream. He was hiding something. Stalling. And there was nothing we could do but wait. Meanwhile the clock kept ticking.

Aaron straightened his tie, though to me I couldn't see that it needed it. "Hannah, think."

"I am bloody thinking. What do you think I'm doing?!" I snapped back.

"Walking."

I stopped. Harris looked at me from his desk. I think he expected some kind of explosion, but I had none to give. Aaron was right. I'd walked some of the energy out, now I needed to stop and think things through. I grabbed a chair from a desk and pulled it to where Aaron had parked himself.

"So what now?" I asked.

"My question to you," he responded.

Harris perched himself on the desk Aaron had claimed. "He's going to stop talking. His solicitor is going to advise him to go "no comment" and that's where we'll be."

"Yes," Aaron accepted.

"So..." I started.

"So?" Harris asked.

"So..." I thought as I spoke. "We don't wait for his solicitor."

Silence dropped in the room as this was worked out.

"PACE states if a life is at immediate risk, and waiting for a solicitor hinders, risks that life…" I began.

"…We can continue the interview without the solicitor," Aaron concluded for me.

"Exactly."

Harris stood again. "The question now is this: is this girl's life at immediate risk?"

As Aaron and I stood in the superintendent's office, surrounded by photographs of what I imagined to be his grandchildren, two boys under five playing on a swing and slide set in a neat garden with smiling faces, the decision was made that the risk to life wasn't immediate enough. The superintendent, Alan Phelan, leaned back in his chair, crossing his stubby fingers in front of him as he explained. We had known about the girl in the photograph for the past few days and nothing had changed what we knew about. He was at great pains to make sure I understood his reasoning. I contained my anger and paced in small circles in the office space in an attempt to keep a lid on what I felt as I would risk my place on the investigation if I blew up at a super in a foreign force now. After being ripped off the investigation following the explosion, it felt as though Walker was waiting for any excuse to take me off and I wasn't going to give it to her. My body throbbed, each breath now burning like fire and the inside of my head felt as though someone was tightening a metal vice around it, one twist of a screw at a time.

"I know how badly you want it, Inspector, but you have to understand, my hands are tied." He unlocked his fingers and linked his wrists together to put meaning to his already frustrating words. "The law is very specific on this, it has to be immediate and I can't justify this as immediate enough." His fingers linked back up. "I'm sorry."

Aaron nodded and ushered me through the glass panelled door. "We have to wait, Hannah. Nothing for it. Look, we're further along than we've been. We could still find her tonight." He was trying to keep me in check and he was also right.

We grabbed a drink, I took a couple of the pills the hospital had provided and waited for the named solicitor, Marr, to arrive.

It didn't take as long as expected, but it was long enough. I was wound up and felt as though my head was about to explode. Marr was pleasant enough when he arrived in the custody suite. He looked tired and as though he'd had a long day. His dark hair was ruffled and untidy, but his clothes were smart, his suit jacket buttoned up and his black shoes, polished. He offered instant professionalism, a smile and a handshake, one that was firm but chilled from the night air. I didn't have time to engage in the usual niceties and I saw my abruptness stop him short a little. We needed to move this along. He put his briefcase down and rubbed his cold hands together.

"Okay, what do we have?" he asked. I handed him Davids' custody record. A quick read through gave him the facts of arrest. After reading, his eyes met mine with a more solemn look than he'd arrived with. He picked his briefcase back up from the floor. "Are you ready to give disclosure, Detective Inspector?"

"If you come this way, Mr Marr." I showed him into one of the consultation booths and handed him the written disclosure, outlining the information we required from his client. "I'm sorry," I said to him, "we don't have time to go over all the details in this interview. What we need to know are the facts as he knows them.

A girl's life is at risk and if he can help, you know it will go on the file that ends up at court."

Marr nodded but gave nothing away. He was here to do what was right by his client, no matter his thoughts on it, but I'd given him the facts and I just had to hope that Marr and Davids had it in them to help.

The interview was hopeless. In the end it really did seem that Jesse Davids knew no more than he'd already told us. The drugs had turned his brain into a long endless landscape of nothingness where the only things visible were the landmarks for obtaining the money for the fixes he needed to keep himself going. How he managed to get young girls to fall for him was beyond me, but then I wasn't a vulnerable teenager with beliefs that no one would love me or that I wasn't worthy of love.

We left Shaun Harris to finalise their end of the investigation. There was nothing further we could do here. I thanked him and his team and I hoped that I'd not left him being too hard on himself for not picking Jesse Davids up earlier. It was an easy link to have missed. He had his homicide detection already wrapped up. He didn't need to look further. Howard had given him all he needed for a safe conviction. I didn't know about Harris beating himself up, I was doing a pretty good job of that on myself.

I felt utterly defeated and burned out. I'd pushed myself and everyone else to the limit and for what? We didn't have anything. We had chased our tails over a single photograph with zero results. The weather reflected my mood perfectly as we drove back to Nottingham. It was dark; the rain was pounding down, lashing the windscreen and bouncing up from the road making visibility difficult. Aaron steadfastly focused on the road as I sunk in the passenger seat, arms wrapped around my ribs trying to hold it together.

"Have you spoken to Anthony or Catherine?"

"What?"

"Anthony, Catherine. You know, the bosses."

I stuck the heel of my hand in my eye and rubbed. "No. I've had my phone off for the interviews and haven't turned it back on." I sighed. It seemed like too much effort. I just wanted to get into bed and stay there for a few days. Instead I leaned into the footwell and rummaged through my bag where I had last thrown my phone as I listened to the persistent and steady squeak of the wipers as they crossed the windscreen. I pushed the button and the screen lit up. I held as it connected, mesmerised as the wipers fought to keep the windscreen clear, oncoming headlights hitting the raindrops and distributing out the glare across the view in front of me.

"Great, twelve missed calls and five voicemails." I scrolled through the missed calls log, I had seven from Grey and five from withheld numbers, but if anyone called from a work landline, they would display as withheld. I went to the voicemail section and hit the key to listen to my messages. "What's the betting Anthony is stressing," I muttered as I waited for it to connect. Aaron nodded, his eyes still focused on the road ahead.

First new message. Message left at one, fifty-one today. "Hannah, it's Anthony. Let me know how you're getting on."

Second new message. Message left at two o three today. "Han, it's me." Ethan. I wasn't expecting that. He must have called from a work landline himself for it to be a withheld number as I hadn't seen his number on my missed calls list. I glanced at Aaron and moved the phone to my left ear. "I miss you. Call me." That's it. I supposed it was more than I'd given him.

Third new message. Message left at two twenty-seven today. Silence. "Great. Another." Aaron furrowed his brow.

Fourth new message. Message left at two twenty-nine today. "Please help me. I don't want to move home again. I don't want to do this anymore. Don't let them do this. If we move, she'll go and then she'll die like the rest. Please."

85

I recognised the voice immediately. It was distinctive in its mousey quiet way. The caller that was pleading for my help on the voicemail hours ago was Caroline Manders. The girl I sat and talked to in front of her parents about her missing friend, Rosie Green. The girl who was too afraid to talk without looking for permission from her father. The father I could see controlling her as I sat there and did nothing, and now Caroline was telling me they were leaving. Leaving and killing someone before going. How could I miss this? The thoughts ran through my head at speed as I replayed the message on loudspeaker for Aaron as we parked at the side of the road, orange hazard lights blinking their rhythmic warning. I'd shouted at Aaron to pull the car over and we were docked up on a grass verge. Caroline's thin voice barely broke through the ticking of the hazards and the beating of the rain as I replayed it yet again.

Any fatigue that had been gnawing away at me was now gone, replaced with a renewed urgency. We had to move and we had to move quickly. I didn't know what was happening in Norwich as we sat here. There was no way to know if we would, yet again, be too late.

"Phone Ross and get him and Sally travelling, they've been in from the start and I want them there when we take this down. Then phone Anthony and fill him in. Ask intelligence to see what they have on the Manders and the address and find out what previous addresses they've had." I shot out directions to Aaron as I scrolled through my phone and dialled out. The call I made was to Clive Tripps.

I briefed Clive of as much as I could considering I didn't have much of a picture myself at the minute, and he said he would ask his team to stay on until we got there. He said he would also swear out the search warrant with the local magistrates while we travelled to them.

The rain was still coming down hard as we walked from the car. I could see Clive as he ran from the doorway of the police station. He had a paper file over his head, which did nothing to protect him. Water was streaming down his face. Down all our faces. Clive held out his free hand towards me as he reached us. "Hannah, good to see you again. Sorry it's under these circumstances."

I shook his hand. Rain ran down my sleeve. "Hi, Clive. Thanks for setting this up so quickly."

Clive turned back towards the building and we picked up our pace and ran for the door.

Martin was in the incident room. "Looks like we have our man then?"

"It certainly does. Ready to come back once this is done? There's a ton of work piling up on your desk." I tried to smile. The tension I felt was too much though and it probably looked like a lopsided grimace.

"Absolutely. Raring to go as always." A more relaxed easy smile came to Martin's face. He took everything in his stride.

Clive grabbed a couple of chairs and sat down in the incident room. It seemed he wanted to be out here with his team. I sat in one of the chairs offered. "Glad to hear it."

I went over what we knew with Clive again, who was as pleasant and accommodating as our previous visit, but with a simmering anger that I knew was probably being directed internally as my own was. This had been a long-winded job, with the senseless deaths of young girls. We had been so close and we had walked away, right out the door.

I called Ross and Sally and briefed them as they continued their drive over. They were making good time and would be with us soon. We were pulling everything together and were not going to take any chances. Nima put a call in to ambulance control and requested an ambulance be put on standby a couple of streets away from the address in the hope that the girl was still there and if she was in need of medical attention, it would be available.

An official briefing was held in the large command briefing room. A bland rectangular room that contained a large oval table and accommodated at least twenty chairs. On a wall at one end of the table was a video conference screen. I could see a couple of cops in uniform sitting in an equally bland room elsewhere in the force and was informed that they were two dog section officers. In the corner of the screen were all the people sat around our table.

The briefing involved Clive's superintendent, Bruce Graham, the homicide investigation team, including Kev and Nima, and several uniform cops needed for the entry and search team. We couldn't take any chances. Everyone was made aware of how dangerous these people were and that the priorities were to secure the offender and locate the girl.

Just as the briefing ended, Sally and Ross were shown in. Quick introductions were made and we were ready. We were going to take down this paedophile ring and my gut twisted into knots as I kept hold of the hope that the girl was still alive.

86

The girl stirred from sleep. Her eyelids were heavy and she struggled to remember where she was. A flicker of knowledge moved somewhere within and she sighed. A sigh which would have been deep and from her soul if her now lifeless frame had the energy to dig that far, but instead a small shudder escaped her and another small grasp on hope slipped away. She forced her eyes open. The wires blurred in front of her and the darkness pressed in, almost suffocating. She couldn't focus and her head screamed. There was a feeling that her eyeballs were being pulled back into her head. Her mouth was dry, her tongue like Velcro against the roof of her mouth. Her eyes closed again. The pain in her head sucked away at her thoughts. She wanted to sleep, to fall into the darkness and leave this pain and isolation. There was a feeling she had lost something but couldn't bring it to mind. Sleep dragged her down, she couldn't fight it and she didn't want to. It was all she had now. Sleep and darkness.

87

The road was quiet other than the sound of the rain on cars and windows. Most of the houses on the street had their curtains closed and lights on. A few were in total darkness. Aaron, Sally, Ross and I were sitting in our car waiting for everyone to pull up. Martin was in a vehicle with Clive, Nima and Kev, and the extra staff required were in a marked van. The dog men were in their cars. We had decided to park at the end of the street and walk the short distance to the house. We didn't want to alert the occupants of the address to our presence before we were ready. This was going to be risky, making sure we secured the offender and safely located any child that may be present. I was concerned but assured. Aaron looked his usual stoic self with maybe a hint of extra determination set in his face. Sally was in the back of our car, straight in her seat, alert and keen. Her hand touched the tip of the asp – metal extendible baton – tucked into her jeans. Ross, also in the back, looked like an excitable family puppy. The nerves that I so often force down as an officer of rank, Ross as a newly qualified detective still openly showed. He was dressed as most plain clothes cops dress when executing warrants of any description. He had on a scruffy T-shirt hanging over his jeans, where he kept his rigid cuffs in his back pocket and dirty, once white, trainers on his feet. While Ross had managed to make the change into jeans, I still wore a dark suit and sensible flat boots. We were so stereotypical if you chose to look at us.

Everyone had their goals and targets. Aaron and I, along with Clive and Kev would go through the front door with an entry team, while Martin, Sally, Ross and Nima would cover the back door.

We left the cars and took to our pre-agreed positions around the old semi-detached. We wore earpieces on our radios to avoid alerting our presence to anyone with the squawking of commentaries through hand-helds. The earpieces usually annoyed me, but I was so hyped up that I barely noticed it. My focus was on finding this girl here, and finding her still alive. I held onto hope. That hope was now mixed with trepidation and anxiety. I realigned my stab vest and looked at the team by the front door. It was impossible to see what was happening inside the house with all the curtains closed. There was a light on in the front window and another upstairs. I was worried about what was in there and how this would play out. I put my hands to my waist and ran them around my belt, feeling for my kit. Everything was there. We were ready.

88

I took a moment and a deep breath. Time slowed. All eyes were on me waiting for the command to go. What were we going to find in there? Would the girl still be alive or would we be recovering a body? I let the breath go slowly, my colleagues were still waiting. I nodded my head, raised my radio and advised the rear team. We were go.

The metal enforcer slammed against the lock and the door shifted and groaned. It didn't give completely. Dan Colson swung his thick-set arms back and, grunting, he slammed the red enforcer back into the door. This time it cracked and splintered under the pressure. I levered myself forward shouting "Police!" as I entered the house. Echoes of "Police!" followed me. I could hear the same sound coming from somewhere in front of me as the rear entry team made their way into the address. Ahead of me were the stairs. To the left was an internal door. I pushed on the handle. Inside the living room our man was raising himself from the sofa, a laptop open on a small coffee table in front of him. Donovan Manders, the man behind all this death and destruction. He was half-sitting, half-standing, his body stooped, his eyes wide and his face white. The couple of seconds it took me to reach him gave him time to right himself; he stood with his shoulders back and his fists clenched at his side.

I was fast. "Don't make a move." I grabbed hold of his wrist, hoping he would decide to try to resist. I didn't need much of a reason to use force to restrain him. Pulling the speed-cuffs out of my belt I pushed one down on his wrist, the metal cuffs locking their jaws securely around it. I grabbed his second wrist and pulled it around hard, his shoulder forced back with the action as I secured him. He was shouting, making protestations I barely registered amongst all the other sounds in the house as officers continued to enter. "Donovan Manders, I am arresting you on suspicion of human trafficking for sexual exploitation and for inciting the murders of Rosie Green, Allison Kirk and Isabelle Thomas. You do not have to say anything, but it may harm your defence if you do not mention when questioned..." I went on with the caution. It rolled off my tongue. We had him. We actually had him. I heard heavy footfalls going up the stairs, echoes of "Police!" still being shouted. Manders decided to pay attention to the caution issued and stopped talking.

89

Sally felt the fluttering in her stomach as she stood in the rear garden waiting for the entry team to make their move on the front door. She didn't know if it was nerves or if she could feel the baby moving. According to one of the books she'd read the first kicks feel like a butterfly, but couldn't remember at what stage that was. It was probably too early. The odd sensation must be nerves. But she wasn't usually nervous at jobs like this. It was an arrest and search, she'd done many. The fact was she knew how upset Tom was going to be. He would be raging when he found out she hadn't disclosed the pregnancy and worse still, was out on a job. It would be okay though. Only being a part of the rear entry team was pretty safe. The only time anything ever happened as part of the rear entry team was if the people inside decided they were going to leg it out the back door before the front entry team could get hold of them. With four of them at the rear door, they were creating a straight barrier anyway and it was unlikely she was going to be involved in any chases. If anyone came out this way, they would run straight into them. She shifted on her feet. The fluttering made her uncomfortable.

"Okay?" Ross asked, looking at her. He couldn't know just

by looking at her, could he?

"Yes, I'm fine, itching to get in."

Ross accepted this and turned to concentrate on the door and his mission.

The fluttering wouldn't give. They were in the house, the nerves were supposed to stop now. The kitchen was quiet, no one was in here. The sounds of the arrest and search team working through the front of the house and up the stairs were clearly heard. She would have a lot of things to explain to Tom later, but confrontation was not going to be one of them.

Doors were opened and checked, including a walk-in pantry and one leading into the dining room. Sally had noticed a door off to the side of the house's main rear entrance. She looked at Ross and Nima as they searched through the kitchen, opening cupboard doors and drawers. Nima even, quite morosely, looked inside the freezer. She knew it had to be done, but it set her butterflies off again. She needed to find this girl alive and save her, not find her pieces shoved into some suburban appliance.

She stepped back out of the rear door. She jumped as she heard, "Leaving already?" Ross grinned like an idiot at her.

"There's some kind of outhouse, I'm going to check."

Ross's smile slipped and he tilted his head as he looked at her. "You okay, Sally? You look a bit off it today. In fact you haven't been right for a few days, but right now, well, I don't know, it's odd you know."

She paused. Amazed by the fact that he had even picked up on it. He gave the impression he wasn't paying attention to much that went on around him. Another relationship she hadn't given credit to. She spent a lot of time with him and she should have figured out she could confide in him. "I know, Ross. I'll explain it all tomorrow. I promise.

"Want me to come with you?"

"No, it's fine. I don't imagine it will be a very large space to check out. I won't be long."

"Okay, shout if you need anything." He smiled again. This time with a more genuine feel to it.

Sometimes his never ending enthusiasm and happiness were a pain in the arse, but sometimes he surprised her and showed her depths she didn't think he possessed. She would have that honest conversation with him tomorrow.

90

My phone vibrated in my pocket. I thought it would be Grey or Walker doing a very untimely request for an update, but an unrecognised number was showing on the caller ID screen. I gripped the rigid bar of the handcuffs between Manders' wrists and twisted them towards me, causing the metal cuffs to dig in. I wanted him to know he was still securely restrained and would not be going anywhere even though I was taking a call. He made complaint but didn't make an effort to move. With my left hand I put the phone to my ear.

"Hello." I was sharp. This wasn't the time.

"DI Robbins?"

"Yes. What?" I kept my eyes on Manders.

"Inspector, it's Tom Poynter, Sally's husband. I'm worried. I've called the station to speak with her as her mobile is turned off and they said she is out on a warrant. Making an arrest?" The concern carried in his voice, but I didn't understand it and I was running out of patience. How had such a personal call had made it through to my mobile at a time like this?

"Yes, Tom, she is here. She's okay, but I have to go."

He erupted in my ear. "What do you mean 'she's there and she's okay'? You're taking her into a dangerous situation in her condition. What kind of supervisor are you?"

Her condition? "What do you mean, in her condition?"

"Her pregnancy. The baby. She told you," Tom's voice was now cracking.

Baby? Sally hadn't told me about a baby. What the hell was going on? I would never have let her come into this if I'd known she was carrying a baby. "Pregnant?" I repeated into the phone. "You're sure?"

"Yes, I'm sure!" A further outburst, then a question, "She said she'd told you days ago."

"There's an unborn baby in the house?" Manders twisted around straining on the cuffs and whispered, the corners of his mouth curling up. I turned the centre bar of the rigid cuffs so hard he squealed. No one in the room paid attention.

My mind was doing cartwheels. How could she do this? I had to get her removed from this house now. Later we would have strong words. "Tom, I'm going to get her out now. Then I will get her to call you as soon as she is. Understand?"

He sounded less angry and more confused, quieter. "Yes. Thank you."

I ended the call and pushed the phone back into my pocket. Damn her. She knew better. Damn!

I pushed on Manders' cuffs forcing him to step forward towards Aaron who was looking through some photographs on the windowsill. He turned to look at me. "Sally's pregnant." It's all I had to say, Aaron grabbed the cuffs holding Manders still and I headed to the back of the house to find Sally and get her out. I'd try not to bawl her out in the middle of the operation. I'd leave that until we got back to the station. What was she thinking? Coming into a live operation like this, carrying a baby.

91

She pushed down on the handle and the unlocked door squealed open. She found herself at the top of some steep steps with a row of small bulbs on the side, lighting the way down. The fluttering grew. She could find the girl. She could be down here. She had to get to her and fast. They had been searching far too long and there was no way of knowing what damage had been caused. Palms flat out on the narrow stone walls to keep her balance, Sally took the steps down. The fluttering in her stomach turned into a knotty uncomfortable feeling. The walls she clung to were damp and cold and the staircase she was heading down steep, the bare concrete of each step narrow with not much in the way of footing; it dipped in the middle from many years of extensive foot traffic. She had to keep going, no matter what she would find there. If there was even the slightest possibility that the girl could be down here, she had to check. She moved her hand from the right wall and steadied herself with her left, putting her right hand on her flat stomach. A habit she now recognised she had formed. She would tell Hannah everything once they were back to their home station. She thought she might even take some time off. Tom was right, the blast had knocked the wind from her sails and a little time getting back on her feet would do her good. It would also make Tom happy.

At the bottom of the stairs was an old rotting wooden door. It had a bolt across the outside, but the bolt wasn't fastened. Sally grasped the handle and took a breath. Was there really anything to fear down here? She was probably overreacting, but she had promised Tom she would be safe, so she pulled out her asp and flicked it, the friction causing the baton to extend to its full length and lock into place. She lifted her wrist upwards, laying the asp back down along her forearm so if there was anyone in there they wouldn't see it and be afraid. She turned the handle. It wasn't as she had expected. She had imagined the space to consist of a bare concrete floor and perhaps old household junk stored, but it was fitted much more like a living room, with carpet and floor length curtains up against a small window near the top of the rear wall. There was a chair in the corner, but it was what she saw in front of her that stopped her in her tracks as her brain struggled to process the sight.

A dog cage was in the middle of the room. Inside it, staring directly at her, was the girl she had seen in the image. She had found her. She was alive. As Sally took a step towards her the girl attempted to push away, eyes wide.

"Hey, it's okay," Sally lowered her voice. She was here. The journey was over. The girl was safe, the man responsible was being held upstairs and she could go home and know that she wouldn't be leaving the station on any other jobs for the next seven months. She crouched in front of the cage and put the asp on the floor at the side of her. Reaching out, her fingertips had barely touched the wire of the cage when she became aware of a rapid movement in the corner of her eye.

92

Martin, Ross and Nima were searching the kitchen and dining area when I pushed through the door from the living room. I nearly knocked Martin over as I barged in, but Martin, on seeing my face, made no comment on my lack of apology. Ross and Nima looked puzzled.

"Where's Sally?"

Nima's look changed to one of confusion. "She went outside to check an external door a few minutes ago. Is everything okay?"

I didn't wait to answer. My concern had ratcheted up a few notches and I had a bad feeling creeping in. Maybe it was the panic in Tom's voice causing me to be so openly stressed, or the anger at myself for not knowing she was pregnant, or not pushing her more when I did know that something was bothering her. I was also angry with her for pulling the wool over my eyes. Doubt and fear travelled the nape of my neck and into my scalp.

I pushed past Ross. I swung the rear door open so hard the single paned glass window gave with the force I'd pushed it into the wall with. It cracked and shattered, hitting the floor with a sound like tinkling bells. I still didn't stop. I needed to find her.

Where the hell was she? I looked to my right and saw nothing but a neatly mowed lawn, dying a little in the poor weather conditions. I looked to my left and saw the second door Nima had mentioned. It wasn't fully closed. I saw light coming from the bottom of the stairs.

"Sally?" I shouted as I started down the stairs sinking deep under the house.

93

She knew what it was as soon as she felt it. The cold slicing its way through her neck. Bringing in the very core of the damp held by the underground hole she was in. Sally brought up her right hand, a slippery warmth under her fingers. Her eyes sought out the girl, who held her gaze, not flinching. She tried to call for help but no sound came other than a small gurgling she didn't recognise. Still the girl held her gaze.

Sally slid off her heels and leaned into the cage allowing it to hold her up. With her left hand she felt around her waist for her radio and tugged at the aerial poking up from her pocket. It didn't move. She needed to keep one hand on her neck. She tugged again, her shoulder leaning into the cage, giving something to help push against. Her pocket gave and she held the radio in her hand. The radio clicked as she frantically transmitted but no sound came from her. She realised all she could do was sit with the girl. She wouldn't leave her now. Sally turned her head slightly, looking for the risk, but movement felt difficult and disjointed. Darkness was playing with the corners of her vision.

Through the blurring edges she could see the woman held some kind of large kitchen knife. The light from the overhead bulb bounced from its blade. Spiking patterns through the darkness. Pretty. She was cold but warmth oozed down her chest. She relaxed into it a little. The fingers of her left hand now curled around the wire of the cage, keeping the child safe. Her other hand, asp long forgotten, held onto the wound.

"You fucking crazy maniacs," the woman hissed. "Think you can come into our home and invade our privacy like this. You wait until Donovan knows. He will sort this out. You'll be sorry." The blade waved in front of her like a sharp silver and red barrier, but Sally wouldn't be going near it. She had the child. She'd done her job. She had to hold on until help got there, then the girl would be safe. She heard her name being called. She tried again to cry out, the only sound little bubbles popping in her throat. The crazy woman waving the shiny blade at her wasn't moving. Sally knew the best place for her was to sit here. With the girl. She was with the girl. She'd found her.

94

The stairs were steep and narrow. As I tried to get down the steps, I fell, my elbow slamming hard into the damp wall as I struggled to stay upright. I swore as I righted myself and continued down. What the hell was I about to walk into? What had Sally walked into? The damp played with my nostrils and seeped into my bones adding to the sense of dread. I heard a high pitched voice scream out from behind the wooden door at the foot of the stairs.

I ratcheted my asp by flicking it out in front of me. The concertinaed metal bars snapped into their locked position. The tip of the asp hit the wall in the narrow space and it echoed around me. My fist wrapped around the handle, I pushed on the door in front of me. The basement was set up with furniture. Sally was down, slumped against a small cage in the middle of the room. I couldn't see past her into the cage and I didn't have time to check. A woman I didn't recognise stood over her. She had a wild look. My mind made the links between the wide-eyed twitching woman in front of me and the perfectly manicured and groomed host I'd previously met, Evelyn Manders. Donovan's wife. She waved a knife erratically. Sally barely reacting on the ground. The woman was screaming but words were difficult to make out. I looked harder and saw a bright red stain down Sally's shirt, seeping down to her stab vest. My heart jumped, filling my throat, constricting the airway. I raised my asp to shoulder height.

"Evelyn. Drop the knife."

Her attention moved from Sally to me, the knife still dancing in front of her. I needed to draw her away. Sally looked bad.

"I will not. This is my home. How dare you!" Her voice shook. The knife quivered in her hand.

"Evelyn. Drop the knife! Now!" I commanded.

She lurched forward towards Sally again. I pulled my elbow back and powered through with the asp as I stepped forward. Evelyn curled around quickly, a loud scream going up. My asp was halfway there when a searing pain sliced its way through my upper arm. My arm dropped but instinct and training to survive kicked in. I pushed back hard again and slammed the asp down, contact with Evelyn's shoulder vibrating through my arm. She fell to the floor screaming. The knife dropped with a soft thwack as it hit the carpet.

I looked at Sally. I needed to get to her. To stop the bleeding. But first I had to secure Evelyn Manders. I reached to my waist for my cuffs but they weren't there. I'd already used them on Donovan. I kicked the knife away and kept a foot on a writhing Evelyn as I leaned over and down to Sally, her eyes nearly closed.

I saw a flicker of recognition. I ran my hand around her waist until I found her cuffs and pulled at them. Sally slid a little further down the cage. Evelyn moved to knock me off balance and I kicked out. The tip of my boot made contact with something soft that gave under the pressure and the scream went up again. Once I had the cuffs in my hand I turned to Evelyn. She was on her side, wailing. I pulled and rolled her so she was face down. I leaned down hard on her. She gave little resistance but the keening sound continued. As I pulled both her arms back I felt her stiffen beneath me and she screamed.

"You fucking evil bitch. Get off me. Get off!"

I yanked harder, ripping her shoulders back and locking her wrists together behind her as she lay on her front screaming. Pain erupted through me, blood streamed down my arm, my ribs pulled tight and took my breath away. Sucking in, I crawled to Sally. I pushed both of my hands onto her neck, releasing Sally's own weak grip on the wound. The white of the fat beneath her skin unfurled like a flower. I pressed harder. Blood seeped through my fingers. I couldn't use my radio to call for help. I needed both hands to stop the flow of blood from Sally's neck. I screamed loud and hard trying to be heard over the banshee sound of Evelyn Manders.

"Help! Officer down! Help!"

95

Sally heard screaming. Maybe it wasn't someone screaming. It was faint and distant, like she was listening through water. Nothing felt sharp or in focus and she strained against the muted feel, but nothing was coming through. Her arm felt heavy as she held it up to her neck. The feeling in her hand was fading. Something told her it was important to leave her hand where it was, no matter how heavy her arm got.

She thought about Tom. About the baby. Their family. Then she thought about the reasons that had brought her here, to this point. She thought about the girl, the child. She'd found her. It was something her own child could be proud of. The weight on her arm pulled more. Tom would be angry. He would be angry that she was hurt and that she had put herself in that position. She loved him so much and she wanted their family more than anything. But she couldn't have done, could she? Look at her now. On the floor, leaning on a wire dog cage, designed to hold small creatures, to keep them safe. She was attempting to protect a child, but in this state what could she actually do? What would Tom make of her decision when he found out? She hoped he would still love her. It hurt to think he wouldn't love her any more. She'd make it up to him. They'd talk about the baby. She would buy a name book and spend evenings curled up on the sofa with him arguing about what kind of name they would have. Old and beautiful like Emily or modern and up to date like India. A beautiful name but Tom was old fashioned. She would love the bickering. They had the time to bicker. Seven whole months ahead of them. If Tom could forgive her this mistake. She curled her fingertips tighter round the wire she was leaning on, hoping the movement would reassure the child within. She couldn't maintain eye contact or voice her reassurance. All she had to offer the girl was a fingertip squeeze and she hoped it was enough. She couldn't tell if there was any response or movement from within.

Sounds dulled. The room around her darkened, the chill invasive. She was aware of someone with her now. She tried to acknowledge them, but she couldn't move. She was so tired, so very tired. She'd sort this mess out later. Now she needed to rest. Just a short rest. Tom would still love her wouldn't he? Sally let go.

96

Blue and red lights sliced through the night as I sat on the step at the rear of the ambulance. My arm was outstretched as a paramedic stitched before wrapping a bandage around it. Words of advice were being spoken but I couldn't hear them. The lights bounced around inside my head and only single words such as hospital and surgery broke through. A concerned look accompanied the words. I had no response.

I'd watched as the girl from the cage was brought out in a chair with a red blanket covering her small, frail frame. Her eyes flickered around, watching. Her body otherwise still. The street was a hive of activity. Police dogs were out, pulling on tight leashes, uniformed officers were knocking on doors and the street was cordoned off. CSIs had pulled up and were suiting up and preparing themselves to enter the home of Donovan and Evelyn Manders. A home where, at first glance, you would see a small family living daily life and going about their business and causing no concern to the neighbours. In fact, I doubted, the neighbours would even know who lived in that house. The ambulance carrying the child had taken off from the scene with its sirens wailing, a mournful sound. A sound that would carry an echo of the evening through the heart of everyone present.

Aaron approached, his tie undone and hanging from his trouser pocket. "The search team are reporting an office of well-filed transactions, names and photographs of children, email addresses, meeting places of offenders and payments to Jesse. It shouldn't take us long to identify the girl now." There was no preamble or emotion. "They ran a well-oiled machine and it looks like it has been going on for some time. Martin has gone with Caroline Manders to the hospital in another ambulance. Children's services are aware and will meet them there. She was perched on her bed listening to all the noise. She's not talking to us. It seems they've had her well-trained to keep quiet and not react to anything." He spoke clearly, giving the facts and the facts alone. "There are a few photographs of Rosie in her school uniform. It looks like they were getting her ready to be moved on and prepared for what that entailed before she even went missing. It explains the troublesome behaviour that started just prior, that no one understood."

I looked at him. He didn't move. He waited.

"Thank you, Aaron." He was what I needed to get through this right now. Here was not the place to break. The lights continued to flash and my head pulsed with them.

"Catherine is on her way."

"I'd expect so." The paramedic taped the bandage and walked away as we stumbled through the conversation. I rested my hand limply in my lap.

"Sally has been left where she is. Scenes of crime will want to process the scene with her there." His tone was matter-of-fact.

Tears sprang to my eyes, unwanted, and I fought to keep them back. I clenched my teeth, locked my jaw tight and stared at the floor. I took a deep breath and looked back at Aaron. He said not a word. The phone in my pocket rang again. Tom.

"Do you want me to talk to him?" Aaron asked.

I took another deep breath. I had work to do. "No. Thanks, Aaron. Give me a few minutes to talk to people here, then I'll go and see him." I clicked *answer* on my phone as I walked towards the house.

About the Author

Rebecca Bradley lives in Nottinghamshire with her family and her one-year-old Cockerpoo Alfie, who keeps her company while she writes. Rebecca needs to drink copious amounts of tea to function throughout the day and if she could, she would survive on a diet of tea and cake.

She lives with the genetic disorder Hypermobile Ehlers-Danlos Syndrome and secondary disorder to that, Postural Orthostatic Tachycardia Syndrome. These are a part of her daily life and she has to adjust her days accordingly, but she still manages to commit murder and will continue to for a long time to come.

Once a month Rebecca hosts a crime book club on Google+ hangouts where you can live chat about a crime book everyone has read. It's great fun. We have members joining in from the UK, the US, France and Australia on a regular basis and have had a German member attend. As it is online, there are no geographical boundaries and you can sit in your home to join in. You can find details of how this works on the blog.

DI Hannah Robbins will return in 2015. Sign up to the <u>newsletter</u> to make sure you don't miss the launch date to find out what happens next and how the team are coping with the events that occurred in *Shallow Waters*.

You can find Rebecca on her blog:

http://Rebeccabradleycrime.com

On Twitter: http://Twitter.com/RebeccaJBradley

And on Facebook: http://Facebook.com/RebeccaBradleyCrime

Please look her up as she would love to chat.

Acknowledgements

This book would not have been possible without the involvement of several people. With my deepest thanks, I am indebted to Denyse Kirkby, Kirsty Stanley and Lauren Turner for their expertise. Any errors, as always, are my own.

Without Simon I may not have made it as far as finishing the first draft and without Keshini I may not have revised it as I did, so thank you both.

There are so many people who have offered encouragement, they are too many to name for fear of leaving someone out and offending, but to you all, I am truly grateful. You are my support network.

Phil, I can't believe you gave me something so precious!

To Jane Isaac and Mel Sherratt for reading more than one draft and providing me with such great encouragement and fabulous quotes. Thank you.

And to Sharon Sant, for the hours you have put in helping hone this into something I am able to put out there, for your patience with commas, thank you.

To Helen Baggott, I can't thank you enough.

Finally to my husband and children who have never once moaned about the time I have left them to sit in front of my laptop to make *Shallow Waters* come to life. This is for you.

6363038R00235

Printed in Germany
by Amazon Distribution
GmbH, Leipzig